KNIGHTS, PIRATES, OUTLAWS, AND ONE BIG HAPPY ENDING

David D. Catalano

First printed in the United States of America
10 9 8 7 6 5 4 3 2 1

ISBN: 1511776358
ISBN 13: 9781511776356
Library of Congress Control Number: 2015906440
CreateSpace Independent Publishing Platform
North Charleston, South Carolina

Dedicated to all who have lost someone in their lives
"Let the peace of Christ rule in your hearts"
(Colossians 3:15 NIV)

TABLE OF CONTENTS

CHAPTER 1
THE BEGINNING

I opened my eyes and turned toward my beautiful wife. "Good morning, beautiful," I said as she opened her eyes and gave me a warm smile.

"Good morning, David." I leaned toward her and kissed her on her soft forehead. Her smile grew bigger as she began to stretch her arms out wide, knocking me in the face.

"Ow! Aida!" I said jokingly. Before she could stretch out her arms again, I pounced on her, wrapping my arms tight around her back. She began to laugh as I rolled around until she was on top. Our foreheads touched as she looked into my eyes with a big smile. "Every morning is amazing with you." My sweet words made her smile turn into a quick peck on the lips.

"David, it's time to get ready for work." She pushed herself off me and began to put on her slippers.

"But baby, do I have to work today?" I said, grinning.

"Those kids aren't going to teach themselves." She slowly picked up a bandana and began to wrap it around her bald head. "Besides, your kids love you!" She turned around and looked at me for approval. I slowly rolled out of bed and stood up, looking into her eyes.

"You look more and more beautiful every day." I kissed her forehead.

"Dad! Mom!" a little voice yelled as tiny footsteps ran across the floor.

"Good morning, Aaron," Aida said as she got down on her knee and gave him a hug.

"You ready for breakfast, bud?" I asked, picking him up and throwing him across my shoulder. He wrapped one arm around my neck in an effort to wrestle me.

"Can I have cookies for breakfast?" he asked with a big grin.

"Cookies for breakfast? Why that's insane!" I said, chuckling as I sat him down at the kitchen table. He ran over to the cupboard and pulled out a box of Cookie Crisp cereal. Aida then pulled out a bowl from the cupboard and poured the cereal into the bowl.

"Honey," she asked, "do you want the usual?"

"Same old oatmeal for me, dear!" She started to heat up some hot water as I sat at the table with Aaron. "You excited for time with Mommy today?" I asked as he shoveled a spoonful of cereal in his mouth.

"Yeah!" he said, crumbs flying. "We're gonna go to the park!" He shoveled another spoonful of cereal into his mouth.

"Alright, son. I've got to get ready for work." I smiled at him as I got up from the table and scuffed the top of his head. I walked back to my room and pulled out some socks, pants, a shirt, and a sweater vest.

After putting on my clothes, I walked toward the front door where Aida and Aaron waited for me. "Bye, Aaron. I love you, son." I knelt down and kissed his head. I then stood up and wrapped my arms around Aida's head. "Bye, Aida. I love you."

"Forever and always?" she said with an even bigger smile.

"Forever and always." I kissed her goodbye.

After I arrived at the school, I pulled up into my parking space and opened my car door. “Good morning, Mr. Benelli,” a student said as he walked by.

“Good morning, Harold,” I said, as I grabbed my briefcase. I then made my way to the front office. I slowly walked in with my briefcase in hand as the front administrator greeted me.

“Ah, Mr. Benelli. How’s your day going today?” she asked as she peeked her head up from her desk.

“Very good, Nancy. How’s your daughter doing?”

“Oh, she’s great! Just trying to make it through college, ya know?” She gave a little wink as I continued past the principal’s office. As I finally arrived at my classroom, the seats began to fill up with high-school kids.

“Shall we begin?” I said, opening my arms in order to gain the class’s attention. “Please bring up the stories you’ve written for homework.” The students began, one by one, to walk toward the front desk.

“I had so much fun writing my story, Mr. Benelli,” one student said.

“I’m so glad, William.” I gave him a pat on the shoulder.

As all the students sat down, I stood in front of the class and watched as many smiling faces waited for the day’s lesson. “Before I begin the lesson, I just want to say I am very proud of all of you for turning in your stories. I hope you enjoyed writing them.” I picked up the pile of papers and began to tap them against the desk. “You see, a story is a powerful thing. It unlocks the imagination and immerses you in a whole new world. In a story, you can be anything. You can be a knight in shining armor!” I began to holster a sword out of thin air and wave it around. “You can become an outlaw in the wild west.” I held my hands at my waist and brought up two “L” shaped guns. “Boom boom.” The class filled with laughter as I blew out the pretend smoke from the end of my index fingers.

"You can be a space warrior fighting off evil aliens. Pew pew!" I put my fingers up and started shooting fake laser guns. "Take me to your leader," I said in an alien voice while spreading my fingers apart. The class began to laugh once more. "But the best stories are what's in here." I held my hand over my chest as most of the class focused on what I had to say. "You see, we may be able to enter into any world, but the best story is the story we make about ourselves." I gave the class a big smile. "Alright, class. Take out your books and turn to chapter five."

As the bell rang, the students quickly began to scurry out of the classroom. Some fist-bumped me, many smiled, some just shuffled past as if they had not yet woken up. "I really enjoyed class today, Mr. Benelli! I have another story for you to read," one last student said as he pulled out a stack of papers from his backpack.

"Thank you, Kyle. I'll definitely read your story and give you feedback. I enjoyed your last one." He gave me a salute as he walked out the door. I sat in my chair as I waited for the next class to come in.

As lunch hour came, I walked into the teacher's lounge and grabbed some food from the cafeteria. "Mm, I love pizza," a teacher said as he sat next to me.

"Ah, Mr. Lite. How's your day treating you?"

Mr. Lite smiled at me as he pulled out a folder. "Mr. Benelli, I read the story you gave me. It was wonderful! Have you thought of publishing it?"

I smiled a little sheepishly. "Well, I haven't thought about submitting it just yet," I said as I took a bite of my pizza.

"I've read your stories. You're an amazing writer! You should try to publish at least one of them. People love reading stories with fantasy and action. And you've got tons."

"You'll be the first to know when I publish one. I'll even get you a copy." I gave him a playful nudge on his shoulder as we both continued to eat. As lunch hour ended, I headed back to my classroom to finish the last three class periods.

Several hours passed and the final bell rang. The class quickly began to leave the room. "Alright, class. Remember, keep writing!" I sat down on my office chair and did one big spin before laying back and stretching out. "Ah, I love teaching," I said to myself as I began to gather papers for grading.

Ring, ring. Ring, ring. I looked at my cell phone to see a number I didn't recognize. *Ring, ring. Ring, ring.* "Hello?" I asked.

"Mr. Benelli?" It was an older man's voice.

"Yes, it's me."

"This is Dr. Hopkins from University Medical Center. We currently have your wife and son with us. Your wife fainted today at the park." I jumped up out of my chair and grabbed my keys.

"Is she alright? Can I come see her?" I was sure Dr. Hopkins could hear the worried tone in my voice.

"Mr. Benelli, your wife will have to stay here for a few days so we can evaluate her. We have to make sure her cancer isn't spreading." My heart fell to my stomach as I felt my knees buckle me back into my chair. I took a deep breath, trying to gain enough air to speak.

"Thank you, Dr. Hopkins. I'll be there shortly." I hung up the phone and rushed toward the front office.

"You alright there, Mr. Benelli?" Nancy said as I swung open the door.

"I'm searching for Mr. Oliver. Is he here?" I tried to seem calm but my heavy breathing from my running gave it away.

Nancy looked at me with worry but nodded her head. "He's in his office," she said softly, trying to soothe my accelerated heartrate. I shook off the tension and took a deep breath. I opened the door and slowly peeked in to ensure he wasn't busy.

"Mr. Benelli, please come in." He motioned me to sit down with one hand as he coursed his other hand through his gray beard. He gave me an old man smile until he saw the expression on my face. "Is everything alright, my boy?"

I took another deep breath as I looked up from my squabbling hands. "Mr. Oliver . . ."

"Please please, call me Jack," he said in a breezy tone.

"Jack, my wife is in the hospital, and I need to leave early to see her . . ."

Before I could finish he quickly chimed in. "Yes, yes, David. Go see Aida. We completely understand. Is she okay?"

"Fine. I mean no. I mean . . . thank you," I said as I opened the door to leave.

"She's in my prayers!" he said softly behind my back.

I shoved my keys into the ignition and shot my foot down on the pedal. My heart raced as my foot began to tap nervously at each red light. *Three more lights. Two more lights,* I thought to myself as I sped down the road. I finally pulled into the hospital and jumped out of the car. "Baby, I'm coming for you!" I shut the door and began to sprint toward the entrance.

CHAPTER 2
TROUBLE IN PARADISE

As I stepped in, my mother greeted me with a big hug. "Dad, is Mommy going to be alright?" Aaron said, his eyes searching mine. I knelt down on my knee and pulled him into my chest.

"Yes, champ. Mom's going to be just fine," I said, trying to sound as confident as I could.

"I'll take care of him, don't you worry. Go and see Aida," my mother said as she grabbed Aaron's hand.

I ran down the hallway searching through each room. "Three oh-nine, three oh-nine, three—ah, here it is." I opened up the door to see Aida lying in a hospital bed with an IV in her arm. Several nurses surrounded her as they continued to hook her up to several devices and check others. As I walked toward her, the nurses quickly moved aside.

"I'll leave you two alone for a bit. She should be all set for now," one said softly as they all walked out and slowly closed the door. I sat down in the chair next to her bed and gently grabbed her hand. The moment I felt the warm touch of her fingers the tension in my body began to ease. I closed my eyes and pulled her hand to my lips. I gave her a small kiss on her hand as I looked into her eyes.

"Sorry you have to see me like this," she said softly.

"Baby, you look more and more beautiful every day," I replied as I stood up and gave her a kiss on her bald head. A smile crept onto her face as she squeezed my hands.

"The results should be coming back any minute." She was trying to reassure me that she was alright.

I looked into her eyes as I leaned my forehead onto hers. "Mr. Lite liked the story I wrote about you." I began to play with her hand.

"I loved that story," she said with a faint smile. I could tell the effort was costing her. "I'm your number one fan." She gave a little chuckle but it soon turned into a heavy cough. She began to cover her mouth as more coughs followed.

"It's alright, baby. Save your energy." I grabbed a washcloth and wiped away the blood on her hand. Suddenly, the door opened and an older man with silver hair and glasses walked in.

"Mr. Benelli?" he asked as he looked at his clipboard and pulled a pen from the pocket of his white coat.

"Yes, that's me." I stood up and offered my hand.

"Dr. Hopkins." His grip was dry but firm. "I believe we talked on the phone earlier."

"Ah, yes. Do you have the results?" I asked gently. There was a sudden quiet in the room. Dr. Hopkins placed his clipboard down and slowly took a seat. He pulled his chair closer to us as he folded his hands together.

"Mr. and Mrs. Benelli, I'm sorry to inform you that the cancer is spreading." His serious tone caused my heart to drop as I looked over at Aida. She closed her eyes as I felt a comforting squeeze from her hand telling me everything was going to be alright. "We're going to have to keep her here and continue further treatment," Dr. Hopkins said as he placed his hand on my shoulder and gave me a strong nod of encouragement. "I'll leave you two alone now." He got up and left the room as I looked over at Aida.

"Aida. I will do anything to make you feel better." I looked deep into her eyes trying to remain strong. She gave a little smile while biting on her lower lip.

"You should write me another story," she said as she held my hand. "Your stories always make me feel better."

I looked into her eyes and fought to bring the best smile I could to my face. "Okay, baby. I'll write you a story."

I left Aida's room and met with Aaron and my mother in the lobby. I told my mother the news as she gave me a concerned look. I held Aaron's hand as we walked out of the hospital together. "Thank you for watching Aaron, Mom." I wrapped my arms around my mother really tightly. She felt the tension in my hug and softly gave me a pat on the back.

"It's alright, David. Everything is going to be alright," she said softly as her hand pressed against my cheek. She looked over at Aaron and gave him a hug and a kiss. "You make sure you get to bed once you get home, okay Aaron?"

"Yes, Grammy!" he said with a smile.

As we got to the car, I picked up Aaron and strapped him into his car seat. "You ready to go, buddy?" I said, giving the seatbelt once last tug.

"Yeah," he murmured. As I opened the door to get into the car, Aaron's head looked up at me. "Dad?"

"Yes, son?" I asked as I turned around and looked into his big eyes.

"Is Mommy going to be okay?" His voice squeaked while his eyes begin to fill with tears.

"She's going to be just fine, Aaron. You want to pray for her real quick?" I said, holding my hand out for him to grab. His soft hand grabbed my mine as we both shut our eyes and bowed our heads. "Dear Lord, I pray for Aida. I pray that you can be with her and us through this hard time and that you can heal her and keep her strong as she continues to fight. Be with her. In Jesus's name, amen."

"Amen," Aaron said as he looked up, a smile back on his face.

"Alright, champ. Time to go home." I started my car and began to pull out of the hospital lot. I turned on the radio to country music as Aaron began to bobble his head up and down while looking out the window.

As I drove, I replayed the moment of Dr. Hopkins coming in and telling the bad news. My heart dropped as I tried to release the memory from my head. The hurt began to build until I saw her beautiful smile. Thinking of her eased my pain. She was so calm and unaffected by the circumstances she was facing. Seeing her strength made me realize everything was going to be alright. I thought about earlier that morning; how being with her made the world seem so much brighter. Then I remembered. I have to write her a story.

I pulled into the driveway and unbuckled my seatbelt. I looked in the backseat to see Aaron sound asleep. I gently unbuckled his car seat and put him over my shoulder. As I made my way to the house, I slowly opened each door as to not wake Aaron. I took off his shoes and pulled the covers up to his chest. His little hands grabbed the blanket and pulled it over his shoulders. "It was a big day for you," I whispered in his ear as I gave him a light kiss on his cheek. "Sweet dreams, champ. I love you."

I slowly shut the door to his room and walked over to my laptop. "Alright, time to write a story." I fervently began to type as I pictured Aida's beautiful smile in my head. I imagined her being with me in the story and developed a whole new adventure with her. I loved writing her stories. The smile she had when she would read them made the hours and hours all worthwhile. I knew this story had to be extra special, because I needed to make sure I could put another beautiful smile on her face. As the hours flew by, Aaron woke up. I cooked a pizza for dinner as we played with his toys. As I played with him, the story continued to be fresh on my mind. After we ate, I brought my laptop into his room and typed away as he played.

"Dad?" he asked, looking up from his set of dinosaurs scattered on the floor.

"Yes, son?"

"Are you writing another story?" He looked at me with a little smile.

"Yes I am, buddy." I grinned. His smile grew even bigger as he went back to playing with his toys. Aaron soon became tired, so I helped him prepare for bed. After brushing his teeth, we knelt down on our knees and began to pray.

"Dear God, I pray that you heal Mommy and make her all better. I pray I get a goodnight sleep and you watch over Mommy tonight. In Jesus's name . . ."

"Amen," we both said. He jumped up in his bed as I pulled the covers over him.

"Goodnight, champ. I love you." I planted one on his cheek.

"Goodnight, Dad! I love you, too." He slowly closed his eyes as I picked up my laptop and painstakingly closed the door. I sat down at my desk and continued to type away at the story.

I typed for several hours until I noticed the sun beginning to come up. I finished several more paragraphs before slowly closing my laptop. I then began to get ready for work as I searched my room for clothes to wear. I had not gotten any sleep, but I knew it was a Friday. I could catch up on some sleep after work.

I woke up Aaron by tickling his armpits. "Wake up, buddy!" I said as he let out several high pitched giggles. Aaron rubbed his eyes and stretched out his arms. I pulled out several different outfits for him to wear. "Put on your clothes. Grammy's coming to pick you up any minute." Aaron let out a sigh as he looked over at the clothes I laid out for him.

"But Dad, I don't want to get dressed."

Uh, oh. What now? I looked at him with a sideways smile. "If you get dressed then I'll watch cartoons with you." His eyes lit up as he ran over and put his clothes on with lightning speed.

I poured Cookie Crisp into two bowls and turned on the TV. Aaron and I ate our cereal as we watched a coyote run into a wall trying to catch a roadrunner. "Ha!" Aaron giggled as food flew out of his mouth. I smiled at him as I put a big spoonful of cereal in my mouth. I made a silly face at him by crossing my eyes and looking at my nose. He stuck his tongue out at me as I swallowed my cereal. I then stuck my tongue out at him as he started to laugh a little more. Soon the doorbell rang. "Grammy!" Aaron yelled as he put his cereal down and ran to the door.

I opened the door, and Aaron leapt up to hug my mother's leg. "Oh, settle down there, Aaron," she said as she patted him on the head. I gave her a smile and a shrug. "Did your father feed you breakfast this morning?" she asked, giving me a motherly glare.

"He sure did! We ate cookies!" he said with a playful smile.

My mother began to laugh as she looked at me with disapproval. "Cookies for breakfast? What is your father thinking?"

"I'll explain later, Momma," I said, giving her a hug and a kiss. I knelt down on my knee and gave Aaron another hug. "Now you be good for Grammy, okay?" Aaron gave me an excited nod. "And we'll visit Mommy as soon as I'm done with work." Aaron's smile got even bigger.

"Yay!" he said jumping up and down.

I got in the car and waved goodbye. It was nice to see Aaron was still able to smile and laugh with Aida being in the hospital again. I began to smile, too, as I thought about how I would continue my story for her.

As I pulled into work, I opened my door and reached for my briefcase. "Good morning, Mr. Benelli!" a student said.

"Good morning, Thomas." I shut the car door and waved. I walked toward the office holding my briefcase. I stepped through the front office to see Nancy perk her head up from her desk.

"Is everything okay, Mr. Benelli?" Nancy asked.

I slowly walked over to her and gently put my hand on her shoulder. I took a deep breath before giving her the news. "The cancer is spreading." I closed my eyes. "But I have faith that she's going to be alright."

Nancy gave a small smile and a nod. "It's always good to have faith, Mr. Benelli."

"Thank you, Nancy." I nodded before turning around and heading for the principal's office. As I stood at the partially opened door, I gently gave a knock.

"Who is it?" a voice asked from behind the door.

"It's me."

"Ah, David. Please, come in." I opened the door to see Jack leaning back in his chair with a pen and paper. "Take a seat," he said kindly as he gestured me toward a chair.

"Good morning, Jack," I said quietly as I took a seat.

"How is everything?" he asked with a worried expression.

I was quiet for several moments as I prepared to tell him the news. "The cancer is spreading," I said in a soft voice.

He tilted back his head and looked up to the ceiling. He looked back at me and put his elbows on the table with his hands in front of his mouth. He looked at me gravely. "If you're struggling or need any time for this, I completely understand."

I nodded my head as I bit bottom lip. "I have faith everything will be alright."

Jack gave me a firm nod. "It's always good to have faith during hard times."

I took a deep breath as I stood up from my chair. I put out my hand and was met with Jack's strong grip. I gave him one strong shake before letting go and walking toward the door.

Students piled in as I sat on my desk typing away. Several students' eyes lit up as they saw my hands steady at work.

"Mr. Benelli?" one student asked as she walked up to my desk.

"Yes, Jessica?" I replied, turning around, trying to smile.

"Are you writing another story?" she asked as the smile on her face grew.

"Yes, I am. Another story for Aida."

Her eyes grew wide as she suddenly turned around and ran to her group of friends. "I told you! He's writing another story for his wife!" Jessica whispered in the background with a huge smile.

"Ah, that's so cute!" another girl said as she covered her mouth. The group of girls began to giggle.

"Alright class!" I said as I typed one more sentence. I slowly stood up and looked across the room at all my students. "Everyone pull out your notebooks. We're going to do a short exercise." The sound of zippers filled the room as students reached into their backpacks. *Whap! Whap!* Notebooks began hitting the desks as student prepared to write. "Everybody, close your eyes," I said as I stood up in front. "Imagine your happiest memory."

A student's hand began to rise. "Yes, Harold."

"What if we don't have a happy memory?" Harold asked as he put his head down.

I gave him a warm smile. "That's alright, just imagine something that you find absolutely beautiful." Harold closed his eyes again and began to smile. "Think about the way it makes you feel, the way this moment or this beautiful thing lights up your world." More smiles began to appear on the students' faces. "Now open your eyes." Everyone's eyes quickly opened as they began to look around. "For the rest of the period, I want you all to write a story while thinking about that memory or beautiful thing that makes you happy." The students quickly opened their journals as the sound of pens scribbling on paper filled the quiet atmosphere of the room. I closed my eyes and thought about Aida's smile one more time before sitting back down and continuing to write her story.

After another period ended, I picked up my laptop and headed toward the teacher's lounge. As I picked up my food and sat down, I opened my laptop and began to type violently at the keyboard.

"Mr. Benelli!" Mr. Lite said as he sat down next to me.

"Mr. Lite, good to see you," I said putting my hand on his shoulder then turning back to my laptop.

"I heard the news about Aida," he said, returning my gesture by placing his hand on my back, but I continued to type. "We're all praying for you."

I stopped typing for a second and looked over at him.

"Thank you, Mr. Lite. I very much appreciate that." I gave him a half-smile. I then turned back to my computer and continued to type.

After school ended, I began to finish grading the different stories the students had left me. Such amazing imagination. I pulled out the story my student Kyle had written and began to read. His story was about a little boy who gained superpowers in order to save his family. I laughed several times knowing Kyle loved to put humor in his writing. I wrote several comments on his paper, encouraging him to continue writing and continued to prepare the following week's lesson plan.

After finally finishing up, I packed my briefcase and prepared to pick up Aaron. I got in my car and sped over to my parents' house, stopping to pick up flowers on the way.

"Mom! Dad!" I hollered as I opened the front door. I gave them both a big hug as Aaron ran into my arms. "Did you have fun at Grandpa and Grammy's house?" I asked as he gave me a big smile and nodded his head.

"Are we gonna see Mommy?" he asked before I could ask any more questions.

"We sure are, champ," I replied while messing up his hair with my hand. "Was he good?" I asked my mother as I handed my father the flowers and watched Aaron climb into his car seat.

"He was good," she said, giving me a small smile. "He misses his mother, but he'll be fine. Now go, your father and I will meet you over there."

"Alright, bud! Time to see Mommy!" I started the car as we began our drive to the hospital.

"Mommy!" Aaron yelled as he stood up on the chair and wrapped his arms around Aida. I came up from behind and wrapped my arms around the both of them.

"I missed you guys," Aida said with a big smile. As she looked at me, she noticed the bags under my eyes. "Ah David, what did I tell you about pulling all-nighters when writing me stories?" She gave me a little slap on my shoulder.

"I just love writing about you," I said, giving her a kiss on the bandana covering her head.

"Aida!" my mother cried as she walked in. "How are you?" She grabbed Aida's hand.

"I'm good! I don't feel too bad today." Aida grinned.

My mother gave her a hug as my father came in and joined in with another hug.

"These are from your husband." He handed her the bouquet of lilies.

"Lilies!" She looked over at me. "My favorite." She pulled me toward her and kissed me on the cheek. "I'm so happy the family is here. It makes me feel so much better." My father put the lilies next to her bed as I sat down.

I grabbed her hand as Aaron climbed on my lap. "How about while we're all here, we pray for you," I said, looking into her eyes.

"That's a great idea!" my mom chimed in.

We all held hands and began to bow our heads. "Dear Lord, I pray for Aida. I thank you for the wonderful mother she is and the wonderful woman she is. I pray that you help her through this hard time and heal her from her cancer. Lord, I pray you place your healing hands down on her and let her know that you are always by her side. I pray that you help our families to be strong. We thank you for being in our lives and blessing us with Aida. In Jesus's name I pray . . ."

"Amen." Everyone opened their eyes.

Aida gave another big smile as she took a deep breath. "I'm so grateful for everyone's support through this." She looked around.

We all began to talk some more as my parents asked her questions about her stay at the hospital. Her smile and carefree attitude made me feel as though everything was going to be alright. She would still laugh and smile as if nothing was wrong. She was the most beautiful thing in the world to me.

After an hour had passed, I looked toward my parents and nodded slightly toward Aaron. "Alright, Aaron. You're spending the night at our house," my father said as he picked up the tired boy and put him over his shoulder.

"Thank you," I whispered to my parents as they both gave me a kiss goodbye. I looked back at Aida with her big smile and pulled out my laptop. "You ready to read my story?" I asked as I opened my computer.

"I think we should do something different," she said as she grabbed my arm. "I want you to read me the story."

I laughed and gave her a quizzical look. "Me? Tell the story?" I said.

"You wrote it! You can read it way better than I can."

"All right, all right," I said motioning her to scoot over. "I'll read you the story but only if—"

She interrupted me with a big kiss on my lips. "I knew you were going to ask for one of those." she said with a giggle.

I scrolled to the top of the page. "'The Knight and the Princess,' by David Catalano."

Aida gave me a confused look. "David Catalano?"

I frowned. "You don't like that pen name?"

She gave me a smile before nodding her head. "Alright, I approve," she said as she snuggled up into my shoulder.

"All right, where was I . . ."

CHAPTER 3

THE KNIGHT AND THE PRINCESS

Part 1: The Battle for Alvernon

His fingers slowly caressed the hard string of his bow.

"David," a voice behind him said.

"Yes, Jon?" David picked up a quiver and slung it over his shoulder.

"You ready for this?" Jon put his hand on David's shoulder while David ran his fingers across the string of his bow once more.

"It's just another battle," David replied as he placed his hand on Jon's shoulder. "May God be with us."

"Man your stations!" a voice yelled as David and Jon scurried toward the front courtyard. David climbed a nearby ladder and overlooked the vast fields in front of the fortress. "Ready your bows!" The voice yelled once more as David pulled an arrow from his quiver and lightly prepared it on his bowstring. He looked over at Jon to see he was also fully loaded and ready for what was about to come. They peered across the vast field once more awaiting the call from the general.

In the distance, several heads began to show from over the hill and soon an army of soldiers on horses began to appear. Big ogre-like monsters with dark gray skin and held on spiked leashes began to rise as well. The loose rocks on the rampart wall began to shake as the army came closer and closer into view.

David looked over to see a fellow soldiers knees quivering as he continued to hold his ground. The general stood on top of the opening gate with his hand up in the air preparing to let the soldiers open fire. David closed his eyes and counted the seconds in which he would have to release his bow.

"Fire!" The general yelled as arrows began to release into the sky. For several seconds, there was only the sound of arrows through the wind. *Grunt!* Arrows began to bombard the enemy soldiers as their march turned into a full sprint. Yelling punctured the air throughout the vast fields as the noise of horses' hooves pounded against the green grass. "Fire!" The general continued to yell as a sea of floating arrows began to drop the enemy forces and hold back their enemy line.

Bang! Bang! As enemy soldiers passed through the sea of arrows, they began to thrust themselves against the wooden gates. "Seal the gates!" A soldier yelled as more and more enemy soldiers began to push through. David looked over at Jon and gave him a nod as they quickly set down their bows. The two soldiers then ran for the ladder and prepared themselves for the enemy line about to break through the wooden gate. "Hold the gates!" The soldier repeated as David and Jon pushed up against the pounding door.

Crash! Within several moments, wood exploded everywhere as soldiers flew back into the courtyard. David unsheathed his sword as he saw enemy soldiers running through with their weapons held high.

A sword flew across David's face as he swung his sword into the back of an unaware enemy. The sound of clashing weapons filled the courtyard as blood began to spatter. David and Jon stood side by side attacking any enemy soldiers that came near. David swung his sword toward another soldier with a loud clinging of blades. David's hard swing caused the soldier to drop his sword as David thrust his sword into the heart of the enemy. More blood splattered into David's face as the smell of tin and dust filled his nostrils. More and more dust was swept up in the air as the two soldiers fought side by side. The air was soon filled with a thick red tint from the blood-drenched dirt.

A ferocious monster was soon released into the courtyard. Its back was covered in arrows as the ogre-like beast began to rip off the heads of any soldier it came across. Its colossal hands carried two large fingers with talons the size of a sword. Its horse-like teeth gnawed human flesh as blood dripped down the sides of its fierce jaw.

"Jon, you get its attention and bring it within range of the ledge!" David yelled as he pointed toward the monster. Jon nodded his head as David approached the nearby ladder.

"Come here, you ugly beast!" Jon yelled. The monster's gnawing teeth stopped as its gaze locked on Jon. It threw the now headless soldier in its hand over its right shoulder as it began to charge toward him. It let out a bloodthirsty roar that caused the other soldiers to cringe in fear as it trampled over several of them. Jon began to sprint toward the ledge, waiting to see a sign of David, but he was nowhere within his vision. The ogre-like beast soon wrapped its colossal hand around Jon's seemingly small body. "David!" he yelled as the monster prepared to bite off his head.

"Ah!" a yell came from overhead as David pierced the glowing eye of the savage beast with his sword. David turned his blade into its eye then dropped down to watch the beast topple backward. Its body slammed against the ground while crushing several soldiers surrounding it. Jon lifted the beast's large finger off his body as he ran over to grab his sword.

"Took you long enough!" he laughed as David ran up to the monster's head and pulled out his sword.

"Well," David jabbed his sword into another attacking enemy, "I was a little—" he spun around just in time to slice the neck of another soldier, "preoccupied!" More barbarous beasts began to come through the gate. "Shoot the eyes!" David yelled as he motioned Jon toward another ladder.

David ran across the upper walls of the fortress, jumping off and preparing to attack. His sword slid into the back of another monster's neck causing it to fall forward. Jon jumped into the air with his sword held high only to have the monster grab him in midair.

David ran toward the beast while slaying enemy soldiers in his path. "No!" he yelled as the monster began to lick its teeth. David jumped up onto the hip of the monster and stabbed its open side. The monster let out a bloodthirsty roar as it tossed Jon up into the air. David was defenseless as the monster prepared to grab him. Suddenly, Jon thrust his sword into the head of the monster as he fell from the sky, causing it to sway side to side.

Boom! As the beast fell over, an enemy soldier began to yell, "The last of our rock trolls has fallen! Retreat!" As the soldiers began to turn away in retreat, David and Jon began to hunt them down, slaying them from behind. The enemy soldiers began to run toward the field only to be shot down by arrows.

The dust finally began to settle as bodies covered in blood littered the battleground. "Victory is ours!" The general yelled as he held up his sword. The soldiers began to cheer as the last of the enemy were shot down by archers. The general walked toward David and Jon and put his hands on the top of their shoulders. "You both fought valiantly," he said as he looked into each of their eyes. "I will see to it that King Kenton knows of your bravery." David and Jon both knelt down on their knee and looked up at the general.

"Thank you, sir." David said as he bowed his head.

"We are honored," Jon added as he lowered his head.

Part 2: The Princess

Her hair gently floated in the wind as she overlooked the outside walls from her balcony. "Princess Aida, it is time," her servant said as he cracked open the door.

"I will be there soon, Benjamin," Aida said as she continued to look beyond the large oak in front of her balcony. The door slowly shut as she took a deep breath. "I want to be free," she said aloud. She closed her eyes and imagined herself escaping the tall castle and running around in the open fields outside the walls. "One day," she mumbled under her breath as she turned around and headed toward the door.

She walked down the long golden hall decorated with paintings and suits of armor. Two servants opened the double doors that revealed a larger hall with three thrones. Her father sat in the middle with his hand stroking his gray beard in thought.

"Ah, Aida," he said as he got up from the throne. "How is my beautiful princess?" He grabbed her hands and gave her a peck on her forehead.

"I am well, Father," she replied with a smile.

The king slowly walked her up to the smaller throne chair and sat her down. He gave her a smile that was returned with a royal nod. Aida looked up at the decorative windows, continuing to daydream about the outside world.

"Your highness, the soldiers are here," a servant said as the large twin doors of the throne room began to slowly open. The general quietly walked in while David and Jon followed close behind. Several other soldiers walked in formation as they began to halt at the steps of the throne. The general knelt down on the smooth red rug as the soldiers behind him did the same.

"Your Highness, we were victorious against the army at Fort Alvernon," the General said in a sonorous voice.

King Kenton nodded his head before standing up and walking toward the general. "You have accomplished a mighty feat, General. You have brought great honor to this kingdom."

The General began to bow his head in respect.

"Thank you, your honor," he said as the king laid his hand on the general's shoulder.

"I ask for one more great battle," he said as he helped the general to his feet. The general gave a firm nod.

"What is it, my king?" the general asked as he stood tall in his heavy silver armor.

"I want to attack King Erik's castle."

The general clenched his jaw as he searched for a reply. "Sire, this will be a difficult feat, but we will come out victorious," he said with a confident grin. The king grasped the general's arm and began to smile.

"Very good. I will see to it that you are given the best armor and weapons for your journey, but tonight, we feast."

The general bowed his head once more before motioning the soldiers to stand up. "These two soldiers fought valiantly, slaying many of King Erik's rock trolls." The general pointed to David and Jon as they stood firm and still.

The king walked in front of them looking up and down at them. "What are their names?" he asked looking over at the general.

"David, son of Victor, and Jon, son of Saul," the general replied as the king placed his hands on each of their shoulders and revealed a gracious smile. "You will both make great generals for me one day if you continue to fight valiantly," the King said as he walked back toward his throne.

David lifted up his head to spot the beautiful princess sitting beside the king. "Who is that?" he whispered to Jon.

"That is Princess Aida. She is the king's beautiful daughter," Jon replied. David's eyes widened as he looked at her beautiful face illuminated by the sun shining through the palace windows.

She had a fluorescent glow as the sun gently pressed against her beautiful skin.

"She is so beautiful," David whispered to himself as he tried to unlock his gaze upon her. *I must meet her,* he thought to himself as they began to march through large twin doors back into the city.

Part 3: Shall We Meet?

Fiddles began to play as people danced around a bonfire in the middle of the courtyard. Several long tables stretched across the area and were filled with assortments of cheese, fruits, and roasted turkey. The fire illuminated the dark sky as the soldiers began to drink tankards of mead.

"Aye!" each soldier yelled as they continued to gulp down full glasses of the frothy liquid. Several soldiers wobbled over to the ladies dancing around the fire and attempted to dance. *Bop!* The giggles of the women were heard as one soldier fell flat on his bottom.

David overlooked the party by standing on a set of steps surrounding the courtyard. He looked once more at his celebrating soldiers before turning around and entering one of the doors leading to the throne room. He silently crouched behind a wall as he heard two voices around the corner. "I told you to get more mead!" one voice said. *Smack!* The sound of a hand slapping someone's face was heard behind the wall. "Go get more mead!"

"Yes, ma'am," the other voice replied as his feet began to scurry away. David peeked around the corner to see the hall was now empty. He began to slowly creep down the hallway as he admired the many paintings and suits of armor decorating the walls. He listened past each door to see if he could hear any sign of the princess he was searching for.

He stopped at a bedroom door and began slowly turning the handle. As the door opened, he glanced in to see a big comfy bed with golden sheets and an empty balcony. "This isn't it," he murmured as he slowly shut the door. *Clank.* Just as he shut the door a servant came around the corner and immediately saw him.

"Intruder!" the servant yelled, turning around to get help. David quickly ran the other way, suddenly bumping into a woman in a beautiful dress. Before she fell to the ground, he quickly wrapped his arm around her back and caught her. His face was within an inch away from hers when he realized it was the beautiful princess.

As he brought her back to her feet, she grabbed his hand. "Hurry, this way!" she said as she pulled him toward a bedroom door. She slowly closed the door behind them and ran over to her bed. "Hide under here!" She pointed underneath the bed as David quickly began to take action. *Knock knock.* Several knocks were heard at the door as David vaulted himself over the bed and rolled under. *Bam!* The door burst open.

"Princess Aida, are you alright?" a guard said as he looked around. "There is an intruder in our midst." Several guards began to search the room.

"I haven't seen anyone," Aida said with a big smile. The guards began to approach the bed. "I've been in here the whole time, and I haven't seen anyone." She began to change her tone. "Now unless you have a reason to bother me, I ask that you please let me sleep." Her tone was stern yet still gentle.

"We're sorry, Princess," the guard said as he motioned the others to come out. "We are only trying to protect you."

"I understand, William," she said in a lighter tone. "Please enjoy yourselves tonight. I'm sure the intruder has been scared off by now." The guard nodded his head as he slowly shut the door. As soon as the door shut, David crawled out from underneath the bed and jumped up.

"Whew, I really thought I was in big trouble!" he said while dusting himself off. "Why did you save me?" The princess sat down on her bed and smiled.

"I know who you are," she replied. "You were with the general in the throne room earlier."

David gave a playful grin. "So you did recognize me?" he replied with a small laugh.

"Yes, David, son of Victor. I also noticed how you couldn't keep your eyes off me." She gave him a playful scowl. David began to turn red as he searched for words to say. "That's alright. You seem sweet." He let out a sigh of relief as he walked toward her balcony overlooking much of the kingdom.

"What an amazing view," he said, looking out across the fields. "Have you ever left the kingdom walls?" He slowly looked over his shoulder into her eyes.

"No, I haven't," she said as she got up and walked toward the balcony. "My father doesn't even allow me to dance at the balls." She put her hands on the railing and began to look up at the tree.

"Really?" David asked as he placed his hands on the railing and examined the tree with her. Aida gave him a nod as she continued to look at the large oak tree. "You know, I was taught how to dance," David said as held out his hand toward Aida, nodding toward the window to indicate the sounds of music and revelry below in the courtyard. "Will you dance with me?" Aida gave him a confused look before finally giving in.

She gently took his hand. David began to smile as he gave her a nod. "Then yes, I would love to dance," Aida said as David slowly lifted her hand and twirled her around. He placed his hand on her back and began to slowly guide her into a dance.

"It's very simple," he said as they both looked down at their feet. "I take a step forward while you take a step back." He slowly lifted his left foot forward as she began to slide her right foot back. "Now, the man always starts with his left." His second step followed as he brought his feet together. "Now, we're going to make a box." He lifted his right foot and stepped backward as she followed each step. They began to make a small box as they continued to take several steps. "You're doing amazingly well, Princess," David said as he looked at Aida, heavily concentrated on her feet.

"I'm surprised," she said with a little giggle. "I'm actually very clumsy." They continued to make a box with their steps several more times.

"If anyone's the clumsy one, it's me. I ran straight into you," he said, winking. "Now, let's spin with it."

Aida began to slowly spin as she put on an even bigger smile. "You're such a good teacher," she said as David spun her around once more.

"No, you are just a fast learner."

She flashed another smile at him as the soft sound of violins from the courtyard began to play in the background. "What's it like out there?" She asked as he continued to twirl her around.

David's eyes looked up as he searched for his answer. "Dangerous," he said with a half-smile.

"Dangerous?" She cocked her head to the side questioningly.

"I've seen ferocious beasts and horrific deaths." David closed his eyes as if trying to block out the picture.

"The whole world can't be dangerous and horrific," she said, batting her luminous eyes.

David looked at her and stopped dancing. "No, because as long as this world has someone as lovely as you, beauty will always exist." He gently ran his hands through her hair and slowly pulled her toward him. She closed her eyes as her hands slowly slid onto his strong muscular chest. She grabbed the cloth of his tunic as their lips began to slowly meet. *Crackle! Crackle!* The sound of fireworks began to explode in the sky as the two interlocked lips. As he slowly moved back, he opened his eyes and looked directly into hers. Her eyes met his with admiration.

She grabbed his hand and softly brought him to the door. "You must go. You have a journey to train for."

David kissed Aida on the forehead once more before grabbing the handle on the door. "Will I see you again?" he asked as he looked into her luminescent eyes.

"Only if you see to it." He gave her a smile as he slowly opened the door and began to inch down the hall. Aida shut the door softly as she leaned herself up against the closed door. "That's what it feels like to be free," she said as she looked up and smiled.

David arrived in the courtyard to see many of the soldiers passed out on the ground. He leaned his back up against a pillar as he began to gaze up at the stars in the sky. "God, thank you for giving me the chance to see something so beautiful," he said as he closed his eyes and prayed.

Part 4: Let the Battle Begin

"Push!" The general yelled as soldiers continued to push large carriages full of horses. Sweat trickled down David's face as he strained mightily. "Push!" The soldiers gave another burst of energy causing each carriage to push forward several more feet.

Cling. Clang. Swords began to clash as David and Jon continued to sword fight. Jon cast his sword horizontally at David only to have David dodge it and kick the back of Jon's knee. Jon collapsed to a kneeling position as David placed his sword against his throat. "You got me again." Jon said as he stood up and prepared for another round. Their swords began to click once more as their shaking arms dripped with muddy sweat.

Bags full of sand were thrust into the air, exploding from the ripples of speeding arrows. David and Jon stood on platforms as they quickly pulled out arrows and began to shoot the flying bags. They shot at the large red targets painted on the floating sacks as they continued to aim with precision. David's strong fingers pulled back on the bow as he closed his left eye for better accuracy. His breathing was rhythmic with each shot as the arrows continued to burst the sacks full of sand. "Good aim, soldiers," a man critiqued as David and Jon shook hands and hit shoulders in excitement

Thump. Thump. Thump. The soldiers' marching had gone on for two days as each pulled with him a large knapsack filled with food and water. David's legs ached as he strove to push himself up the final large hill. He soon saw the outreaching valley as they reached the top. "All right men," the general said as he came to a sudden halt. "We camp here." The soldiers slowly began to unpack their bags and prepare their rations. Each soldier pulled off his boots and began to set up his camp. As everyone began to eat, David quickly finished and retired to his bedroll. As he lay down, David closed his eyes and thought about his last encounter with Aida. A smile came on his face as he replayed the memory of dancing and kissing her. He soon felt himself fall fast asleep.

"Get up, men!" the general yelled as the sun began to peek over the horizon. David opened his eyes and prepared to put on his boots for marching. "We must continue to train," the general bellowed as the men prepared to trudge down the path. He then began to lead yet another march as the soldiers followed closely behind. David and Jon trudged next to each other as David walked in a daze. Jon looked over at David to see him smiling and looking at the sky.

"Still thinking of Aida?" he whispered quietly.

David looked over at Jon and gave him an innocent nod. "I pray to God that I may see her again," David whispered back as they continued to march down the long dirt road.

After many miles, the soldiers soon arrived back home to the kingdom. The general then released them to their tents as they trudged toward their beds. Several hours passed until night came. As the soldiers continued to sleep, David grabbed his bow and arrow and began to sneak out of the tent. He ran smack into Jon.

"David," Jon whispered, "where are you going?"

David gave a smile and looked toward the castle. "I'll be back soon," David said as he lightly punched Jon's arm. "I must see her one more time before we leave for battle." Jon nodded his head in understanding.

"Go, my friend. Do what you must, for tomorrow we begin our march." David grasped Jon's inner forearm as he put his arm around Jon's back.

"Brothers in arms," David said as their shoulders came in contact.

"Brothers in arms," Jon replied before returning to his tent.

Above on the balcony Aida overlooked the courtyard as she gazed out over the vast field. Suddenly, she saw an arrow with a long rope penetrate the brick wall next to her. She jumped back in surprise until she looked down to see David climbing up the rope. After several moments, David hopped onto her balcony and looked at her with a big smile. "Aida," he said as he took a step closer. Aida jumped onto him unexpectedly with her arms wrapping around David's strong shoulders.

"I'm so happy to see you again!" she said, closing her eyes and resting her head against his neck. David squeezed her tightly as he closed his eyes and felt her warm body push up against his.

"I go to war tomorrow," he whispered in her ear. "I wanted to see you one last time before I leave." Her radiant eyes looked into his as he leaned in for a kiss. Their lips slowly touched as David's heart began to beat even faster. Their lips soon let go as he began to turn back toward the rope. "I must go," David said as he prepared to propel down.

"Wait!" Aida said as she grabbed his arm. "Promise me you'll be back?" She looked deep into his eyes.

"I promise," he said as he leaned his forehead against hers. "I promise." He slowly kissed Aida's forehead and jumped on the rope. He began to propel himself down as Aida waved goodbye.

As the sun began to rise, the soldiers' heels clicked against the winding dirt road. They continued to march carrying their heavy weaponry and armor. Hours went by as the men continued to trudge through the scorching heat. The sun began to slowly fall as the soldiers continued to strain through the long march. "Halt!" the general yelled as they saw the tall stone castle in the distance. "Rest up, for in the morning we begin our battle." The general lay his weapon down as the men began to settle. The soldiers began to spread apart as they pulled out their bedrolls and prepared to sleep.

"Are you ready for tomorrow, brother?" David asked as he lay down on his bedroll and looked over at Jon.

"Yes. We should pray for God to be with us." David nodded as he faced Jon and grabbed his inner forearm.

"Lord, may you be with us tomorrow and protect us through battle. May we live to glorify you another day. May we be grateful for all the things you have given us in our journies. In God's name . . ."

"Amen," they both said, opening their eyes. David rolled back over into his bed as his heavy eyes slowly began to close.

As the next morning came, the men prepared their weapons and horses as the general prepared to lead them to war. The general stood in front of his army on horseback, pacing back and forth. "Today, we fight for our kingdom." His voice echoed throughout the forest behind. "Today, we protect our families and our future from the threat against this kingdom!" The soldiers began to cheer with their fists held high. "May we fight for God's glory!" The general thrust his sword forward as the soldiers began to march toward the castle. A sea of arrows began to fly in the air as the general and his army continued to march.

"Cover!" the general yelled as the soldiers covered their heads with cross-painted shields. The army continued to make its way down the long grass field as arrows flew into their wooden shields. Suddenly, a catapult shot out an enormous boulder. "Stay in formation!" the general yelled as the rock flew into the ground and crushed part of the advancing army. Arrows continued to fly until the army breached the front gate. "Push!" the general yelled as the soldiers began to bang at the large wooden door.

David and Jon carried a long wooden ladder as they shoved it against the back castle wall. They began to climb as several soldiers followed. "The courtyard should be clear of soldiers," David said to the soldiers following below. "We have to find the throne room." They continued to climb the back wall and hopped up to find the courtyard bare of soldiers. "Let's go," David whispered as he motioned for his soldiers to follow. He unsheathed his sword as he crouched down and silently walked along the enemy walls.

An enemy soldier appeared; David instantly stabbed him through the neck. They then continued to walk into the courtyard. "To the front doors!" David pointed as his men followed close behind. They ran to the door to find it wouldn't open. *Boom!* David kicked the large double doors open causing wood to fly everywhere. Royal guards began to come out as David and Jon quickly rolled to dodge the flying arrows of the enemy archers. David and Jon began to run across the sides of the room, slaying the shooting archers as the royal guards fought the following soldiers. King Erik sat on his throne with heavy gold armor. He then stood from his chair and grabbed his long golden sword.

"You are but mere boys," he sneered as he prepared his fighting stance. Jon ran toward the king only to have the king's sword slice across his chest. Jon flew across the room as the sword slashed across his breastplate. David stepped toward the enemy king, slashing his sword forward only to have it blocked. "Ah, a strong boy you are." The king laughed as he began to throw a wave of attacks toward David. With each strike, David's arm began to shake trying to absorb the heavy blows. David then quickly dropped to his knee and swung toward the king's shins only to have the king jump in the air and slash David across the arm. Blood began to seep through David's armor as he gripped his sword even tighter. The king lunged forward with a heavy thrust as David quickly slid to the side and cut off the king's hands. "Agh!" he groaned as he fell to the ground gushing blood from his severed forearms. David flipped his sword before catching it and cutting off the king's head.

David looked over to see Jon on the ground with a large gash through his chest. Jon began to cough up blood as he lay on the cold brick floor. "Jon?" David ran over and knelt next to him as he placed his hand upon his comrade to feel the deepness of the wound.

"It's alright," Jon said weakly as he held his chest. "We fought a good fight for the Lord." Jon gave a small smile as his eyes began to fade.

"Jon! Don't die on me!" David said, grabbing his shoulders trying to keep him awake.

"I'm going home to the Lord," Jon replied as his breathing began to slow. David looked at his motionless body for several moments before quickly picking up Jon and throwing him over his shoulder. He ran toward the courtyard, passing through the broken twin doors with Jon on his back. As soon as he ran through the doorway, an army of men greeted him with bows and swords. David's lip quivered as he saw the severed head of the general held up high by one of the horsemen. He fell down to his knees, releasing Jon to the cold hard ground in front of him.

He looked at Jon and began to clench his jaw. One of the soldiers got off his horse and walked toward Jon's motionless corpse. He gave the motionless corpse a small kick. The soldier started to laugh before kicking David and forcing him to fall face forward onto the ground. Several other soldiers were brought to the ground next to David as he began to groan in agony. "Brother," he said painfully under his breath as he looked at the lifeless face of his best friend.

Part 5: Time to Escape

David lay silently in his jail cell with his head up against a moist wall. His arm continued to sting as he filled the open wound with wet mud. He looked at his toes as drops of water continued to drip onto his head from the ceiling. "I have to escape," he said quietly as he stood up and leaned against the cold iron bars. He sat back down and closed his eyes, thinking about a way to get out of his prison.

The sound of keys jingling on a chain opened his eyes as a guard began to patrol the room. "Hey you," David quietly whispered. The guard looked over at him and hit the iron cell with the hilt of his sword.

"Shut up, you worthless criminal!" he yelled before turning back around.

"Excuse me, sir." David continued to bang on the cage trying to get his attention.

"Shut up!" he yelled again, slamming his sword against the iron bars of the cage. David was persistent.

"Hey you," David whispered again in a teasing way.

The guard looked back at him, infuriated. "What?" he roared.

"You look really fat in those pants," David whispered as the other prisoners began to laugh.

"That's it!" the guard said as he opened up David's cell. The guard quickly threw the door open and aimed a hard punch at David. David quickly grabbed his arm and thrust him into the iron bars. As the guard groaned dazedly, David held his palm over the guard's nose and mouth, waiting for him to slowly quit breathing. He felt the guard's body become motionless. He quickly began to disrobe the man to steal his uniform.

"Let us out. Please!" several voices whispered as David held the keys in his hands. David nodded his head and began to unlock each of the prisoners' cages.

"Follow me," he said as he clenched his sword and began to sneak up a set of stairs. Several other soldiers began to rush toward David as he approached the top. He slew each one quickly, holding his sword with both hands and striking with violent force. David pointed to the following prisoners to grab the enemies' swords. David sheathed his sword as he picked up a bow and quiver full of arrows. "Pick up all you can find. I need two people who can shoot a bow behind me." Two prisoners stepped up as David searched through the room for two more bows. He opened a chest to find several bows and arrows at the bottom. "Take these." He tossed the bows at the two prisoners as they quickly caught them with their dirt-covered hands. He handed them both a quiver full of arrows and placed his hands on their shoulders. "I need you to follow me and shoot any soldiers that come in our path," David said as he indicated to both of them to follow directly behind him and motioned for the other soldiers to proceed as well.

David and the prisoners ran up several more stairs before appearing in the courtyard of the kingdom. "We must find the stable," he whispered as they began to crouch alongside one of the brick walls. "Go!" David yelled as the prisoners ran toward the double doors leading into the lower castle. David and the two prisoners prepared their bows as several soldiers stood watch on the upper deck of the courtyard walls.

"The prisoners are esc—" An arrow flew through the soldier's heart before he could finish his words. Enemy soldiers began to arm themselves with bows as David and his two bowmen began to shoot the arising archers. They then ran through the double doors with the prisoners behind them and continued to shoot down the enemy. They soon approached a large set of gray-bricked stairs and ran down as the prisoners continued to run through the lower city.

"To the right!" David yelled as they approached several soldiers preparing to attack. David and the two bowmen began to shoot the enemy soldiers while they ran toward the prisoners. "Run!" he yelled as the soldiers began to come closer. One prisoner kicked open the door to the stable as others began to quickly jump on horses. Just as David and the two bowmen ran through the door an arrow pierced the back of one of his bowmen. David quickly turned back and helped pick up the bowman just to receive an arrow into his right shoulder. He groaned with pain as he quickly put the bowman on his shoulder and ran over to a remaining horse.

Dust began to kick up in the air as the prisoners burst out of the stable. David threw the bowman over a horse and jumped on. *Schwuuf!* An arrow flew across his face as he began to hit the side of his horse and grab the reins. The horse quickly galloped out of the stable as arrows flew at David and the prisoners. The half-broken wooden door leading out of the castle came nearer as the men continued to race toward the exit. "Stop them!" one soldier yelled as the enemy soldiers ran into their barracks and grabbed bows.

David soon felt his horse's feet pounding against the green grass of the open field. He looked back at the kingdom one last time as he took a deep breath. He watched as the immense brick fortress became smaller and smaller. He closed his eyes then looked forward trying to move past the death of his best friend Jon.

Part 6: The Knight

The throne room was filled with cheering townspeople as King Kenton stood over David. The king reached out his hand to grasp a thin gold sword brought in by a servant. He held the sword high for all to see as David lowered his head and rested on one knee. "I name thee Knight of Tuscania," he said as he tapped David's right shoulder and then his left. The crowd cheered loudly as David stood up. The king wrapped his arms around David and then grabbed his arm and held it high. The crowd continued to cheer as the king looked back at David. "You have defeated King Erik and have brought the prisoners of war back to us." He placed his hand on David's bicep, grasping it tightly. "You have fought valiantly. As Knight of Tucsania, you will have the duty of being my personal guard." David nodded his head in honor as he looked into the king's eyes.

"I will do all I can to protect you and your family," David said as his eyes turned to Aida. She gave him a quick smile as he looked back out at the cheering crowd.

As the ceremony ended, a servant brought David through the hall to a closed door. David slowly opened the door to his new room in the kingdom as he looked around in admiration. "Thank you," he said to the servant. The servant gave him a quick nod before walking off. He walked toward two wooden doors revealing a balcony. He looked out to see a large oak tree standing nearby his window. David smiled as he turned his head to see the beautiful princess standing on her balcony looking at the sun beginning to set. "Aida," he said as he pressed his hands against the railing. She turned to him with her gleaming white smile and placed her hands on the railing facing him. "I fulfilled my promise," he said with a smile. "I made it back to see you."

A smile came on her face as she closed her eyes and took a deep breath. "I was so happy to see you made it back." She leaned against the castle wall. "I prayed that I would be able to see you again." David's heart began to skip several beats as he watched her open her shining eyes. "I want to hear to about your wondrous adventures," she said as she put her elbows on the ledge and looked into David's eyes.

David shied away as he thought about the loss of his best friend. "My stories are full of agony and pain." He looked away at the sun beginning to fall behind the mountain.

"David," Aida said in a comforting voice, "stories may be filled with agony, but that doesn't mean they don't always have happy endings."

He gazed back at her, enthralled by her response. "A story wouldn't be a story if it didn't have any pain or agony would it?" David looked at her with a half-smile.

"Well. I'll have to find a way to give my stories happy endings."

As David stayed in the kingdom, he began to spend a great amount of time with Aida. David and Aida became very fond of each other. As David watched over the king, he would retire to his room every night and talk with Aida across the balcony. He would tell her stories of the many battles he faced and stories of when he was a little boy in his village.

Aida would listen carefully, closing her eyes and imagining every detail of the places he had been. Each night, Aida would sing beautiful songs as David rested his head against the brick wall of the castle. Her voice was calming and beautiful as David would close his eyes and relax his tired body. Through their many nights together, David and Aida began to form a friendship. David looked forward to each night when he would be able to talk with Aida. Aida began to open up to David and sing him different songs she had been practicing throughout the day. She would sing songs she had learned from the temple. He loved the way she would sing hymns of the Lord as her songs began to help him fall asleep.

One night as the moon shined bright throughout the sky, Aida continued to sing a beautiful hymn. "You are more and more beautiful to me every day," David said right after she had finished singing.

She smiled at him and began to look up in the sky. "David?" she asked as she continued to look up at the stars.

"Yes, Aida?"

"Do you think there's a happy ending with us?" she peered over at David, looking at him with her luminous eyes.

"Why of course," David said gently as he looked over at her growing smile. "I'm going to take your hand, and we're going to escape on a real adventure." He tried to imagine how such an adventure would play out. Aida jumped up and down trying to hold in her excitement.

"Let's run away together, David," she said as she looked over at him. "Let's make our own happy ending."

David looked at her for several seconds before his smile began to disappear. "I'm sorry, Aida," he said as he began to come to his own realization. "I can't escape with you." He looked away trying to not see the upset in Aida's eyes.

Aida looked down as she sat down against the wall of the castle. "I understand," she said quietly. "I guess I'll just be trapped here forever."

Boom! Boom! Suddenly several hard crashes were heard against Aida's door. David looked at Aida before grabbing his sword and bursting out into the hall. Several royal guards lay on the floor as men dressed in black stood at the door. "Assassins," David said under his breath as they looked at him and prepared to attack. They began to run toward David as he jabbed his sword forward. The assassin jumped over his head as David kicked at the enemy's chest. The assassin flew back as David ran toward the second assassin trying to open the door. He thrust his sword forward as the assassin quickly fell back and rolled across the floor.

The assassin threw a dagger at David, just to have the dagger brush passed his shoulder. "Aida!" David yelled as the assassin ran toward David. The door flew into the assassin's face as Aida stood in the middle of the doorway. She looked over to see the assassin on the ground as David ran over and drove his sword in his chest. "Perfect timing!" he said with a crooked smile. The second assassin began to approach as David motioned for Aida to close the door. Another dagger flew toward David as he hit it away with his sword. The assassin threw another dagger just as David dropped to the ground and threw the dagger that had fallen to the floor. *Zing!* The dagger flew across the air and pierced the chest of the assassin; he fell to the ground, motionless. David opened the door to find Aida up against her dresser. She ran toward David, wrapping her arms around him.

"Aida?" King Kenton called as he appeared around the corner. He came around to find Aida in David's arms. David let go as the king began to approach.

"It's alright, Your Highness," David said as he bowed his head. "I defeated the assassins." Aida ran toward King Kenton and wrapped her arms around her father.

"Thank you, David," he said, holding his daughter tight. "You have fought valiantly once again." The king saw David looked toward Aida and the smile she gave him in return. David bowed his head once more before he retired to his room. The king kissed Aida on her forehead and pulled her tight toward him. "I'm so happy to know you're alright," he said. "I will have more guards on watch immediately." He slowly closed the door as Aida lay down in her bed and thought about how David had bravely saved her. As she pondered it more, her heart began to throb as she thought about how they could never be together.

The next couple of days, David began to patrol the kingdom at night making sure it was safe for the king and the princess. As he walked across the upper deck of the courtyard, he looked out over the castle walls and the far green fields. He imagined running away with Aida. He then thought about the other night and how that could never happen because of who he was, a lowly soldier. David's heart hurt as he thought about how much he had fallen for Aida and her beautiful voice. He wanted to see her again. He had to see her again.

The night came when David was finally able to see Aida. He went outside to his balcony to find Aida in tears. "Aida, what's wrong?" he asked as she continued to look straight ahead at the big oak tree.

"My father wanted to protect me and has arranged for me to be married to a prince." She looked over at David with tears streaming down her face. "I will have to live in their kingdom away from here." She looked back at the oak tree and began rub her eyes. David pressed himself up against the railing of the balcony facing her.

"What? When are you to leave?"

Aida closed her eyes as more tears began to run down her cheeks. "I am to be taken tomorrow," Aida replied as David clenched his jaw. He sat there quietly as she continued to look out over the balcony.

"You can't leave!" he said, hitting his fist against the balcony railing.

"Why?" she said angrily while looking over at him.

"Because I love you!" he yelled. There was a moment of silence before her lip began to quiver. She then began to shake her head as she quickly opened the door and slammed it behind her. "I love you," he whispered again, knowing she couldn't hear him.

Aida sat on her bed with her back against the headboard. She began to cry with her head between her knees as she thought about leaving the man she had grown so close to, the man she realized she was in love with. Tears continued to fall down her face as she fell asleep, heartbroken by the fact that she might never see David again.

The next morning, Aida prepared herself. She wore a beautiful dress and began to brush her hair. She suddenly heard several knocks on the door. "Be right there." She put the brush down. As she opened the door, she saw David standing there in shining silver armor.

"I need you to come with me," he said as he gently grabbed her hand.

"Where are we going?" she asked as he slowly glided her along.

"Trust me," he said with a smile. The guards waived at the princess as they walked across the hall. David continued to walk her through the courtyard and down the castle steps holding her hand. She clenched his hand tighter as they began to run at a faster pace. A horse appeared at the bottom of the steps as David stopped beside it. "Get on!" He lifted her up as she swung her leg over the horse. David quickly hopped on the horse as she wrapped her arms around his waist. They then began to gallop through the lower city.

A smile came on her face as she asked once more, "Where are we going, David?" David continued to hold the reins before turning his head over his shoulder. "I'm taking you on an adventure!" he said with a smile

She grabbed his waist tighter as they began to gallop faster and faster toward a large wooden gate. As they approached the gate to leave, the king's men all began to appear, blocking them from leaving. "Stop!" a loud voice yelled as David came to a sudden halt and turned his horse around. King Kenton trotted down with his big white horse resting his hand on the hilt of his sheathed sword. "Where do you think you're going?" the king said with a stern voice.

David closed his eyes and took a deep breath. "Your Honor, I'm giving Aida a happy ending. I will protect her till the day I die. I will make her the happiest woman in all the land. Your highness, I love Aida with all my heart. Truly, you must understand."

The king lifted his head high as he glared into David's eyes. He then clenched his jaw and looked over at Aida. He saw Aida pull herself closer to David as she rested her head on David's strong shoulder. There was a long moment of silence as the men pointed their arrows directly at David's neck.

The king looked up once more and then back at David. "Open the gates," he said just loud enough for the guards to hear. David watched as the large wooden gates began to open. He looked back at the king as the king gave him one last nod. David nodded back before turning his horse around and slowly trotting past the moving soldiers. "May God be with the both of you," he called out as David began to gallop out of the gate.

The horse's hooves began to pound against the green grass of the open field once more. "Where are we going now?" Aida asked softly.

"We're going on an adventure, for our journey has just begun." He grabbed her hand on his waist and turned his head back. "Time to make our own happy ending." The horse continued to gallop into the horizon, and the knight and the princess . . .

CHAPTER 4

BACK TO REALITY

". . . Lived happily ever after." I closed the laptop and looked over at Aida's smile. She looked over at me with adoration as she kissed me on the cheek.

"That story was amazing," she said as she tightened her grasp around my hand and looked into my eyes. "But not nearly as amazing as our story." I gave her a smile before gently grabbing her cheek and giving her a light kiss on the lips. As our lips parted, I pushed my forehead against hers and gave her one more smile before slowly pulling myself up from the hospital bed.

"I will let you rest," I said as she wiggled her head deeper into her pillow. Aida's eyes began to look heavy as she tried to keep them open. "Goodnight, Aida. I love you."

"Forever and always?" she asked as her eyes opened once more awaiting my answer.

"Forever and always," I replied as I turned out the light. All the way home I continued to think about Aida's adoring smile and how much I had enjoyed reading to her. It still hurt knowing she wouldn't be coming home with me that night.

As the next morning came, I parked in my usual spot at the school and prepared to grab my things. "Good morning, Mr.

Benelli!" a student yelled as I began to grab my briefcase from the back seat.

"Good morning, William." I said with a half-smile. I then made my way to the office and walked in to see Nancy sitting at her desk.

"Good morning, Mr. Benelli," she said gently with her usual smile.

I tried to give her the best smile I could. "Good morning, Nancy," I said quietly, giving her a quick wave and continuing to hurry through.

As I arrived at my classroom, I sat in my chair with my head back looking up at the ceiling. I continued think about Aida as the classroom began to fill up with students. "Alright, class," I said as I stood up and gathered their attention. "Before we start, I want to give a lesson on the importance of imagination." The class watched me as I walked toward the front of the room. "I have noticed many of you have begun to release your imagination through your stories." I picked up a stack of graded papers and plopped them down on my front desk. "Imagination is more important than simply stories. You see, imagination can even be more powerful than knowledge, for knowledge is what's known while imagination is the exploration of the unknown. Imagination is what fuels creativity." I looked around at the students as I felt their full attention. "Keep exploring in your writing," I said with a smile. "Go places you've never gone. Explore worlds you have only imagined." I slowly leaned against a desk as I motioned for the class to get out of their seats. "Now come up and get your papers." The class quickly began to get up out of their seats and stampede my front desk. They all began to gather around the front desk, reaching in and looking through the stack of papers. "After you grab your paper, please sit down and share your story with a partner in the class!" I yelled as the students finally began to walk back to their seats. I sat down and monitored each student as he or she sat and spoke with their partners.

I walked around each desk listening to the room fill with vibrant chatter of different stories and themes. Some students acted out scenes from their story as others watched. I stood by one student as she began to read a heartfelt story she had wrote.

"I was a warrior. I had survived. Although I had faced the hardships of a broken home, I had found another among the city of elves." A smile came on her face as she finished her story. Several of us began to clap.

I gently put my hand lightly on her shoulder and began to whisper words of encouragement. "Thank you for sharing your story, Kayla. You are very brave. I have seen that you are the warrior of your own story."

"Thank you, Mr. Benelli. Thank you for helping me with my story." I gave her a pat on the back.

"Keep writing. Keep being the hero of your story."

After listening to several more stories, I heard the bell ring for lunch. The students began to rush out the door as I grabbed my briefcase and followed them out toward the teacher's lounge. I opened the door to see Mr. Lite saving a seat for me at one of the large round tables.

"Mr. Benelli!" he called across the room. I gave him a nod as I got in line waiting for food. After I got my tray, I quickly sat down in the chair beside Mr. Lite.

"Grilled cheese and tomato soup is my favorite," he said with a chuckle as he adjusted his glasses. I gave him a half-smile as I dipped my grilled cheese into the tomato soup and took a bite. "So how is your wife?" he asked as he gave me a concerned look.

"She's going to be in the hospital longer than she was last time," I said, trying to act positive.

He nodded as he put his hand on my shoulder. "It'll be alright, Dave. Just keep praying."

I nodded. "That reminds me. I wrote another story." I pulled out a stack of papers from my briefcase and placed it on the table. "I wrote this for her." I slid it over to Mr. Lite as his eyes lit up.

"I'm excited to read it!" he said. "I really enjoyed your last one."

"Writing is what keeps me going right now," I said as I continued to slowly eat my food. Mr. Lite gave a strong nod as he picked up the papers and began to read.

After lunch, I taught for several more periods. As school ended, I sat at my desk and continued to grade papers and prepare my lesson plan. After several hours, I leaned back in my chair and looked at all the papers on my desk. I looked over at the clock to see it was finally 5:00 P.M. I took one deep breath before getting out of my chair and packing up my briefcase. After I gathered all my things, I quickly ran out the door and down to my car in the parking lot. "Time to see Aida!" I said aloud as I opened the door and got in.

As I arrived at my parents' house, I got out of my car to see Aaron and my parents waiting for me outside.

"Dad!" Aaron yelled as he ran over to me and jumped into my arms.

"Hey, champ. You ready to see Mommy?" I said gently as I picked him up and hugged him tightly. He nodded excitedly as I put him down. He then opened the door to the back seat and crawled in. "Thank you, Mom and Dad, for watching him," I said as I wrapped my arms around the both of them. As I let go, I turned toward my mother as she held onto my arm.

"It's alright, son," my mom said as she looked into my tired eyes. "Stay strong. We love you." She softly patted my cheek before letting me go.

"I love you both, too," I said valiantly. As I got in the car, I looked back to make sure Aaron had properly strapped himself in. "You ready, buddy?" I asked as we pulled out of the driveway.

"Time to see Momma!" he said loudly. I grinned at his enthusiasm as I started the car and began our drive to the hospital.

"Momma?" Aaron said softly as he walked in. Aida's eyes remained closed as we continued to approach her. I grabbed Aaron's hand as we came closer to her bed.

"Aaron?" she said, barely able to tilt up her head. Her skin was very pale as she tried to lift her weak arm up toward Aaron. I lifted up Aaron and placed him on the side of her bed. He leaned in and kissed her on the forehead. She tried to open her eyes, but they quickly closed again as her breathing continued to slow. I grabbed her hand to feel the weak grasp of her fingers.

"Is Momma okay?" Aaron asked, looking at me with teary eyes.

"She's alright. She's just very tired," I said as I picked him up.

Her pale body was motionless as Aaron sat on my lap looking at his frail mother resting. It was very quiet in the room as we continued to sit by Aida. She lay peacefully with her arms by her sides and her eyes quietly closed. She wasn't wearing her bandana, so her white bald head sank into the flower decorated pillow.

My mother knocked on the door and slowly walked in to see us quietly sitting by Aida. "How is she?" my mother whispered, trying not to disturb Aida. I pulled my lips in unable to answer.

"Dr. Hopkins should be coming in any minute now," I finally replied as I put Aaron down. My mother grabbed Aaron's hand as I nodded for her to take him out. I sat next to the bed for several more moments until I heard a light knock at the door.

"Can I come in?" a voice asked. Soon the door opened revealing Dr. Hopkins carrying a clipboard. He sat down in a chair with wheels and rolled his chair over to me. "Mr. Benelli, we have some unfortunate news." His tone was very serious.

"What is it, Doctor?" I asked as he continued to look up at me.

"Your wife's cancer is spreading and has entered into stage III cancer." Dr. Hopkins put his hand on my shoulder. "We're doing all we can."

I felt my stomach drop to the floor while daggers of pain stabbing my insides overcame me. I began to breathe heavily as I looked over at Aida. I clenched my jaw and turned my head trying to gain strength to say something.

"Thank you, Doctor," I said, barely able to speak. Dr. Hopkins gently patted my arm before standing up and walking out the door. I grabbed Aida's hand and began to bow my head. "Dear God, please be with Aida and our family through this hard time. Send your love and peace upon us." I looked at her resting face. "In Jesus's name, amen."

I left the room to find my mother and Aaron sitting in the waiting area. My mother took one look at my face before realizing what had happened. She wrapped her arms around me as Aaron tugged at my leg. "Dad? Is everything okay?"

I knelt down on my knee and softly wrapped my arms around him. "Everything's alright. Mommy is going to be just fine. We just need to keep praying for her." Aaron's lip began to quiver as he closed his eyes and bowed his head. I closed my eyes and pressed my forehead against his.

"Dear God, I pray that Mommy is all better and . . . and that she can come home, in Jesus's name, amen." Tears rolled down his cheek as I picked him up and put him over my shoulder.

"Time to go home, champ," I said as we kissed my mother goodbye. We walked over to the car as I opened the door and helped Aaron climb in. The pain in my stomach still raged as I got into the driver's seat and tightened my hands around the steering wheel with all my might. I clenched my jaw and began to breathe slowly. I exhaled one last time before starting the engine and beginning my journey home. As we arrived home, I prepared dinner for Aaron and silently ate with him at the table. After we ate, I gently tucked him in as we said one more prayer together. Then I pulled up his blanket and gave him a kiss goodnight.

"Mr. White? Is Mrs. White with you?" I held my phone close to my ear as I leaned against my kitchen wall.

"Yes, David. What's wrong? Is everything okay?" Mr. White said through the phone. There was a moment of silence as I tried to come up with the right way to tell them the news.

"The doctor told me Aida's cancer is spreading. She now has stage III cancer." As soon as the words left my mouth, my lip began to quiver. The other end of the phone was silent for several moments as I awaited the reaction.

"We'll be flying down," her father said, trying to show strength in his voice. The sound of crying was heard in the background as the pain in my stomach continued to wail at me.

"Kenton and Theresa, you can stay with me again if you need to. I'll need some help with Aaron anyway." The phone was quiet as Mr. White consoled his crying wife.

"Thank you. I'll book a flight as soon as I can," Mr. White replied.

I opened the door and peeked into Aaron's room.

"Aaron will be happy to see his other grandparents," I said as I slowly closed Aaron's door.

CHAPTER 5

WRITE AWAY

My eyes slowly opened as I leaned up in my bed. I looked over to see Aaron lying silently next to me. I softly rubbed his head before getting up and standing at the window. I looked out at the dark sky as I pressed my hands against the windowsill. I took several breaths trying to release the constant pain of my churning stomach. I closed my eyes trying to think of Aida and how she must feel in that hospital bed all alone. I sat down on my bed and looked up to the ceiling as I tried to close my eyes. Another sleepless night.

Aaron rolled over as I watched him peacefully rest. He was too upset to sleep alone and had come into my room the last couple of nights. I got up from my bed and walked into the hallway toward my office. My laptop lay open on my desk. I looked at the dark screen before finally turning on the blinding light and beginning to type. I closed my eyes as my hands typed away. I began to write another story.

Aida was constantly on my mind as a smile finally came across my face. I could see every detail in my mind's eye as if it were really happening and imagined Aida's smiling face. I continued to type rapidly as I frequently stopped and thought about what this story would bring. My mind was so focused that many hours passed. I realized I needed sleep for work the next morning.

I slowly closed my laptop and walked back over to my bedroom. I lay my head on my pillow as I continued to imagine the new story I was going to present to Aida. My stomach churned once more as I thought about news of her cancer, but the pain eased as I imagined writing her another story and lying with her as I read it. I felt my eyes soon become heavy as I finally drifted off to sleep.

My eyes opened to the soft light of the rising sun shining through the window. "Time to get up, champ." I nudged Aaron as he began to stretch out and roll over. I got up from the bed and walked over to the sink. I splashed my face with warm water and looked into the mirror. A beard had begun to cover my face. My scraggly hair needed combing.

I rubbed my eyes before nudging Aaron again. "Come on, champ. Time to get up." He opened his eyes and slowly began to get out of bed. I picked out clothes for him and set them down before making my way to the kitchen.

I opened the cupboard and grabbed a box of Cookie Crisp cereal as I began to heat up some water. Aaron came in all dressed as he slumped into his chair. "Here you go, champ, your favorite!" I gave him a half smile as I put a bowl of cereal in front of him. I sat down next to him as we quietly ate our breakfast. "You want to watch some cartoons?" I asked as Aaron as he slowly put cereal in his mouth. His head looked down as he shook his head.

The doorbell rang as I grabbed his hand and walked him to the door. I opened the door to find my mother waiting outside. "Hey, Aaron!" she said as she knelt down and gave him a hug.

"Thank you for taking care of him." I gave her a hug. "Aida's parents should be down tomorrow to help take care of Aaron while I'm gone." She gave me a nod of understanding as I knelt down and kissed Aaron on the head. "I love you, son," I said as I wrapped my arms around him. His little arms squeezed me tight as I felt a tear roll down his cheek.

"I love you too, Dad."

As I arrived at the school, I tried to make it seem like everything was just fine. After every period, I would pull out my laptop and type more and more on of the story. A smile would creep on my face as I imagined Aida and her excitement when I surprised her with another story.

As lunch approached, I stayed in my classroom continuing to write the story. Time flew by as I waited to get off work and see Aida. As the clock hit 5:00 P.M., I got out of my chair and grabbed my briefcase. I waved goodbye to several teachers as I walked through campus toward my car.

"David!" Aida greeted me when I walked into her room. My face lit up as I saw a big smile come on her face.

"Hey, baby," I said softly as I grabbed her hand and softly kissed her lips.

"I'm feeling much better today," she said as she placed her palm on my cheek and looked into my eyes.

I held her hand as I took in the wonderful moment of being so close to her. "Aida, you look more and more beautiful every day." I said with a big smile.

She began to giggle as she sat up even more in her hospital bed. "And you are growing out the beard, I see." She began to slide her fingers across my face. "Are you getting enough sleep?" She looked at me worriedly.

"I'm writing you another story."

Her face lit up. She leaned over to the side of her bed as she picked up a small set of papers. "I've been reading the last story you wrote me every night." She grinned.

I gave her a smile as I pulled up a chair and sat next to her bed. "Your parents will be here tomorrow."

Aida knew why they were coming. Nonetheless, she said excitedly, "I can't wait to see them. Are they staying in our extra room?"

"Of course! They're staying there to help with Aaron."

She looked off into the distance. She tried to hold the smile as her eyes began to water. "Is he okay?"

"Yeah," I said, looking into her eyes. "He took your place in our bed."

"Ah," she said sadly. "Well, you tell him Mommy loves him."

"I do, every night after we pray."

Aida closed her eyes as she leaned her head back. "I'm so happy God gave me an amazing husband like you." She opened her eyes and looked at me.

A big smile came on my face as I leaned closer to her. "I'm so happy God blessed me with an amazing woman like you." Her eyes began to water again as she wrapped her arms around me and kissed my neck. "I love you, baby," I whispered into her ear.

"I love you, too." She squeezed a little tighter.

"Forever and always?" I asked, leaning my forehead against hers.

"Forever and always," she replied, looking into my eyes.

The next morning, I sat down at home waiting for the doorbell to ring. When it did I quickly got up as Aaron ran to the door. "Dad, they're here! They're here!" he yelled.

"Kenton and Theresa! Please come in!" I grabbed Mrs. White's luggage as she walked through the door.

"Kenton! Make sure you bring my other suitcase!" she yelled as she walked into the door. "Oh sweetie, it's so nice to see you." She wrapped her arms around me and gave me a kiss on each cheek.

"Nice to see you Mrs. White," I said with a smile as Mr. White followed slowly behind. "Mr. White," I said, holding out my hand. He grabbed my hand as we closed in for a hug. "I'm so happy you guys made it. How is the weather in Ohio?" Mrs. White continued to kiss Aaron on both cheeks and wrapped her arms around him.

"It's very nice this time of year." She let go of Aaron and looked at him up and down. "When did you get so big?"

"I'm almost four!" Aaron said as Mrs. White patted him on the head. "Grandpa!" Aaron said as he jumped up in his arms. Mr. White picked up Aaron and pretended to steal his nose.

"Where'd it go?" he said jokingly as Aaron slapped his hand.

"You don't really have my nose, Grandpa!" Aaron replied playfully. We all began to laugh as I gathered up their luggage.

"Thank you guys for coming." I led them down the hallway. "Here's your room. Make yourselves at home." They both gave me smiles as I took Aaron and walked back over to the kitchen. "You excited to see Mommy today?" I asked Aaron as we sat at the table.

"Yeah!" He hopped up in his chair.

Aaron and I continued to talk at the table as we waited for Mr. and Mrs. White. As soon as they finished unpacking, we all got in the car and prepared to see Aida.

"Aaron's all strapped up!" Mrs. White said as she tugged at the straps on his car seat. I started the car and began to make my way back to the hospital. As soon as we arrived, we quickly checked in with the front and walked toward Aida's room.

"Mom! Dad!" Aida said as a big smile came on her face. Mr. and Mrs. White each came over and kissed her forehead.

"We're so happy to see you, honey." They stood close to the bed. We all sat and talked together as Aida began to laugh at the stories her parents were telling.

"Yeah, our life is pretty simple up in Ohio," Mrs. White told Aida as she poured a cup of water. "Your father's church is doing very well. He still counsels the pastor and makes sure everything is running smoothly."

"The job of a pastor is a lifelong commitment," Mr. White said jokingly as he reached into his bag. He slowly pulled out a Bible and put it on her counter. "David said we should bring this. It's your Bible from back home."

"Thank you, Daddy." She leaned over and ran her hands across the cover.

"Mr. White, I was hoping you could lead us in prayer," I said as I put my hand on his shoulder.

"It'd be my honor!" He grabbed my hand as well as his wife's. Mrs. White continued to hold Aaron on her lap as she grabbed Aida's hand. "Dear Lord," he started, "Thank you for the wonderful fellowship today and the gift of having my beautiful daughter Aida with us. I pray that you may take care of her and be with her through this hard time. Lord, I know the plans you have for us are not to hurt us but to give us hope and a future. Help us understand your will and your plan for us. We love you. In Jesus's name . . ."

"Amen!" we all chimed in. We opened our eyes as Aida gave a hopeful smile to her father.

"I know He's with me through all this," she said. Her calm composure made me feel at ease as I watched her continue to demonstrate a positive attitude.

"That's my girl." Her father said. Mr. White soon began to stretch out his arms as he looked over at Mrs. White. "Well, we're going to get some rest," he said as he picked up Aaron and helped Mrs. White out of her chair. He gave me a nod as he made his way to the door. "I'll come pick you up after you're done, and we'll go get dinner." I gave Aaron and Mr. White a hug as they walked out the door. I kissed Mrs. White on the cheek as she looked at me with a smile.

"She's going to love it," she said as she patted my cheek and walked out the door.

"I'm going to love what?" Aida said as soon as Mrs. White walked out the door.

"I have a surprise for you," I said as I sat down in the chair next to her bed. I pulled out a stack of papers and placed it on my lap. She smiled as she clapped her hands in excitement.

"Another story!" she said excitedly.

"Yep! I finished last night."

Her smile made it worth all the late nights I had spent typing the story.

"Well, come on!" She began to move her pillows around so she could sit up. "Read me the story!"

I sat back in my chair and began to read the words on the page.

"'Pirates of the Great Sea' by David Catalano."

CHAPTER 6
THE PIRATES OF THE GREAT SEA

Part 1: The Legend of Scylla and Charybdis

"They're gaining on us!" Jon yelled as the men held the ropes to the sails. Rain poured down on the pirates as the ship continued to rock back and forth viciously.

"We have to pass through the Strait of Messina!" David yelled as he began to violently turn the ship's wheel.

"Are you mad?" Jon yelled over the pounding rain. "We'll never make it through in this weather!" The ship began to tilt as it changed course.

"They won't follow us in there!" David yelled over the rain as he continued to steadily hold the wheel. His legs were spread wide as he tried to keep his balance through the heavy rain.

Schhwaff! A large iron bolt flew across the top of the wooden ship. Several more bolts were seen flying from the following ships as the pirates continued to sail through the monstrous storm. "They're firing at us!" Jon yelled as the other men began to hold on tighter. "Captain?" David held steady as he focused the bow of the ship forward.

"Almost there! Stay mid-ship!" David yelled as the wooden ship began to turn into the strait.

"They're turning back!" Jon yelled as the men continued to hold the sails. The ships began to turn away as the men stood silently watching. The men were quiet as the rain continued to pour down on the deck and the sea began to calm. David looked over at his men as they stood calmly holding the ropes waiting for what was to come. Only the sound of rain hitting the deck was heard as the men looked around in fear.

A large rock began to appear on their right as the ship began to pull left. David tried to hug the nearby rock, but the noise of spinning water and lightning soon instilled fear into his men. A raging whirlpool spun beside them, pulling the ship toward it. "Charybdis!" A man yelled as the ship began to tilt into the whirlpool.

"Keep the sails strong!" David yelled as the ship continued to turn slightly. The men held on to the large ropes for dear life as the sail began to flap violently in the strong wind. Suddenly several large waves began to knock the ship toward the whirling whirlpool. Movement was seen behind the nearby rock as even larger waves began to crash against the side of the ship.

"Scylla!" One of the men yelled as a dragon-like head hissed over the large rock. Several more appeared until six hissing heads began to make their way toward the ship.

"Captain?" Jon yelled as the rope continued to lift him up from the ground.

"The legend is true," David said under his breath as the monster swam closer and closer to the wooden ship.

"Captain! We're not going to make it!" Jon yelled as the monsters' heads rose out the water, showing several rows of teeth. The heads began to hiss with snake-like tongues as the pirates continued to pull the ropes.

"Hold on!" David yelled as he spun the wheel toward the ravenous splashing of the whirlpool. The Scylla hissed loudly as its heads went under the water. The men held on for their lives while the ship began to turn sideways.

"Where'd it go?" one of the men yelled as the men began to look around.

"Over there!" Another pirate yelled as red fins began to appear in the sides of the spinning whirlpool walls. A massive red blob followed the ship until it disappeared under the boat.

Hiss! The Scylla's six heads suddenly appeared on both sides of the ship. "Captain! It's here!" Another man yelled as the heads began to show their vicious rows of teeth.

David looked into one of the Scylla's heads as its serpent-like eyes prepared to strike. As it did so, David quickly straightened the wheel and shoved his sword through the wheel into the wooden mass. The wheel was unable to turn as the sword halted the spinning wheel. As the ship began to turn sideways, it immediately lost speed, leaving the Scylla to fly forward. David ran to mid-ship as he grabbed Jon's sword. "What're you doing?" Jon asked as David jumped up on one of the ropes.

"Saving my ship!" David said as he swung his sword underneath his feet, cutting the rope and projecting him forward. He flew across the ship rotating the sail and causing the ship to turn completely sideways. "Hold on!" he yelled as the ship slid into the raging Scylla.

Thump! The Scylla began to hiss viciously as the ship collided into her. As the ship hit the Scylla, it caught the storming wind and flew out onto the calm ocean. The Scylla tried to regain its balance but found itself sucked up into the spinning whirlpool. Twelve webbed feet were seen as the Scylla tried to squirm away from the pulling whirlwind. Its long tail was soon sucked in as the six heads screamed and hissed. The men watched as the Scylla's enormous body disappeared into the deep dark abyss.

As the ship began to settle on the calm water, David let go of the rope and landed back onto the ship. As his black boots hit the wet deck, he immediately somersaulted to his feet. As he stood up, he threw the sword in his hand to the ground and started to wipe off the collected water on his black vest. "Now that's what you call being stuck between a rock and a hard place," he said as the pirates began to cheer.

Jon looked at him with a playful scowl. "Captain, I'm not sure I'd want to go through that again."

David laughed as he walked up the stairs to the upper deck. He pulled out his sword from the wooden mass and sheathed it to his left side.

"Why Jon, this is expected in the life of a pirate." He gave Jon a quick grin as he grasped his hands around the wooden rim of the steering wheel. Jon walked over and picked up his sword as David began to slowly turn the ship.

"Where to now, Captain?" Jon asked as he sheathed his sword and leaned against the wooden railing. David pulled out a cylinder from his side and opened it to reveal a rolled up piece of paper. He eyed the map for several moments.

"We're off to find the White Mare," he replied while quickly rolling up the paper and shoving it back into its cylindrical case. "We sail northwest." He quickly turned the wheel some more as the ship continued to smoothly sail across the calm seas.

Part 2: Aida's Capture

"Aida, are you ready?" a man asked as Aida threw the strap of a brown satchel over her shoulder.

"Yes," Aida replied as she took in a deep breath. She turned around and wrapped her arms tightly around her father. "Will I see you again?"

Her father took a deep breath as he slowly let go and put his hand on her cheek. "Nero's soldiers are coming. I will try and hide, but you must leave Salerno. It is not safe here anymore."

Aida's eyes began to water as she looked behind her at people packing a large wooden ship. "Goodbye, Father. I love you," she said as he wrapped her in a giant bear hug.

"I love you, too." He wiped a tear from her cheek with his thumb before beginning to walk away. "May Christ be with you!" he yelled as he continued to wave goodbye.

Aida stepped onto the wooden walkway to the ship as several men walked by carrying crates full of supplies. She looked around the dock to see men preparing for the long journey ahead. She continued up the walkway until her feet hit the wooden planks of the large boat.

"All aboard!" the captain yelled as bells began to ring. Aida began to hear the sound of a crank pulling up a large chain. She peered over the wooden railing of the ship to see a large anchor being pulled from the deep water. "Set the sails!" the Captain yelled as several men began to pull on ropes. A large white sail began to drop down as the wind began to pull the ship away from the dock.

"We head west to Oblia!" the Captain hollered as he began to turn the large wooden wheel. The ship continued to separate from the dock as people waved goodbye to their families. Aida waved at her father across the increasing gap as the ship began to turn toward the vast sea.

As the wooden ship calmly sailed across the blue ocean, Aida stood with her arms up against the railing looking far off into the sea. "I'm going on an adventure!" she said to herself with a smile. She looked far off into the distance as the sun reflected off the calm blue ocean. She closed her eyes as the wind flew through her long hair. She opened her arms and began to feel the cool breeze of the ocean caress her body.

She soon opened her eyes and thought about her home. She thought about her father and the life she had in Salerno. She thought about how she might never see her home again. Her heart sank as she realized her adventure would mean letting go of the known for the unknown.

The ship continued to sail for two days across the Tyrrhenian Sea. Aida waited in the lower chambers by sitting on a chair and reading a book. She quietly imagined herself in the story as she thought about her new adventure. She closed her eyes and pretended she was swept up by pirates and became a part of their crew. She imagined herself fighting alongside them looking for lost treasure. She began to laugh as she thought about how that could never happen.

Crackle! Suddenly a large hole opened up in the lower chamber as an iron bolt penetrated the wooden wall and exploded in splinters across the room. Aida jumped up as she looked through the large hole to see another wooden ship. *Crackle!* Another iron bolt pierced through the wooden wall as Aida ducked her head. More broken wood exploded into the room as more iron bolts began to pierce through the ship. Aida quickly ran toward the upper cabin as water began to fill up the lower chambers.

As Aida climbed she began to hear sound of pirates boarding the ship. "Agh!" someone yelled as swords began to clink against each other on the main deck. As Aida peered through the cabin window, she saw several men killed by the pirates, who fought with sabers. She watched a pirate with yellow teeth and a feathered hat then began to walk toward the upper cabin door. Aida saw the door handle turn as she pushed herself up against the wall in fear. She quickly grabbed a feathered pen lying on the ground as she waited for the pirate to open the door.

Whoom! The door burst open as the dirty pirate kicked open the door. Aida quickly stabbed the pirate with the feathered pen in his neck causing the man to squeal in agony. She ran out onto the open deck only to run straight into several more pirates. "Now hold on there, missy!" A pirate with a long gray beard began to walk down the upper deck stairs. He held his thin sword over his shoulder as Aida fell to the wooden deck. She began to back herself up against the wooden railing of the ship as the gray bearded man stood tall in front of her. He coursed his hand through one of the braids on his long beard as he examined Aida. "Looks like what we have here is a nice treat, boys!" The men began to cheer loudly as the gray bearded man motioned for another pirate to take her.

"You're coming with us," the pirate said as he went to grab her. Aida quickly kicked him in the shin as she got up and tried to run. Another pirate quickly caught her and threw her over his shoulder while she kicked and screamed.

"Let me go!" she yelled as the pirate threw her on the other boat and jumped aboard.

"Are we all loaded up?" the pirate with the gray beard asked as they began to pull away from the sinking boat.

"Yes, Cap'n Graybeard," one pirate replied, giving a quick salute. Captain Graybeard began to grin, revealing a set of rotten yellow teeth. He quickly grabbed another pirate's arm and looked over at Aida.

"Bring her to me," he hissed as the pirate went over and pulled Aida to her feet.

Aida began to struggle as the pirate dragged her unwillingly over to the captain. She stopped struggling once she saw the captain's dark eyes look into hers. He ran his dirty black hands across her face as he began to smell her hair. He took one long sniff before licking his teeth. "We sure found ourselves a beauty," he said as the other pirates began to laugh. Aida smelled his pungent breath; her eyes began to water from the scent. "Take her to the prison cell," he continued as he raised his upper lip once more showing off his yellow teeth. He began to bite his lower lip as the other pirate dragged her down to the lower chamber of the ship.

Slam! "Stay in there!" he yelled after he locked the barred iron door. Aida sat in the corner holding her satchel as her lip began to quiver. She felt afraid as the moist air from the musty cell began to make her sick. She laid her head against the iron cage and closed her eyes. She started to pray. *What on earth will happen now?* She thought fearfully.

Part 3: Saved by a Pirate

As David stood at the helm, he continued to navigate the ship across the calm sea. "Captain?" a man yelled from the eagle's nest.

"What is it?" David yelled, looking up.

The man continued to peer through a small telescope. "We're approaching another ship!" he yelled.

David tilted his head back in thought. "What kind of ship?" David asked.

"A pirate ship." David's eyes widened as he pulled out a telescope from his belt. He walked over and placed his right foot on the wooden railing. He extended his telescope and peeked through the tiny lens. A small smile came on his face as he quickly shut his telescope and tucked it in his belt.

"Jon!" David yelled as Jon opened the cabin door.

"What is it, Captain?" Jon asked as he peeked his head out the cabin door.

"Man the ballistae. There are pirates ahead."

Jon adjusted his glasses and gave a salute. "Aye aye, Captain!" Jon quickly shut the door and ran down into the lower chambers. "Man the ballistae!" he yelled.

David quickly turned the wheel as he maneuvered the ship toward the pirates. Suddenly the large pirate ship in the distance began to turn toward them. *Schhwaff!* Iron bolts began to fly through the air as they splashed into the water. David continued to maneuver the ship around as more bolts began to fly through the sky. The ships continued to close in on each other as David patiently waited to give the signal.

"We're within range!" David yelled as the ship neared the approaching pirates. "Fire the ballistae!" Jon repeated the order in the lower chamber as bolts began to fly at the enemy ship. Iron bolts continued to splash into the water as each of the ships maneuvered away from the shooting ballistae.

"Arm the catapult!" David yelled. The men on the deck prepared an iron hook into the large catapult. "Steady now . . ." David said to himself as an arrow pierced through the side of his ship. "Fire!"

Sving! The catapult projected a grappling iron far off into the air toward the enemy ship. *Boom!* The grappling iron broke into the large wooden frame as David's men grabbed the attached rope. "Pull!" David yelled as he ran down and joined his men in pulling the large ship toward them. Several more men joined as the enemy ship began to pull closer and closer.

Crack! The ships soon collided against each other. "Attack!" David yelled as his shipmen began to swing to the other ship on ropes. David quickly grabbed a rope and swung across rolling onto the upper deck. He unsheathed his sword and stabbed an attacking pirate through his chest. Another pirate ran toward David, but he knocked the sword out of his hand and slit his throat. A third pirate swung violently; David blocked each attack. David fenced with the pirate until his swift feet knocked the pirate's saber out of his hand. David then kicked the pirate in his chest, causing him to fly off the ship. As he fell, he was crushed in between the colliding ships. David jumped down to the lower chambers as several more enemy pirates began to charge at him. Iron bolts continued to pierce through the wooden walls as David and his men fought the enemy.

"The ship is sinking!" Jon yelled from across the ship as water began to seep into the lower chambers. David killed several more men before looking over at Jon.

"Take all you can!" David yelled to his men as they jumped down into the lower chambers. *Thump!* Black boots hit the ground as Captain Graybeard jumped off the upper deck, landing in front of David. He drew his sword as he looked at David with a horrific grin, showing his crooked yellow teeth.

"You will die with my ship!" he yelled in fury as he ran toward David. David ducked under his swinging saber and ran up the stairs to the upper deck. Captain Graybeard ran after him as their swords began to clash. Captain Graybeard's feet were quick as David tried to use his footwork to hit him off guard. David stabbed forward just to have his sword knocked out of his hands. Captain Graybeard took another huge lunge toward David as he jumped back and grabbed a hanging rope. Captain Graybeard grew angry as he slashed his sword at David once more. David quickly jumped over him using the rope and kicked him in the back. Captain Graybeard began to lose his balance as David gave him another violent kick. Captain Graybeard flew over the railing and was soon crushed by the colliding ships. David looked over as he watched the captain fall to his doom.

"Hurry, Captain!" Jon yelled as the ship began to sink further, beginning to tilt backward into the water. David grabbed his sword and jumped down to mid-ship. He wrapped his arms around a rope and prepared to jump back across to his ship.

"Help!" a voice screamed from the lower chambers. David looked up at Jon and slowly began to let go of the rope. Jon gave a quick nod as David ran toward the lower chambers and quickly jumped down. He waded through the waist-high water as he followed the screaming voice. "Help! I'm in here!" the voice continued to yell. David approached a wooden door and began to violently kick it until it flew open. As David walked in, he saw Aida locked up in an iron cellar. "I don't know where the key is, but please help me," Aida said as her hands grasped the iron bars.

"Hold on," David said as he unsheathed his sword. *Clang. Clang. Snap!* David's sword broke in half as the door slowly opened. "Come with me," he said as held out his hand. Aida quickly grabbed his hand as they waded through the rising water. The water continued to rise as the ship began to tilt even more. They began to swim through the lower chambers until they finally reached a ladder. "Go!" David said as he pushed her up the ladder. When she reached the top, David disappeared under the rising water. Aida looked down at the water for several moments waiting for David come up. She became nervous as the ship continued to tilt even more. Suddenly David's wet head rose from the water as he jumped up onto the tilted deck. He coughed out some water as he grabbed her hand and ran toward the edge of the boat.

"Jon! Throw me some rope!" David yelled as the ship began to sink, further drenching their feet. Jon threw down a long rope as the ship continued to tilt down deeper into the water. "Hold on!" David said as Aida wrapped her arms around his shoulders. David quickly grabbed the rope with both arms as Jon and several of the other men began to pull him up.

Aida climbed over the wooden railing and fell to the ground as David jumped over the railing and began to catch his breath. The men gathered around as David leaned up against the wooden railing gasping for air.

"Victory!" David yelled with his hand up high as he continued to breathe heavily. The men cheered as David helped up Aida. She quickly wrapped her arms around him as he slowly accepted her gesture. When she let go, he held her hands and looked into her beautiful eyes. "What is your name, my lady?"

"My name is Aida from the city of Salerno. I was captured by those pirates on my way to Oglia."

David looked over at his men. "Welcome. I am Captain David of the *Christ's Crusader* and these are my men." Aida looked around as the men began to wave. "We were all once part of the Roman Empire, but Nero ordered all followers of Jesus to be killed. We had to flee from the Roman Empire."

Aida looked around at the wooden ship as debris and wooden shards covered the ground. "Can I be a part of your crew?" she asked.

David looked around at his men and raised his right hand. "All in favor?" he yelled.

"Aye!" one said.

"Aye!" several more began to yell.

"Aye as well, Captain," Jon said with a nod.

"Well, I present to you our newest member. Aida." David turned toward her as he gently shook her hand. "Welcome to the *Christ's Crusade*."

Part 4: *The White Mare*

David stood at the helm of the ship looking off into the horizon. His eyes became heavy as he continued to sail across the sea. He soon looked over at one of his men standing on the main deck. "Kyle, will you please fetch Jon for me?"

"Aye aye, Captain!" Kyle said as he saluted and ran into the cabin. David's arms felt fatigued as he watched the sun sink down into the blue sea.

"You called for me, Captain?" Jon said, opening the cabin door and looking up at David on the upper deck.

"I need you to take control of the helm," David said as he began to release the wheel.

"Aye aye, David," he said, walking up the steps. David walked toward Jon, and they grasped forearms.

"You have been a great co-captain," David said as he looked into Jon's eyes. "Thank you for being such a great friend."

Jon nodded his head in appreciation. "Thank you, Captain. May the legend of our journeys pass through the ages." David let go of Jon's arm and strongly grasped his shoulder. He nodded at Jon before continuing down the stairs. Jon stepped up to the helm and placed his hands on the wooden wheel. He held it tightly, giving David a salute as David went into the cabin underneath.

As David walked into his cabin, he saw Aida sitting at his desk reading a book.

"Oh, I'm sorry," she said as she rose from her seat. "Jon said this place was—" David quickly put up his hand to quiet her. "It's alright, Aida," he said, looking into her eyes. She smiled at him as she sat back down in the chair. David slowly took off his doublet vest, revealing a loose black shirt underneath. He lay his head down in the hammock strung near his desk as Aida silently read her book. It was quiet for several moments as David closed his eyes and began to relax. "What book are you reading?" he asked sleepily from his slightly rocking hammock.

"*The Knight and the Princess,*" she said with a smile.

David began to chuckle as he opened his eyes and looked over at her. "*The Knight and the Princess*, eh? Sounds terrible." He looked back up at the ceiling.

"And you think you could do better?" she said with a smirk.

He tilted his head in thought. "Do you know how to use a sword?" he asked. David then slowly started to get out of his hammock.

"Well, no," she said, looking over at him.

David quietly got up and walked over to a chest. "Here," David said. He opened the chest and set down a thin sword in front of Aida.

"What is this?" She slowly put down her book.

"It's a saber," he said, unsheathing his sword from his side. "It's the chosen sword of a pirate." Aida began to pick up the blade and examine it. "Sabers are light and for those with quick feet." He began to get in a stance holding his sword forward. "En garde," he said charmingly as she held the blade and began to mimic his stance.

"En garde," she replied with a smile. He slowly lunged at her with his sword as she knocked it down.

"Very good, but you need to stay light on your feet and hold your blade properly." He quickly did another lunge, knocking her saber from her hand. She became frightened as her saber flew across the wooden floor. David walked over to the fallen saber and picked it up from the ground. He then walked back and gently placed her hand correctly on the blade. He looked into her glowing eyes as he placed his right hand on her waist. "That's how you properly hold a saber," he said with a smile so charming it made her lose her breath. He lifted her hand with the saber and began to point it forward. "Bend your knees and keep light on your feet." Her head rested against his strong chest as she began to focus her blade. He slowly let go of her hand as she began to lunge forward in a stabbing motion. "Very good," David said. "That's enough for today."

David quietly walked back over to his hammock and rolled in. He pulled his hat over his face and closed his eyes. Aida continued to practice lunging as she circled around with her feet. After practicing several lunges, she slowly put the saber down on the desk and sat back in the chair. She looked at the open book on the desk before closing it and pushing it aside. "It's time I make my own adventure," she whispered as she looked over at David sleeping on the hammock.

The ship continued to sail for several days; Jon and David took turns steering the ship. When David would retire to his cabin, he would continue teaching Aida how to use a blade. Several more days passed as David was once again steering the ship. "Land ho!" the man in the eagle's nest shouted as land began to appear in the distance. The pirates began to climb out of the lower chambers as an island came into view.

"Anchor the ship!" David yelled. The men began to release the anchor. The anchor dropped into the water with a splash as the metal chain holding it continued to fall deeper and deeper. Suddenly the anchor stopped and the men began to climb down long ropes dangled over the sides of the ship. David jumped on a rope and slowly propelled himself down. Aida appeared beside him as they hit the water and began to swim toward shore. Once ashore everyone gathered around David. David pulled out the piece of paper from his cylindrical case and began to look around. "Welcome to Archimedes Cove," he said, looking at the lush green trees in front of them. "Follow me!"

Aida followed close behind as David and his fellow pirates began to walk toward an enormous cave. The middle of the cave was filled with water. David pushed himself up against the wall and began to cautiously inch his way up a tight ledge. Aida and the men followed when they reached flat rock and began to walk deeper into the large cave.

Light from small holes in the cave's ceiling illuminated the area. David walked into a large open cove. Suddenly David saw it: the *White Mare.* The pirates' eyes opened wide as they saw a beautiful white boat floating within the illuminated cove. David continued to walk toward the overhanging rock connecting to the *White Mare*'s deck. As he came closer, he heard the echo of mellifluous voices coming from a hidden cave across from him. He began to look around as the echoing became louder and louder. As David reached the ship, his men heard the beautiful voice as well and began searching for its origin. Suddenly shadows were seen moving from the cave across the ship as David and his men pulled out their sabers and prepared for battle. As the shadows came closer, they took on a human form. Soon the light cove lit up the shadows and several lovely women began to appear.

"Hello there," one of the women said as she walked up to the men. The woman had long blonde hair and eyes that were bright blue. Her voice was piercingly beautiful as she slowly walked toward the pirates. "We are inhabitants of this island," she said with a white smile that dazzled several of the pirates. Aida began to look around as she saw the men drooling over the comely women in front of them. "Follow me . . ." she said softly as more beautiful women began to appear from the shadows. David and the men began to follow until Aida grabbed David's arm.

"David. I don't have a good feeling about this," Aida whispered, watching the men follow in a line as if in a trance.

"They seem harmless," David said, looking back over at the beautiful women taking the men into the cave. He began to walk toward the cave until Aida grabbed his arm again and leaned herself up against his chest.

"Kiss me," she said, looking into his eyes. David looked over once more as he tried to refrain from walking away. He looked back into Aida's eyes and saw how lovely she was. He slowly placed his hand on her cheek as she held onto his chest. He closed his eyes and leaned in for a kiss. As their lips locked, Aida grasped his doublet vest tighter as David pulled her closer. Suddenly David opened his eyes and realized the trance the women had put him in.

"Aida. We have to save the others!" he said as he grabbed her hand and ran toward the dark cave. "Wait!" David yelled at his men who paused and looked back. David looked in the dark cave and saw the true lizard-like form of the creatures that were surrounding his men. He quickly unsheathed his sword and stabbed one in the heart. The creatures began to growl, revealing sharp teeth as they jumped onto the walls. David grabbed another one of his dazed men's swords and threw it to Aida. Aida quickly caught it and turned toward the menacing creatures. She quickly lunged toward the creature, stabbing the blade into its heart as it let out a loud screech. The men continued to follow the leading scaly green creature while Aida and David began to fight off the creatures crawling along the walls.

Hiss! "The *White Mare* is not yours to take!" the leading creature screamed as she opened her mouth, revealing long sharp teeth. The creatures filled the walls as David ran over and stabbed the green monster in the heart. The monster screeched loudly; David kicked the dying creature onto the ground.

"Aida! Run!" The men began to wake from their trance as they saw the creatures climbing down the walls with their sharp teeth. "Run!" David yelled as he continued to fight off several more green reptilian beasts. Their screeching echoed throughout the cave as the pirates ran down the long rock ledge and jumped onto the white ship.

"Pull up the anchor!" Aida yelled. The men cranked up the anchoring device. The ship began to drift away from the rock platform as David continued to fight off the violent creatures. "David! Hurry!" Aida yelled. David looked behind to see the *White Mare* slowly drifting away. He turned around and sprinted across the platform as several of the creatures followed close behind, running on all fours. As he approached the ledge, David jumped off the rock, reaching out toward the ship. Aida quickly threw him a rope as David hovered in the air, the creatures nipping at his heels. Suddenly, his hands grasped the rope as he flew into the side of the moving white ship. He pulled out his blade and swung at the two creatures next to him, knocking them off the ship's side.

Aida waited as the men continued to pull up the anchor. David's head began to appear as he grabbed the white wooden railing and climbed onto the ship. "Set the sails!" David yelled as the creatures hissed at the ship drifting out of the cove. David ran up to the helm as he began to steer the ship toward the opening of the cove.

"We're not going to make it!" one of the men yelled as they began to pick up speed from the opened sail and move toward the rock wall. David continued to turn the white wooden wheel as the creatures pursued them. The ship nearly hit the side of the opening as it grazed through. The green creatures hissed as the ship passed into the open sea.

The open sky and warm sun calmed the men. David took a deep breath and looked up into the sky. He glanced back at the dark cove to see the creatures retreating from the warm sunlight. The pirates began to cheer as Aida walked up to the upper deck. David looked at her with a smile; she gazed at him with bashful eyes. "Thank you, Aida."

"You're welcome," she replied before turning around and walking down the stairs to the lower deck.

David swiftly began to steer the ship down the island in search of their old ship. As he approached their wooden ship, he saw the ship engulfed in flames. "No!" he yelled as the ship came closer into view. David quickly pulled out his telescope and leaned over the wooden railing to get a better look. He saw the ship in flames and a body lying motionless on the white sand beach. "Anchor the ship!" David said to one of the pirates as he jumped out and swam toward shore. As he waded through the water, he saw Jon lying on the sandy floor with an arrow in his lung. "Jon! Are you okay, mate?"

Jon began to cough up blood as he looked up at David. "It's alright, Captain. I'm going to heaven to be with Jesus." More blood seeped out of his mouth as David held onto his hand.

"Jon, I need you. I need you to help navigate the *White Mare*."

Jon's eyes began to slowly close. "It's alright, David. You're the best navigator in all the Mediterranean." His breathing began slow as a smile came on his face. Soon Jon's chest completely stopped moving. David looked at Jon; his heart hurt. Suddenly an arrow flew into the sand. David looked up to see a man with a painted face holding a bow. Several more began to appear as David quickly ran toward the ship. *Splash!* Arrows flew into the water as David swam toward the large white boat. He quickly grabbed the large rope on the side and climbed onboard as more arrows flew into the water behind him.

"Set the sails!" David yelled as he ran over to the helm and began to turn the ship toward the sea. The men pulled the ropes to the sails as the *White Mare* began to pick up speed. David clenched his teeth and grasped the wooden wheel tighter as he looked behind at the island. He watched the small island disappear as the ship continued to sail into the open sea. His heart began to ache as he thought about the loss of his best friend.

Part 5: Time to Build an Alliance

"We lost several great men today," David said as he stood in front of his sailors. There was a moment of silence as David looked up at the sky. "They rest with our Lord now." Everyone began to bow their heads in mourning as David slowly walked back to the upper deck. Aida watched as David grasped the large wooden wheel and began to stare off into the sea. His face was devoid of emotion as he focused all his attention on steering the ship.

For two days straight, David continued to sail the *White Mare.* His eyes fixed on the open sea as he stood still looking off into the horizon. David soon began to feel weak as the hours continued to pass. Aida would occasionally come out and watch David stare off into the distance. She saw the pain in his eyes from the loss of his best friend as she watched him silently steer the ship. The rest of the ship was also quiet as the men mourned the loss of those they had left behind.

"Land ho!" a pirate in the eagle's nest yelled as they began to come closer to a large dock.

"Where are we?" Aida asked, looking at the large city in front of them.

"This is Citta Nascosta," David answered from the upper deck. "It is the rebellion's hidden city."

Several other large ships were docked as the *White Mare* pulled in. The anchor splashed into the water as the chains began to unwind. A large wooden platform was placed against the ship as the pirates began to walk down. Several other pirates waited at the bottom as David walked down the plank.

"The Legendary *White Mare*!" One of the pirates yelled as David stepped onto the dock.

"The ship designed by Archimedes himself!" another pirate said aloud; the crowd began to whisper. David unsheathed his sword and tapped it against a large bell dangling above. The surrounding pirates quickly became quiet as David and his men stood in front of them.

"I have found the *White Mare*," David said, as he placed his foot up on a nearby crate. "We will use it to defeat the Tyrrhenian Cetus that has been haunting the sea." The pirates began to look around in confusion until a man with a long black beard and black eye patch stepped out from the crowd.

"And how do you suppose we do that?" he said in a deep voice.

David took a good look at him; the man had a wooden peg for a leg. "Captain Victor, I'm sure you've heard of the *White Mare*'s weaponry."

Captain Victor began to laugh, and the surrounding pirates started to laugh with him. "I once got into an entanglement with the Tyrrhenian Cetus," Captain Victor said as his face became very serious. "The creature ate my ship and most of my crew." He looked down at his wooden leg. "Even the strongest ballista couldn't penetrate the tough skin of the monster."

David crossed his arms as he looked back at his ship. "I do not have just any ballista on this ship," David said, looking back at Captain Victor with a smile. "I have Archimedes' Bolt."

Captain Victor's eye widened as he nodded his head. "Archimedes' Bolt?" He ran his fingers through his beard in thought. "If this is true, me and my men will aid you in your conquest."

David looked around at the gathered men. "We will need more pirates then just yours and mine," David replied, eye to eye with Captain Victor. "We must convince the rebellion to join our cause."

Captain Victor looked back at his men then back at David. "We will meet with Lord Alpheus tonight," Captain Victor said. He then turned around and walked back toward the city, taking his entourage with him.

David's men continued to load the *White Mare* with supplies before retiring to the nearest tavern. His men began to order drinks and sing songs as they played different card games. David watched the men drink bottles of rum and soon became too drunk to stand. They sang songs as they hung on each other trying to stand up without wobbling. David liked what he saw of the men enjoying themselves in the tavern. He soon walked outside and leaned up against a nearby wall. He looked up at the stars and began to think about the hard journey ahead.

"David?" a voice asked.

David looked over to see Aida standing outside looking across the open bay. David gave Aida a smile as he walked over to her. "Would you like to take a walk with me?" David asked as he held out his arm. She agreed with a smile as they latched arms and began to walk across the docks looking at the lit up lanterns hanging from the ships. It was quiet as the admired the beauty of the hidden city illuminating in the night. The stars lit up the sky as they continued to walk down the docks.

"Aida?" David asked as he stopped and looked into Aida's eyes. "When you kissed me at the Archimedes' Cove, you knocked me out of that trance."

Aida gave him an innocent smile as she began to blush. "I had to save the crew," she said nervously as David pulled her closer. David gently put his hand on her cheek.

"You were so brave back there, and you fought so well with your sword." David looked at her in admiration. "I just never knew whether that kiss was real." He slowly turned away and bit his lip.

"What do you mean?" she asked as she gently put her hand on his shoulder.

David looked behind at her and took a deep breath. "I've never felt this way about a woman before," he said, clenching his jaw. "Someone as beautiful and amazing as you deserves someone better than a dirty pirate like me. I'm not capable of the kind of love you need."

Aida leaned her head against his muscular shoulder and looked up into his eyes.

"I think you have it all wrong." Her smile made David's heart beat even faster. "Love has no boundaries." David turned toward her as she placed her hands on his chest. "Love is never about who deserves who, but who is most willing to fight for the one they love."

David looked deep into her eyes as a smile crept on his face. "Then I will fight with all my heart for you through all the obstacles we may face." Aida's fingers grasped his shirt as David pulled her in for a kiss. Their lips met; butterflies began to flutter around in Aida's stomach. She had truly found the adventure she was hoping for.

David and Aida walked back to the *White Mare* with their arms linked as he opened the cabin door and let her walk in. "I must meet with Lord Alpheus," David said as he kissed her forehead. Aida smiled at him and gave him a nod. David then shut the door and walked back toward the city.

As he entered the city, he walked up many stony steps until he arrived at a large red door. The door slowly opened as David walked in to see a heavy man with a gray beard sitting on a massive throne. "Lord Alpheus," David said with a bow as he walked midway up the steps to the throne. Captain Victor stood next to him as Lord Alpheus began to stand up from his chair. His large red cloak dragged across the floor as he greeted David.

"Welcome, Captain David," he said, extending his hand. "I heard about your adventures and your encounter with Scylla and Charybdis." He squeezed David's shoulder in approval. "That's a pretty feat for a pirate." Lord Alpheus then walked back to his throne and sat down. "But the Tyrrhenian Cetus is a much more dangerous foe." He placed his hands together in a steeple.

"Yes, but I have Archimedes' bolt," David replied.

Lord Alpheus' eyes grew wide as he tilted his head back. "Archimedes' bolt?" Lord Alpheus looked over at Captain Victor for confirmation. The captain simply nodded.

"Its density is unmatched," David said confidently as Lord Alpheus began to course his fingers through his long gray beard.

"Hmm," Lord Alpheus mumbled as he sat in thought. He continued to twirl his beard around his index finger. "I will give you several ships of my men to aid you. Eliminating the Tyrrhenian Cetus will allow for more access to the ocean and easier travel for our rebellion." He stood up and looked into David's eyes. "If you fail, it may be the end of the rebellion."

David nodded. "I understand."

"I will prepare the men," Captain Victor said as he began to walk away. "We shall have them ready in two days."

David nodded his head once more at Captain Victor. He looked back at Lord Alpheus and gave him a salute.

"May God be with you in this great battle," Lord Alpheus said.

"May God protect us," David replied. He turned around and walked back toward the large red doors. Lord Alpheus watched as David disappeared down the stony steps.

As David walked down the stone steps, he looked up at the sky and closed his eyes. "Dear Lord, may you follow us into this battle."

Part 6: Battle of the Tyrrhenian Sea

A fleet of ships led by the *White Mare* began to sail across the open sea. David stood at the helm controlling the wooden wheel as he stared into the distance. "Aida!" David yelled as she walked up the stairs to the upper deck.

"Yes, Captain?" she asked as she leaned against the wooden railing.

"I need you to steer the ship."

Aida gave him a confused look as he walked over and grabbed her hand. He stood behind her as he placed her hands on the wheel. "I need you to learn how to steer this ship in case something happens." He began to slowly turn the wheel with her as the ship began to sway left. "Always keep both hands on the wheel. Your hands will go over and under like this." He began to turn the wheel right as the ship began to sway right. "Your turn." Aida began to turn the wheel left following his instructions. "Very good." He said letting go of her hands and letting her steer the boat on her own. He held his hands on her waist as she continued to steer the ship. "Now, hold the wheel steady and try to keep her going straight." She continued to steady the wheel from side to side trying to keep the boat balanced. "You're a quick learner," David said as he pulled out his compass. "Continue to keep the ship going east." He pointed to the compass as she began to straighten the ship once more.

David showed Aida how to sail as the many pirate ships followed behind their leader. They sailed for several days.

"Captain!" the sailor in the eagle's nest yelled.

"What is it?" David asked looking up at the pirate as he peered through his telescope.

"We have a problem," the pirate replied as David pulled out his telescope and peered over into the vast sea.

"Darn," David said as he stood at the top of the upper deck. "Prepare the ballistae! A Roman fleet is approaching!" The men quickly began to run toward the lower chambers. Aida followed them down into the lower chambers as David continued to steer the *White Mare* toward the Roman ships. The other pirate ships had men scurrying around as everyone prepared their weaponry. A pirate stood on the front ballista of the *White Mare* as they began to edge closer to the approaching ships. "Wait for my command!" David yelled as the tension continued to grow. Large wooden boats with the emblem of the Roman Empire on their sails came into view as David unsheathed his sword and held it high.

"Fire!" David yelled as large iron bolts began to fly through the air. Bolts began to rip through the large white sails of the *White Mare* as flying iron filled the sky. *Crack!* An iron bolt pierced through the front of an enemy ship as it began to tilt into the water and sink.

"Abandon ship!" those soldiers yelled as the ship began to sink into the water. David continued to steer through the mess of the approaching fleet as the pirates behind began to take them down.

Aida helped aim the ballista as it shot into another enemy ship. She helped load until an iron bolt exploded into the side of the *White Mare.* Wood flew everywhere as the pirates continued to shoot the ballistae. Another enemy ship fell as Aida shot it straight into the front end. Suddenly the ships began to rock back and forth as a monstrous wave began to form in the middle of the battlefield.

David watched as a gigantic tentacle wrapped around one of the Roman ships and crushed it in half. *Screech!* A monstrous roar came from the sharp-teethed mouth of an eight-tentacled monster. Each of its large teeth was the size of a full-grown man as it opened its mouth and let out another bloodthirsty screech. It slammed another one of its enormous tentacles against the water and a huge wave rose to knock over several ships.

The *White Mare* continued to steer through the splashing tentacles until David saw the enormous eye of the atrocious creature. "Arm Archimedes' Bolt!" he yelled as the pirate on the front ballista ran toward the lower chambers. *Splash!* The ship began to tilt as a giant tentacle hit the water beside the boat. A pirate flew overboard as David steered into the large wave. "Aida!" David yelled as the tentacles continued to grab ships and empty the men into the beast's mouth. Aida ran out of the cabin holding onto the door as the ship began to sway violently. "Take the wheel!" David commanded as Aida ran to the upper deck.

"Aye aye, Captain." Aida saluted as she grabbed the wheel.

David jumped down to the lower chambers to see men shooting bolts at the tentacles of the beast. "Where is Archimedes' Bolt?" David yelled as he ran through. A pirate quickly pointed to a wooden door. David ran over to the door and kicked it open to reveal a large silver bolt. He picked up the bolt with both hands and ran toward the ladder. Water began to spray in as another wave tilted the ship. David held onto the ladder as he threw the bolt onto the deck. He climbed the ladder and saw them continue to come closer to the hideous beast. He picked up the Archimedes' Bolt and ran toward the front of the ship. "Aida! Get us closer!" he yelled as Aida turned the ship head on toward the beast. David threw the heavy bolt into the front ballista and tugged with all his might to load the bolt.

The monster let out another bloodthirsty roar as it opened its mouth and began to swim toward the *White Mare*. "Steady . . ." David said as he began to aim toward its massive eye. *Schwuuf.* The arrow flew into the air at an accelerating speed. Aida quickly turned the ship as the arrow flew into the eye of the approaching beast.

Screech! The monsters tentacles flew up in the air as David ran toward the helm. The monster's head flew into the water as a huge wave knocked the *White Mare* backward. David held onto a rope as the ship tilted sideways and almost flipped from the enormous wave. He saw Aida holding on to the wheel as the ship continued to be pulled by the wave. David let go and ran toward the upper deck as the ship violently swayed. He saw Aida's hands slipping as he grabbed another rope and jumped toward her. She let go, almost flying off the ship until David's hand grasped hers. He hung off the ship holding the rope with one arm and her forearm with another.

"David, you can't hold on!" Aida yelled as David tightened his grip on her forearm. He slowly felt his hand continue to slip from hers as he strained to hold on.

"I love you too much to let go!" David yelled as his hand began to slip down the rope. Water continued to splash his face as he struggled to hold on. The ship then abruptly hit the flat sea as David and Aida flew into the ocean.

Aida's eyes were closed as she felt the sea continue to pull her under. Suddenly an arm wrapped around her as she felt herself pulled up to the surface. She gasped for air as David held her in his arm and swam toward the *White Mare.* The long rope he had held on to was dangling on the backside of the ship. He grasped it with one hand as he held onto Aida. "Help! Pull us up!" Several moments passed until a few pirates came out onto the upper deck and began to pull at the rope.

Aida held onto David as his men pulled him up onto the upper deck. He climbed over the wooden railing with Aida only to fall on his knees and gasp for air. Aida lay on her back trying to gasp for air as well. The men began to cheer. David slowly got up and helped Aida up as they looked off into the sea. The large body of the Cetus floated motionless in the ocean as David wrapped his arm around Aida.

"The Tyrrhenian Cetus has fallen!" The men began to cheer, hugging each other and throwing their hands into the air.

David wrapped his arms around Aida as they looked at the dead monster floating and bobbing lifelessly in the water. "Wait!"

a pirate yelled as he pointed. "The Roman ships!" The remaining Roman ships lay still in the ocean. They watched the ships for several minutes until suddenly they began to turn around.

"They're releasing us," David said as the men looked at each other in confusion.

"We're free to roam the seas!" one pirate yelled as the men began to cheer once more.

David held Aida closed to him as they watched the men pop bottles of rum in celebration. "Well, Captain. What do we do now?" Aida asked as she turned toward him. David looked off into the ocean for several moments.

"We go to Oblia," he said.

"And what are we going to do there?" Aida asked, leaning in closer.

"We're going to find a home," David answered, kissing her on the lips. He looked into her eyes one more time before letting go and walking toward the wheel. He grabbed the wooden wheel and began to turn the ship. The men looked up at David and gave a strong salute as David stood at the helm. "We're off to Oblia!" he yelled as the *White Mare* continued to sail across the open sea. Captain David and Aida lived . . .

CHAPTER 7

DAY BY DAY

". . . Happily ever after." I closed my laptop and looked over at Aida. Her eyes were closed as she began to smile.

"That story was amazing," she said as she opened her eyes half-way. "But our story is still better."

I gave her a smile as I stood up and kissed her forehead. "I love you, Aida," I said as I placed my forehead against hers and grabbed her hand.

"Forever and always?" she asked. I pulled her hand up to my lips for a small kiss.

"Forever and always," I replied, gently kissing her hand.

I left Aida to rest as I got in back into my car. Mr. White placed his hand on me as I looked up. "It's alright, David," he said as he patted my back softly.

"It's so hard seeing her like this," I said, still looking up. Mr. White pressed his lips in as he tried to give me more comforting words.

"All we can do is pray," he said as he patted my shoulder once more and put the car in drive. The car was silent as I looked out the window and pondered what was going to happen next. I closed my eyes and began to pray some more as my stomach began to ache from seeing Aida so weak.

As we arrived at the house, we opened the door to the smell of fresh chicken. I grinned when I saw Mrs. White pull a glass tray of chicken out of the oven. "Time to eat, everyone!" she said as we all grabbed plates and sat at the table. Mrs. White dished each of us a portion of chicken and spaghetti as I cut up Aaron's food.

"Alright, champ. Use your fork not your hands." Aaron nodded as he began to shovel food into his mouth. I cut up some chicken and rolled spaghetti around my fork. I pulled a bite into my mouth and slowly started to chew.

"This is delicious," I said.

"It is indeed. Thank you so much, honey, for cooking for us," Mr. White added as he slurped up some spaghetti causing sauce to splatter on his face.

"Grandpa!" Aaron said, giggling in horror. We all began to laugh at the sauce on Mr. White's nose.

After clearing my plate, I got up to clear the table. I pulled out some Tupperware and filled it with homemade chicken and spaghetti. Mrs. White looked at me with concern. "She may not be able to fully enjoy it," she said as I began to pop the lid on.

"I know," I said as I put my head down. "I just want her to feel like she still is part of the family." I slowly put the food in the refrigerator and closed the door. Mrs. White nodded as she placed her fingers on my chin and lifted my head.

"Cheer up. She's still so happy—even in her condition." She wrapped her arms around me as Mr. White took Aaron to bed.

Mrs. White cleaned the kitchen as I peeked through the door of Aaron's room. "Come in," Mr. White whispered as Aaron lay sound asleep. I slowly pulled the covers over Aaron and kissed him on the forehead.

"Good night, champ," I whispered as I walked out the door with Mr. White.

"Everything alright?" he asked as we walked into the kitchen.

We both pulled up chairs as Mrs. White came and sat down at the table with us. "I'm okay," I said, trying to keep my head up. "I just haven't been able to sleep or eat as much." Mr. White nodded and gave me a concerned look.

"I know this is hard," he said, clenching his jaw. "You've got to have faith that this all in God's hands."

I nodded before looking back up at Mr. White. "I trust in Him," I said with a half-smile. "Sometimes it just hurts." I held my hand on my chest as I felt my heart drop into my stomach once more.

"We're here for you, David," Mrs. White said as tears began to roll down her face.

Mr. White began to comfort her as he looked over at me. "We're always here if you need us." Mr. White said as he held Mrs. White's hand.

"As am I for you," I said as I held out both my arms to accept theirs. "Shall we pray?" I asked. Mr. White nodded. We all bowed our heads as the room became completely quiet. "Dear Lord, I pray you be with our family through this hard time and continue to give us strength. Be with Aida as she faces this illness and help to heal her. We love you and are grateful for all you've given us. In Jesus's name, amen."

"Amen," Mr. and Mrs. White chimed in.

"Time for bed," Mr. White said as he helped up Mrs. White and held her close to him.

"Goodnight."

I opened the door to my room and took off my socks and shoes. I threw off my vest and button-down shirt and fell back onto my bed. I took a deep breath and closed my eyes. *Knock knock.* I slowly opened my eyes and walked over to my bedroom door. As I opened the door, Aaron stood rubbing his eyes, holding a stuffed penguin. "Can I sleep with you tonight?" he asked as he put his arms up for a hug. I nodded my head as I picked him up and lay him in the bed next to me. I rubbed his head and kissed his forehead as I pulled the covers over us.

"Good night, champ," I whispered as I heard his breathing begin to slow. I lay in bed with my eyes open, looking at the rotating fan. My eyes began to close. I thought about the story I had written Aida and the smile she had after I had read it to her. Thinking about her always helped me fall asleep. I continued to think about her beautiful face until my eyes closed, and I began drift off into the night.

The next morning was hectic as I tried to get Aaron dressed. "Come on, champ! We've got to look nice for church!" Aaron pulled on his shoes as we entered the kitchen.

"Good morning, you two!" Mrs. White said as she poured a bowl of cereal. "I don't know how you eat this Cookie Crisp," she said with a laugh as she placed Aaron's bowl on the table. I smiled as she placed a bowl of oatmeal in front of me.

"How'd you know?" I said with a grin.

"You need to eat healthier," she said with a scolding smile.

After we ate, we all got in the car and buckled up for church. "You all ready?" I asked.

"All ready, Cap'n!" Aaron said with a salute. I started the car and began to pull out of the driveway. We listened to Christian music on the radio as we drove to church. After several minutes we pulled up to the church and got out.

"Good morning Mr. Benelli!" A man said as we began to approach the entrance.

"Good morning, Pastor Pearson," I said as I shook his hand.

"Mr. and Mrs. White, it's so nice to see you both again," Pastor Pearson said as he gave each of them a hug. "I would love to see all you after the service for prayer." He placed his hand on my shoulder and gave me a comforting nod. He looked down at Aaron. "Well hey there, little guy." He mussed Aaron's hair.

"Hey, Pastor Pearson," Aaron replied as he wrapped his arm around his leg in a pint-sized hug.

Pastor Pearson gave me a smile as he patted Aaron's back. "You excited for Sunday school?" he asked Aaron. Aaron nodded his head in excitement as he grabbed my hand.

"I love snack time!" he said to a chorus of laughter. I waved to Pastor Pearson as I walked Aaron down through the double doors.

"You guys go find seats," I said as I walked Aaron over to another open door. "Alright, champ. Have fun in Sunday school." I rubbed his head and waved goodbye as he ran over to the other kids in the room. I walked into the main church to find Mr. and Mrs. White sitting in their chairs waiting for me.

"Mr. Benelli!" another voice said as I turned around.

"Ah, Mr. Henkel! Nice to see you," I replied as Mr. Henkel shook my hand and gave me a smile.

"My son is really enjoying your class," he said as I smiled back.

"I'm glad to hear that. These two are Aida's parents, Mr. and Mrs. White."

"Pleasure to meet you both!" Mr. Henkel said excitedly as he shook their hands. "Aida is an amazing woman. She's done a great job in the children's ministry." Mr. Henkel looked over at me as he placed his hand on my arm. "She is still in my prayers."

"Thank you," I whispered as he waved to Mr. and Mrs. White and walked off.

Music started to play as people began to sing. I stood up and closed my eyes, trying to suppress the pain in my stomach. I began to let out my voice in worship as I continued to feel weak in the knees. I pressed myself against the chair in front of me as I closed my eyes in prayer.

"You may all take a seat," Pastor Pearson said as everyone began to sit down. Everyone became attentive as Pastor Pearson began to read several scriptures from the Bible. His arms moved and his body swayed as he conveyed his message through stories accompanied with mild theatrics. "Now everyone, bow your heads." We all bowed our heads as Pastor Pearson ended the sermon in prayer.

"Amen," we all said as people began to get up from their seats. I walked over to the front with Mr. and Mrs. White as several people gathered around in a circle. Pastor Pearson nodded his head as we all began to hold hands.

"Dear Heavenly Father," he began, "please be with Aida and her family as she faces her illness. Lord, we pray that you heal her and have your will with her. Keep them strong as they face their hardships. May they feel your love and peace through it all. May they know that everything is in your hands. In Jesus's name we pray, amen."

"Amen." We all sat and talked for several minutes more. I looked at my watch and motioned toward the exit.

"Thank you all for your prayers," I said as we began our goodbyes. We then walked down the hall to see Aaron waiting at the door. I signed him out and waved goodbye as I grabbed Aaron's hand. "Time to see Aida," I told Aaron as walked toward the car.

"I can't wait!" Aaron yelled. "I want to tell her what I learned in Sunday school!" He gave us a big smile as we all began to get into the car.

It was a short drive as Aaron continued to fidget in excitement. We quickly checked in and walked toward Aida's room. The door began to creak as we peeked in to see Aida lying on her bed. "Good afternoon, Aida," I said as I walked over and kissed her on her forehead.

Her eyes slowly opened as she began to reveal a smile. "Good afternoon, David," she said, grasping my hand. The rest of the family began to walk in. Aaron jumped up on my lap.

"Mommy!" he yelled as she turned over and looked at him with a smile.

"Hey, baby," she said softly as she brushed her hand gently across his cheek.

Aaron smiled at her as he began to jump up and down in excitement. "Momma! I learned about Jonah today in Sunday school!" Aaron could hardly hold his excitement as he held her hand to his cheek. "It's about this prophet who was eaten by a big fish!" He began to pretend his hands were the characters as he clamped his right hand on to his left. He told more of the story as he began to act out the characters on the boat and impersonate different voices. "And then he was spit out after three days and three nights!" He stuck three fingers up with both hands as he smiled at his mother. Aida began to gently giggle until she began to cough.

"You tell the story so well, Aaron," she said, smiling at him and looking over at me. "You take after your father." She gave him a kiss on the forehead as he turned around and jumped on my lap again. I reached out my hand and slowly grabbed hers as she began to sit up.

Cough cough. She used her right hand to cover her mouth, leaving behind a red substance. I quickly grabbed a nearby towel and quietly wiped the blood on the back of her hand. Her mother began to hold Mr. White tighter after seeing the blood; Aida's mother's eyes began to water. Aaron looked at me with wide eyes as I set the towel onto the counter. "Mommy, are you okay?" He asked, leaning onto the side of the bed and looking at his mother.

"Mommy's fine," she said, reaching out and rubbing his head. Aaron put his arms out as I lifted him up and let Aida wrap her arms around him. Her eyes began to water as she was finally able to hold her baby boy again. We sat with her for several more hours until it was time to go.

"Time to go, champ," I said as she kissed his forehead. He began to puff out his lower lip.

"I wuv you, Momma."

"I love you too, baby," she said as a tear rolled down her cheek.

I put down Aaron as he ran over to Mr. and Mrs. White. As they waited for me, I slowly leaned in and kissed her forehead. "You look more and more beautiful every day," I said. She started to cry in earnest.

"I love you," she said as I stood up.

"I love you, too," I said, grabbing her hand and looking into her eyes.

"Forever and always?" she asked.

"Forever and always," I replied as I slowly let go of her hand. I nodded to her parents to come forward as I picked up Aaron and left for the waiting room.

I sat down with Aaron as he began to quietly play with the toys. He had an empty expression on his face while he held two dinosaurs and began tapping them against each other. His eyes looked lost, and I felt the pain in my stomach begin to inflame. My heart hurt for Aaron as I thought about how he must feel. His mother whom he adores was stuck in a hospital bed barely able to handle his energy. I closed my eyes trying to calm myself. The ferocious flame in my stomach began to burn as I continued to see Aida lying in that hospital bed, weak and frail. I clenched my jaw tightly, trying to remain strong as I carefully watched Aaron continue to play with his dinosaurs.

CHAPTER 8

TRYING TO REMAIN STRONG

It was time for another day of school. I opened the door of my car and reached for my briefcase. "Good morning, Mr. Benelli!" a student said, walking by. I waved my hand slightly and nodded toward the student as I began to walk toward the front office.

I opened the door to see Nancy at her desk. "Good morning, Mr. Benelli. Is everything alright?"

I stopped next to her and looked up at the ceiling. "I don't really want to talk about it," I said, looking straight ahead. I felt like if I did I might bawl.

She nodded her head. "I understand."

I walked into my classroom and sat in my chair. Students began to pile in as I sat quietly looking down at my briefcase. I stood up in the front of the room and looked around at the students as they settled in their chairs. "Alright class, pull out your book, *Of Mice and Men,* and read chapter eight." I sat back in my chair, opened my briefcase, and pulled out papers.

Each class period was completely silent as the students continued to read. Soon the bell rang for lunch hour, and the students began to bolt out of the classroom. One student stood at the doorway looking over at me holding a stack of papers trying to show me his story. I continued to look down at the papers in front of me as he looked down, discouraged. He slowly walked out as I peered through the corner of my eye at him. My heart sank, for I knew Kyle wanted me to read another one of his fabulous stories, but I just couldn't find the strength. I took a deep breath as I slowly got up and headed to the lunchroom.

As I waited in line, I avoided all eye contact with people. I grabbed my tray and walked toward the corner of the room so I could sit alone. I began take several bites until I felt a hand on my shoulder.

"Mr. Benelli!" Mr. Lite said as he sat down right next to me. I gave him a small nod and began to clench my jaw. "Is everything alright?" He looked over at me and lowered his glasses.

"I'm fine!" I said, irritated, as I continued to eat.

Mr. Lite continued to look at me with a worried expression. "Are you sure, David?" he asked.

I began to grow impatient. I closed my eyes trying to hold in my pain. "I'm fine!" I yelled, slamming the table and causing the whole room to look at me. My clenched fist lay on the table as I took a deep breath. I slowly got up and grabbed my tray. I felt everyone's eyes watching me as I closed the door behind me.

"Three more periods," I said aloud as I sat in my chair and leaned on my desk. People began to sit down as I tried to keep myself calm. The pain from seeing Aaron so empty and Aida so frail continued to churn my stomach.

As the final period passed, it was finally quiet in my lonely classroom. *Knock knock.* I looked over at the door before taking a deep breath. I didn't want to be bothered. "Come in," I said reluctantly. The door opened to reveal Jack with his long gray beard.

"David. Let's have a talk," Jack said as he grabbed a chair and sat next to me at my desk. I looked up at the ceiling again, trying to gather fortitude.

"I'm sorry, Jack. I'm just having a very tough day," I said.

Jack nodded his head in understanding. "David. I want you to take some time off. Spend time with Aida."

I looked away from him as I considered his suggestion.

"Just give me a couple more days," I said, looking back over at him. "I don't want to leave my students just yet."

Jack nodded as he began to get up. "Remember, have faith. It's all in God's hands."

I nodded as he began to walk out the door. I closed my eyes and recited to myself, "It's all in God's hands." The ferocious flame in my stomach began to ease as I tried to push away the worry. The flame continued, but I began to feel a little more at ease thinking about God's sovereign hand. I turned back to my desk and went back to work.

Ring ring. Ring ring. I closed my eyes and looked over at my cell phone. It was another unrecognizable number. *Ring ring. Ring ring.* I clenched my jaw as I placed the phone up against my ear.

"David Benelli, how may I help you?"

A woman's voice came on the phone. I heard children playing in the background.

"Hi, Mr. Benelli, this is Chelsea Moore from daycare. Your son Aaron got in trouble today. We're sorry, but we need you to pick him up."

I bit my bottom lip trying to remain calm. "I will come get him immediately," I said before hanging up the phone and slamming my desk. "Dammit!" I said aloud as I began to pack up papers and put them in my briefcase. I then quickly walked out of my classroom and toward my car.

I threw my briefcase in and slammed the door behind me as I began to pull out of the parking lot. I tapped the steering wheel violently as I felt my heart continue to pound against my chest. I felt filled with anger. After driving for several minutes, I finally pulled up to the daycare.

"Mr. Benelli, thank you for coming," a woman greeted me as I got out of the car.

I followed her into the building. As we opened the door, I saw Aaron sitting on a chair on top his hands hanging his head.

"What happened?" I asked calmly as she began to hand me the sign-out sheet.

"He pushed another kid over in daycare today. The other boy must've said something. Is everything okay at home?" Her eyes were filled with worry as she awaited my answer.

"My wife is dealing with cancer," I said softly as I handed her back the signed clipboard. I looked over at Aaron as he watched with sad eyes as the other kids continued to play. "It's really hard seeing his mother in the condition she's in."

The woman nodded as she looked over at Aaron. "I'm sorry to hear that, Mr. Benelli. I wish we could do more."

"It's alright," I said, looking back at her. "His grandparents can take care of him these next few days. I'll be getting off work soon as well." I shook her hand softly. "Thank you for watching him." She gave me a smile as I walked over to Aaron and gave him a scolding look. "Alright, son. Come with me." I grabbed his hand and quickly walked him out.

I opened the door to my car and began to strap him into his car seat. He looked down in guilt as I walked over and got in. "Aaron, I am very disappointed in you," I said sternly as I started the car and began to drive home. The car was silent as Aaron began to sniffle, tears running down his face.

When we arrived home, I picked him up from his car seat and walked him into the house. Aida's parents were waiting as I brought him in. "I'm going to have a talk with him," I told them.

"Don't be too hard on the boy," Mr. White said as he looked over at Aaron. I nodded as I sat him on the couch.

"Aaron, I have taught you better than to hurt other people. Why did you push that other boy today?" My voice was stern as he looked up at me in tears.

"I'm sorry, Dad." His voice squeaked as he tried to speak. "He said Mommy was going to die because all people who have cancer die." My heart sank as tears continued to roll down his face.

"Come here, son," I said as he ran into my arms. I picked him up and placed his head over my shoulder. "It's alright, champ," I said as I patted my crying son's back. "Not all people who have cancer die." I felt him continue to sniffle as I closed my eyes trying to stay strong. I sat Aaron down on my lap as he looked into my eyes. "Violence is never a way to solve things, son. You mustn't take out your anger on others."

"I know." Aaron said with his head down.

"You want to go get something to eat?" I asked as he continued to sniffle. He nodded his head as I held his hand and walked toward the front door. Mr. White came out from behind the door and gave a small wave.

"I'll see you guys when you get home," Mr. White said quietly.

As we got in my car, I drove us down to McDonald's down the road. Aaron and I sat in the car as I watched him take several bites of his chicken nuggets and shove a couple fries down his throat. "No telling Mama, now," I said with a little chuckle as I took a deep bite into my burger. He finally gave me a smile as we quietly ate our food together. It may have only been several minutes, but the little smile on his face while eating in the car was a moment to remember. After we finished I started the car and began to drive home. As we drove home, we began to sing songs to the radio.

When I finally parked, I pulled out Aaron from his seat and threw him on my shoulder. I spun him around several times before opening the door and walking in. He ran to his room. I walked over to Mr. and Mrs. White and gave them both a hug.

"How's she doing?" I asked them as we all sat at the kitchen table.

"She's alright," Mrs. White said in a soft voice. "She had a little more energy today."

"That's good," I said putting my elbows on the table. "Does she know about Aaron?" I looked over at his room. I saw him playing with several figurines, clashing them together and making sound effects.

"No," she said as she looked over at Mr. White.

"She has enough to worry about," Mr. White said softly. I nodded my head in understanding as I sat and talked to them about my day.

Several hours later, I found myself sitting on Aaron's rug running a triceratops figurine across the top of his head. "Dad!" Aaron said pulling my hand down to the T-rex he was holding. We continued to make them tap against each other as if they were fighting a battle. Several other figurines scattered the room as he pretended to move them around and use them as characters.

Aaron and I continued to play until we smelled food cooking in the kitchen. "Yum. What's that smell?" I said to Aaron as I sat him down and pulled up a chair. My nose soon picked up the delicious smell of garlic and tomato sauce.

"Lasagna!" Mrs. White said as she pulled out a pan from the oven with red oven mitts. Steam began to slowly rise from the dish as the whole room was filled with the smell of lasagna. She placed the hot lasagna on the table and grabbed a spatula, revealing a cheesy layer filled with Italian sausage.

"Mm," Mr. White said as he licked his lips, "yummy." Aaron began to laugh at Mr. White as Mrs. White plopped a small piece of lasagna on his plate. She continued to serve everyone as we all sat at the dinner table ready to eat.

"Shall we pray?" I asked as Mrs. White began to sit down. Mrs. White gave a nod as we all grabbed hands and bowed our heads. "Dear Lord, thank you for this delicious meal. May you bless the hands that prepared it. I know Aida cannot share this meal with us, but I ask that you help her recover and so that one day she can." I tightened my grip around Mrs. White and Aaron's hand as I continued. "We thank you, in Jesus's name . . ."

"Amen." We began to eat. The dinner table was quiet as we dug into the cheesy lasagna. As we ate, it was hard thinking about Aida and how she would miss another meal with her family.

The rest of the night continued in solemn quiet. I pulled out all the papers from my briefcase and began to finish the work I had from earlier. Another hour passed and I heard little footsteps tapping on the tile floor.

"Dad?" I looked over to see Aaron in pajamas holding a stuffed bear in one hand and his blanket dragging across the floor in the other. "I can't sleep," he said with big eyes. I felt my heart drop as I put down my pen and walked over to him.

"Alright, champ. I'll tuck you in." I picked him up with his blanket and bear and walked him back over to his room. I slowly placed him in his bed and wrapped the blanket around him. I tightly tucked the blanket underneath him until he was unable to move. Aaron began to laugh as he started to wiggle around.

"I love when you wrap me up," he said with a smile. I smiled back and gave him a small kiss on his forehead.

"You ready to pray?" He nodded his head. We both closed our eyes and bowed our heads. "Dear Lord, I pray that you protect us tonight and help us to better serve you. I pray for Aida that you heal her and be with her as she continues to face her illness. Lord, be with us in all we do." I opened my eyes and looked over at Aaron. "And Jesus said . . ."

"Amen!" he yelled. I gave him a smile before standing up. "Dad?" I looked back at him to see his big eyes looking up at me. "Can you to tell me a story?" I pulled a chair next to his bed.

"All right," I said, rubbing his head. I then picked up several figurines lying around and began to tell him a story. "There once was a dinosaur named Aaron." I walked his T-rex figurine across the top of his dresser. "He was the strongest and biggest dinosaur in all the land." I began to use the figurine to lift up the lamp on his dresser and then slowly set it down. "Now, although he was very big and strong, all of the other dinosaurs made fun of him." I picked up two other dinosaurs and placed them in front of the T-rex. "Ha! You're too big! You don't fit in with the other dinosaurs!" My voice was higher pitched as I pretended to be one of the talking dinosaurs.

"Aaron became very upset. Everyone was making fun of him for being big and strong." I looked over to see Aaron's eyes focused on the figurines I was holding. "Aaron was so upset he ran off into the night." I slowly walked the dinosaur over to the other side of the room. "He never wanted to return because so many had made fun of him for who he was." I pretended to walk the dinosaur up in the air and make him look discouraged. "But suddenly, Aaron saw a mirror." I put up the T-rex to a mirror and pretended the dinosaur was looking at itself through it. "Aaron realized that what the others were saying wasn't true and that his strength and size were wonderful gifts from God." I walked the T-rex over to the dresser and placed him next to the other dinosaurs. "You see, Aaron may have been different but different only meant he was unique. For his strength and size were beautiful gifts from God that he learned to appreciate." I sat back down in the chair as I looked at Aaron's big eyes. "And the other dinosaurs' insults never upset him again, because Aaron now knew being different only meant he was unique."

Aaron began to smile as he pushed his head deeper into his pillow. "Dad?"

"Yes, son?"

"That dinosaur is me, isn't it?"

I smiled at him and leaned forward in my chair. "Yup, and just like that dinosaur you have many special gifts that make you different from anyone else." Aaron looked up at me with a smile and closed his eyes.

"Goodnight, son. I love you," I said as I kissed his forehead and pulled the covers over his shoulders.

"Goodnight, Dad. I love you, too."

I then turned out the lights and slowly shut the door. A smile remained on my face as I walked back to my desk and put my things away. I started to yawn as I finished packing my things and got ready for bed. As I lay in bed, I stared up at the ceiling thinking about my day. My eyes continued to stay wide open as I tried to force myself to sleep. "Another sleepless night," I said aloud, turning over and looking at the moonlight filtering in through the window. "Another sleepless night."

CHAPTER 9

A THIRD STORY

As I lay in bed, the ferocious flame in my stomach continued to burn. I clenched my jaw as my hands began to grasp the bed. I jolted up, breathing heavily as I tried to calm the storm raging in my stomach. I then slowly slid out of bed as I looked out the window at the stars. I placed my hands on the windowsill and closed my eyes trying to calm myself. I began to slow down my breathing as the emotions continued to burn within me. I couldn't make it stop. I quickly let go of the windowsill and walked toward the door. "I know what to do," I said to myself as I walked back to my office.

I sat down in my chair and opened my laptop. The feeling in my stomach continued to pound at my insides until my fingers hit the keyboard, and I began to type. I felt the pain in my stomach rush into my fingers and release into the keyboard as words began to form on the page. I closed my eyes and imagined Aida's smile. More words began to quickly appear on the page. I immersed myself in another story as I imagined Aida's beautiful smile. It was the only way I knew of keeping a smile on her face.

My hands stayed steady at work as I continued to pound at the keyboard. My mind was focused as the raging pain in my stomach seemed to be thrown into my writing.

After several hours, my eyes grew weary. Sunlight began to peek through the window. I rubbed my eyes with one hand as I sat back in my chair and admired my progress. I soon heard ruffling in the kitchen. I got out of my chair to find Mrs. White preparing breakfast.

"Good morning, Mrs. White," I said softly so as not to alarm her.

"Good morning, David," she replied while pulling out a box of instant oatmeal. She turned around and looked at me with a scowl. "Did you pull another all-nighter?" Her voice was motherly as I gave her a half-smile.

"I just couldn't sleep." I pulled up a chair and sat down as she began to heat up some water.

"David," she looked at me with concern, "you need rest." She began to pour hot water into a bowl and mix it around. As she approached the table, she took another hard look at me. "When was the last time you shaved?" I began to run my hands through my now long, coarse beard. She set the bowl next to me and began to sniff me.

"Hey!" I said with a chuckle as she cringed.

"Or showered!" She looked at me with a worried look. "I know it's hard, David. But you've got to take care of yourself." I gave her a nod as I slowly began to eat my cereal.

"Dad!" Aaron yelled as Mr. White came into the kitchen holding him on his shoulders.

"Good morning, champ." Aaron quickly ran over to me and gave me a hug. His hugs were my favorite part of the morning. As we all sat down, Mrs. White placed a bowl of Cookie Crisp cereal in front of him.

"Your favorite," she said with a smile as she kissed his forehead.

"What do you say?" I said to him as he grabbed his spoon and prepared to dig in.

"Thank you, Grammy!" I rubbed his head as he shoveled a spoonful of cereal into his mouth.

"Good morning, Mr. White," I said as he sat down across from me.

"Good morning, David." Mrs. White placed a bowl of oatmeal in front of him.

After breakfast, I got ready for work and met Aaron and Mrs. White at the front door. "Thank you for taking care of him today," I said as I gave Mrs. White a hug.

"That's what we're here for," she said with a smile.

"Alright, champ. You be good." I rubbed his head before picking him up and giving him a hug.

"I love you, Dad!" he said as I put him back down.

"I love you too, champ." I grabbed my briefcase and opened the door.

After I arrived at the school, I slowly got out of my car. "Good morning Mr. Benelli!" a student said as I grabbed my briefcase.

"Good morning, William," I said softly. I made my way to the front office.

As I entered through the door, Nancy peeked over her computer. "Good morning, Nancy," I said, giving her a small wave and a smile.

"Oh, good morning, Mr. Benelli," she replied giving me a smile then turning back to her computer.

As I got to my classroom, I quickly pulled out my laptop and began to type away. I felt more relaxed as I continued to type. The classroom quickly began to fill as I closed my laptop and prepared for the day's lessons.

The class periods went by quickly; it was then lunch hour. I didn't leave my classroom as I continued to type away at the story. I couldn't eat. The feelings inside my stomach were continuing to build, but I continued to focus on the story at hand. Writing on my laptop seemed to dull the pain as I continued to write all through the lunch period.

The hours continued to fly by as the bell rang for my last class to leave. There was no time to ponder as I dug straight into work. I continued to finish the lesson plan for the rest of the semester as I steadily wrote down the different topics and lessons. I dropped my pencil and looked at the clock to see it was already six o'clock. I quickly grabbed my laptop and briefcase and headed out the door.

"Sorry, Mrs. White, I was finishing up work so I could take some time off," I said as I held my phone to my ear and started my drive home.

"It's alright, David. We'll see you soon."

I quickly pulled up to the house and waited for everyone to come out. Mr. and Mrs. White slowly came out the front door as Aaron followed quickly behind. I rolled down the window and gave them a smile as they got in. "You guys ready!"

"Yessir!" Mr. White said with a smile as he walked around, getting into the passenger seat. Mrs. White helped strap Aaron in as we made our way to the hospital.

When we arrived at the hospital, Aaron was bursting with joy. "Momma!" Aaron yelled as he ran over to her. Aida closed her Bible and gave him a big smile.

"Hey, baby," she said, rubbing his head softly. I sat down on the chair next to her bed and placed Aaron on my lap. "Hey, honey." She smiled at me as I grabbed her hand.

"Hey, beautiful." I began to play with her hand as she looked over at her parents.

"Mom. Dad." She had an excited expression on her face as Mr. and Mrs. White gave her big smiles. Each gave her a kiss on her forehead as they sat down at the end of her bed. We all sat and listened as Aida told us stories about the hospital and how her treatment was going. She finally had more energy.

I began to bounce Aaron on my lap as Aida continued. "The nurses have been so nice to me. They always try and make me smile by talking with me and making sure I'm comfortable." Her smile eased my pain as I continued to hold her warm hand.

"Aida, don't you think David's beard is getting a little too long?" Mrs. White looked over at me with a playful smirk. Aida examined me for a second as I leaned in and let her grab my long beard.

"A little scruffy, but I still think he looks handsome." She took another close look at me as she held her hand on my cheek. "Honey, are you getting enough sleep?"

I looked away with a half-smile. "I'm writing you another story."

"Oh! I'm so excited." She clapped her hands. "You better not be pulling all-nighters writing it, though!" She gave me a scolding finger as she squinted.

"Uh . . ." I gave her a shrug as she gave me a little smack on my hand.

"David," she said with a scolding look, "you need your rest." I nodded as I continued to play with her hand.

We sat and spoke with her for another hour before she began to lean her head back and close her eyes. Mrs. White gave me a nod as I put the sleeping Aaron over my shoulder and stood up.

"Good night, Aida," Mrs. White said, kissing her daughter on the forehead.

"Goodnight, Mom and Dad," Aida said as Mr. White came over and gave her a kiss. I then grabbed Aida's hands and signaled everyone to bow their heads.

"Dear Lord, I thank you for letting us have another day with your beautiful daughter. Thank you for blessing us with her presence. Lord, we pray that you heal her and bring her back home. In your stripes, she is healed." I squeezed her hand tightly as I said those words. "In Jesus's name . . ."

"Amen." We opened our eyes. I leaned in and quickly kissed Aida's lips.

"Goodnight, babe. I love you."

She smiled at me as she softly ran her hand across Aaron's back. "Forever and always?" she asked with her beautiful eyes and smile.

"Forever and always," I replied. She then laid back and closed her eyes as we turned out the lights and shut the door.

It was quiet the rest of the night after we drove home. I quickly put Aaron to bed. He'd had a long day. I went into my office and continued to type away at my computer. My eyes were tired, but I could not fall asleep with the pain that continued to inflame in my stomach. Seeing Aida's smile made it completely disappear but another lonely night made the flame slowly return.

My hands typed away as the night grew long. My eyes focused on the screen as I would occasionally wipe my eyes to keep them open. I wrote for hours until before I knew it, the sun began to rise. I heard Mrs. White in the kitchen again as I slowly got up from my chair. My legs wobbled as I walked toward the kitchen. My body felt weak as I sat down at the kitchen table. I felt my head begin to sway as I tried to focus on getting ready.

Mrs. White placed a bowl of oatmeal in front of me as I slowly pulled several bites of food to my mouth. My arm shook with each bite as I tried to gather up energy to eat. My bowl was still half full before I got out of my chair and began to walk toward my room. "Thank you, Theresa," I said, before continuing to walk away. As I continued toward my room, I met Aaron and Mr. White in the hallway as they began to excitedly walk toward the kitchen.

"Good morning, Dad!" Aaron said as I walked by.

"Good morning, champ," I said quietly as I looked over at Mr. White. "Good morning, Mr. White."

"Good morning, David." He continued his way to the kitchen as I got dressed and ready for school.

After getting ready, I said goodbye to everyone before getting in my car. As I arrived at school, I felt very weak trying to make it through the day. Through each class period, I continued to type away at the story.

As lunchtime came, I sat in my classroom and stayed in to write the story. My typing continued all throughout the day until the final bell rang. I waved goodbye to my students as they all began to exit the classroom. I sat in my chair and leaned my head back, admiring my accomplishment. I couldn't wait to read it to Aida. I took several breaths as I looked up at the ceiling. I closed my eyes and stretched out my legs and arms, feeling the blood rush through my fingertips and toes. I cocked my head side to side as I leaned over my desk and began to finish up the semester's lesson plan.

As the clock hit five, I slowly got up and packed my briefcase. I wobbled my way over to my car as I drove over to the hospital. I carried my laptop in with me as I checked in at the front desk. It was just me this time. It was hard taking Aaron to the hospital every day, and Mr. and Mrs. White had decided to give me some alone time with Aida.

I walked into her room to see her smiling face reading her Bible. As I set down my laptop, she slowly closed her Bible and gave me her full attention. I walked over and gave her a big kiss on the lips. "I missed you, baby," I said as I held her cheek. I slowly took her Bible with my other hand and placed it on the nearby counter.

"I missed you, too," she said, giving me another kiss. She then looked over at the laptop in my hand, and smiled hugely. "Did you finish the story?" I nodded with a smile, sat down, and opened my laptop. I soon felt another burst of energy as I prepared to read her the story.

"You ready, baby?" I asked as she looked at me with her beautiful eyes. She nodded her head excitedly as I began to read the story. "'The Outlaw and the Reverend's Daughter' by David Catalano."

CHAPTER 10

THE OUTLAW AND THE REVEREND'S DAUGHTER

Part 1: Don't Mess with an Outlaw

The saloon door swung open as a dirty man covered in mud-brown clothing walked in. The spurs on his boots clanked with each step. In his hands were two revolvers held up and ready to shoot. His dirt-brown beard and missing teeth were almost as scary as the stench of his clothing. His eyes began to violently search the room as his top right lip raised into a sneer.

"I'm looking for an outlaw!" he said as he hit off a glass from the top of the bar. Glass and whiskey went everywhere as the man held his gun up to the bartender. "Now you tell me where I can find him," he said in a rusty voice. The bartender held up his hands as the man shoved his gun into the bartender's chest.

"Do you at least know his name?" the bartender asked in fright as he began to back up against the shelves of alcohol behind him.

"I don't know his name, but he wears a black mask." Before the bartender could move his hand, there was a hoarse voice behind him.

"You lookin' for me?" His cowboy hat covered his eyes and both cowboy boots rested up on the table. The man looked over at him and sat down in the empty chair across from him.

"Are you the one who killed my brother?" he said in a voice laced with anger. The outlaw lifted up his hat revealing a black mask across his eyes. The saloon was quiet as people looked at what the mysterious outlaw would say.

"Depends. Were your brothers tryin' to rob some innocent people?"

The man was angered in his response and pulled the trigger. The outlaw rolled onto the floor, dodging the two gunshots and holstered his revolver, releasing a string of bullets into the chest of the dirt-covered man.

The man fell back on the floor as the outlaw got up on his feet. He brushed off the dust on his chaps before walking over to the bar. He quickly picked up a glass of whiskey and gulped it down. He slammed down a piece of paper with the words WANTED across the bottom before gently placing the empty glass on top. "This guy's name is William Baker. Take this paper to the sheriff and see to it you get your reward." The outlaw tilted his hat at the bartender before walking toward the swinging doors.

"Wait!" the bartender yelled. "What's your name?"

The outlaw stopped in his steps as he turned his head over his shoulder. "The name's David." He then swung open the doors and hopped on his horse. "Yah!" he yelled, as the horse began to gallop out of the city.

Spit hit the dirt has a large boot began to twist over it. David now stood several miles outside of a nearby city overlooking the dusty road from atop a nearby hill. "David, you sure they're comin' down this way?" David looked over the ridge with his foot propped up on a mossy rock while his hand spun his revolver.

"Don't worry, Jon. They should be passin' through any moment now." He took off his hat and combed his hair back before putting on his hat again. Jon sat down on a rock as he twisted off the top of his canteen.

"You ever grow tired of running around huntin' outlaws?" Jon asked as David continued to peer over the ridge.

"Well, there ain't exactly any place for wild boys like us," David replied, holstering his revolver.

"Yeah, but what if we found a place?" Jon began to steadily drink from the canteen. "I mean wouldn't you like to actually have a place called home?"

David's eyes continued to look far off in the distance. "Jon, we've never had a real home. I just don't think men like us are meant to have a home." His gaze switched over to Jon, giving him his full attention.

"David, one day we will find a home. We won't be wild boys forever." David gave Jon a smile before stepping back up and looking over the ridge.

"Let's just hope God has mercy on us."

A carriage carried by four horses began to appear on the long dirt road. "Jon, they're here." David said as they quickly ran over to their horses and hopped on. Their horses' heels clicked against the sandy pebbles as David and Jon galloped away toward the moving carriage.

A woman sat quietly in her carriage as she looked out the curtain. "Dad, is this next city going to be nice for us?" she asked, looking over at her father.

"You're going to love Tombstone, Aida," he said in reassurance as he smiled at her across the carriage. Suddenly the carriage stopped and the sound of neighing horses was heard outside. Numerous hooves began to stomp around until a gunshot made the carriage accelerate at a much faster pace.

"Reverend," a voice said on top the carriage in a faint voice. The reverend peeked his head out the carriage to see several men riding alongside them and the coachman bleeding from a gunshot wound. The coachman continued to hold on to the reigns for dear life until the carriage hit a rock and they began to rock side to side with the wheels lifting off the ground. Gunfire filled the air as the horses became more and more frightened. Suddenly the carriage flipped on its side and the horses fell over with the carriage. The carriage dragged for several feet until the halters broke off and the horses ran down the dusty road.

Dust filled the air as several men dismounted their horses and began to open up the back of the carriage. "See who's in that carriage," a man said as two men began to climb on top. As they opened up the carriage door, they lifted up the reverend and threw him to the ground.

"Hey boss! Look who we have here!" They picked up Aida in her now dust-covered dress. "Looks like will be having fun tonight!" The boss smiled as one of them slung Aida over his shoulder. The boss walked over to the reverend as the man placed Aida on the ground. The reverend looked over at Aida to see her unconscious. He knelt down with his hands together looking up at the sky.

"I don't think this man has any reason to live," the boss said as he pulled out his gun and aimed it at the reverend's head. The reverend began to bow his head.

"Lord, please be with me," he whispered as the boss pushed the gun right up to his head.

"Silly reverend. You think God's gonna save ya?" The men all began to laugh as the boss put his finger on the trigger.

Boom! The boss' gun flew out his hand as another bullet hit him in the chest. Gunfire began to ensue as the men pulled out their guns and shot several rounds. David jumped off his horse and began to fire while running around the bandits. Two more men were shot in the back as Jon came up from behind and hid next to the carriage. David ran forward as one man remained dodging several bullets before sliding on the dirt and shooting the man right in the head. Blood splattered onto the ground as David got up and dusted off his brown chaps.

"You alright, sir?" David asked as he helped the reverend up. Jon soon came out from behind the carriage and holstered his gun.

"Thank the Lord!" The reverend bellowed as he got up and gave David a hug. His hands remained on David's shoulders as he looked into David's eyes. "It's by God's grace you were here to save me," he said, flashing David and Jon a smile.

David and Jon looked at each other in confusion. "Where were you headed, Reverend?" David asked as he walked over to Aida resting on the ground.

"I'm going to Tombstone," the reverend said as he knelt down next to Aida.

"Jon, throw me my canteen," David yelled. Jon quickly tossed David his canteen; David lifted Aida's head and began to splash water on her face. Her eyes slowly fluttered open as the reverend held her soft hand.

"Aida! You're okay!" the reverend said with relief as he pulled her toward him.

"What happened?" she asked as the reverend began to lift her up.

"We were attacked by bandits, but by God's grace these two men saved us."

As she stood up, David looked into her eyes, and she locked onto his gaze. Aida wrapped her arms around David as a large smile grew on her face.

"Oh, thank you," she said as she hugged him tightly. She then wrapped her arms around Jon as he walked next to David. "Thank you. Thank you." She let go and stood next to her father.

"So Tombstone, huh? What business you have in that town?" David asked as Jon began to gather up the bandits' horses.

"I'm spreading my ministry there," the reverend said as Jon handed David the reigns of one of the bandits' horses.

"I see. Well, we're also headed to Tombstone. Hop on and you can come with us." The reverend nodded as David helped the reverend and Aida up on a horse. David and Jon then began to pack up the bandits' bodies onto the horses.

"Why are you doing that?" the reverend asked as David and Jon hopped on their horses.

"These men are outlaws," David said as he looked over at Jon.

"We almost didn't come get ya. That's way more men then we usually take on," Jon continued as he looked back at David. "But David said he couldn't let ya die." David quietly nodded his head as the reverend gave him a smile.

"Thank you for saving us," the reverend said once again as David gently nudged his horse and began to trot down the road. The other horses began to follow as they began their journey to Tombstone.

As their horses walked down the long dirt road, David continued to glance over at Aida. She held her back up straight and even though her dress was covered in dirt, she still had a lady-like composure. Suddenly, their eyes met as David quickly turned away hoping she hadn't noticed. A smile came on her face as he peeked at her from the corner of his eye.

"Are you guys believers?" the reverend asked as their horses continued to pick up dust.

"We were raised together in the town of Yuma," David said as he looked over at Jon. "Our parents were killed when we were real young."

"One of the men that helped raise us taught us a lot about the Word and God," Jon said as he looked off into the distance.

"We don't know much, but we have faith that He's always with us. We have the stories to prove it." David looked forward with a little laugh.

"Well, you can add saving me and my daughter to that list," the reverend said as he looked over at Aida. "You guys should come to one of my services."

David and Jon looked at each other and began to chuckle to themselves. "Reverend, I don't think God wants us in a holy place like your church," David said with a crooked smile.

"If you ask me, that's exactly where God wants you to be," the reverend replied. David's face became serious as he looked up and thought about the reverend's response.

"Why would God ever love wild outlaws like us?" Jon asked looking over at the reverend.

A big smile came on the reverend's face as he prepared to answer. "Do you know who Jesus is?"

"He's the son of God," David chimed in.

"Precisely. Well, Jesus died on the cross so that you and I could be free of all our sins."

David laughed, "Well he's sure got a lot of sins to cover."

Jon began to think about what the reverend had said. "Yeah, but why would God send his son to die for us? We ain't worth much."

The reverend's smile grew even bigger. "God loves you. He sent his son to die for your sins because He wanted to be with you, and Jesus wanted you to be with his father." David and Jon looked at each other as they tried to understand what the reverend was saying.

"So all we got to do is believe?" David asked.

The reverend nodded. "If you believe it with your heart that Jesus can save you from your sins, then God will always be with you."

"I want to believe," Jon said as he trotted his horse closer to the reverend. "What do I have to do?"

David watched as the reverend grabbed Jon's hand and bowed his head. "Repeat after me. Dear Lord." Jon bowed his head and began to repeat the reverend's words.

"Dear Lord."

"I accept that Jesus Christ died on the cross so that I could be cleansed of all my sins." Jon repeated the words as David continued to look over curiously. "I know that through Christ I am saved and I am holy. Today, I begin my continuous journey toward knowing you." David looked over at Aida to see a big smile on her face as Jon repeated the reverend's words. "In Jesus's name we pray, amen."

Jon opened his eyes with a smile. "It's amazing, Reverend. I feel it in my heart." The reverend gave him a smile before looking over at David. David quickly looked away and continued to trot forward. "It's alright, David. It's all in God's timing," the reverend said as David looked back and nodded. He looked once more at Aida as she gave him big smile.

Part 2: Tombstone

Their horses trudged passed a sign with the words TOMBSTONE and several words underneath saying TOO TOUGH TO DIE. The town was dusty as the streets filled with people walking around and carriages rolling by. David and the others began to walk down the streets with their horses as the reverend began to trot ahead.

"It should be right up this way," he said, pointing toward the open street. They continued down the road until they stopped at a wooden building with broken windows. "This is it!" the reverend said as he got off his horse and walked toward the building. He walked through the open doorway and began to look around. Aida followed as she got off her horse and began to explore the wooden structure.

David and Jon looked at each other as Jon gave a shrug and got off his horse. He began to walk around the structure as David slowly followed. "It needs a lot of work. I could use your guys help," the reverend said as he looked over at Jon then David.

"I could stay and help," Jon said, looking over at David.

"I could help as well," David said. "But we got to turn in these bodies first." The reverend nodded as they walked out the door. David took once last look at Aida as she flashed him a smile. He tipped his hat toward her as Jon and David walked toward their horses.

"We've got four of them," David said as he put several papers on the sheriff's desk. The sheriff looked at the papers and then walked outside to see the bodies on the floor.

"I'll give you a hundred each," he said after looking at all the bodies. Jon nodded as David reached out his hand.

"Deal," David said as the sheriff shook his hand and walked into the back. He came back with a pouch full of gold coins.

"Four hundred dollars all in gold coins. Just as promised." He dropped the pouch in David's hand. David tossed it over his shoulder to Jon. Jon quickly caught it as David tipped his hat at the sheriff and began to walk off.

"Thank ya, Sheriff," David said over his shoulder as he proceeded to walk out the door.

Jon juggled the pouch as he smiled at David. "This is a large sum of money. We can finally buy our own place with this."

David looked at him with a crooked smile. "I don't think I'd want to sleep in a cozy home just yet," David said jokingly.

Jon gave him a serious look. "I don't want to hunt down bounties anymore. I want to find a place I can call home."

David looked up at the sky as he kicked up some dirt. "But we been movin' around since we were able to hold a gun."

Jon placed his hand on David's shoulder. "I think it's time I give up that life. I can stay here with the reverend and get a good job huntin' meat."

David kept his head down in thought before looking back up at Jon. "I understand. You've always wanted to find a place you could call home." He began to look around. "I think this place will serve you well."

Jon patted David's shoulder as they both mounted their horses. "Let's go see the reverend," Jon said as he looked at David with a smile. "And Aida." He gave David a wink as David began to laugh. "I see the way you look at her." David looked at him with raised eyebrows. "Don't deny it," Jon said, giving him a smirk.

"Alright, ya caught me." David looked up at the clear blue sky. "She's just so beautiful. How could a woman like that ever be with an outlaw like me?" He looked straight ahead.

"You know, you don't have to be an outlaw forever. You could settle down in this town with me."

David looked over at Jon with a smile. "I don't deserve a life like that," he said as they finally arrived at the reverend's structure.

Jon scowled. "God sent His son to die for us so you could have a life like that." David turned away. "It's alright. Like the reverend said, it's all in God's timin'." As David and Jon stood out front, the reverend soon came out with a piece of paper.

"I need your fellows' help," he said as he handed the paper over to Jon. "I'll give you fellows money and you can ride on over to Tucson. The church there said they have some supplies for us. Tell 'em Reverend Paul sent you." Jon nodded his head as he looked over at David.

"You ready to ride?"

David took off his hat, combed his hair back, and placed his hat back on his head. "Let's ride." David replied, mounting his horse. Before Jon could hop on his horse, the reverend grabbed Jon's arm.

"Why don't you guys set up camp with us tonight in our church? I could use your help cleaning up the place a bit." Jon looked over at David as David nodded back with a smile.

"Alright, we'll stay," Jon said as he began to unbuckle his sleeping roll from his horse. David dismounted and began to tie up the horses to the hitching rail outside the building.

"Guess we'll have a roof over our heads tonight," David said to Jon with a laugh.

As nighttime rolled around, the city was lit up with fire-lit lanterns. Several lanterns lit up the building while David and Jon began splitting up gold coins. "Four hundred dollars, Jon? What're you plannin' on doin'?"

Jon smiled as he looked out a broken window. "I'm gonna start my own business. I'm gonna start a family." He looked over at David. "You ever plan on doin' more than what you're already doin'?"

David raised an eyebrow. "Sure, I've thought about it," he said as he looked over at Aida. "If I could, I'd have a family and raise 'em with you." He gave a soft punch to Jon's arm. "Uncle Jon sure has a ring to it." Both of them began to laugh until Jon began to look away in thought.

"Well, what's stoppin' ya?" Jon asked as he looked straight into David's eyes.

David again looked over at Aida. "I just ain't good enough for that life," he said in a low tone. Jon gave him a half-smile as he softly hit him again on his shoulder.

"It's alright. You'll find you're worth it soon enough." Jon then crawled onto his sleeping roll and placed his head on his pillow. "I'll see ya in the mornin'. Now get some sleep."

Soon both Jon and the reverend were sleeping soundly. David eyes stayed open as he looked over to see Aida still reading a book by her lantern. David walked over to her as he leaned up against the wall next to her. "What're you reading, missy?" He asked softly as she stared at the book for several more moments.

"It's a book called *Pirates of the Great Sea*," she replied.

David was unable to resist her radiant smile. "What's it about?" He sat down across from her.

"Well," she said excitedly, "it's about a pirate who falls in love with a beautiful woman, and even though they are from two different worlds, they still find a way to fall in love." The lantern began to reflect light upon her eyes causing David to look right into them.

"I could understand that," he said with a little laugh. She began to shake her head with a smile. She got up and began to walk outside the front as David followed her.

"I heard you say you don't normally sleep under a roof. Why is that?" David took a step closer to her as he looked up at the sky.

"I like to count the stars when I sleep." She began to giggle.

"So you're sayin' you'd always sleep outside over inside on a comfy bed?" David looked at her with a smile as her eyes continued to stare into his. "If I had the beautiful stars in your eyes next to me, I'd never need to sleep outside again." His gentle voice made her lose her breath. David took a step closer as he held her hands.

"David, don't you be tryin' your flattery on me." David gave her a smile that caused her to turn away. She looked out into the lightly lit town. "I noticed you wear that black mask." She turned around and looked into his eyes. "Why is that?" He ran his fingers across the mask covering his eyes.

"I'm a wild outlaw," he said in a gentle voice.

"Then why doesn't Jon wear one?" she asked as she stepped forward and rubbed her fingers on the side of his mask.

"'Cause Jon's a good man. He ain't a killer like me." David put his head down as she lifted his head back up with her hand.

"There's good in ya, David. I see it."

David clenched his jaw as he looked away. "You don't know what I've done." Her hand pressed against his chest. "I may not know what you've done, but I've seen the good you've done for me and my father. You're like a courageous knight. It took a lot of bravery to take on all those men."

David closed his eyes trying to hold back the feelings her hands on his chest brought to him. He gave a half-smile before grabbing both her hands softly. "I ain't worth nothin'. God can't use a wild outlaw like me."

Aida looked down and squeezed David's rough hands. "It's all in God's timing. You'll see." She slowly let go as she began to walk back inside. David's eyes followed her as she blew out her lantern and crawled onto a cot. David then looked up at the stars and closed his eyes.

"God. What would you have from a man like me?" he prayed.

Part 3: Let's Ride!

As morning came, the sun slowly rose over the distant mountains. The Arizona sky was orange and purple as David and Jon began trot down the desert road. Cacti of all kinds scattered across the desert and several lizards scurried across the hot rocks. As the sun began to rise, a scorching heat baked the two outlaws. David grabbed his canteen from one of his saddlebags and began to pour the warm water down in his dry throat. After each rise in the road, the illusion of water seemed to form at the top of the next hill. With each gaining step, the water slowly disappeared like a mirage and showed nothing but rocks and sand.

David and Jon's revolvers reflected the bright sun as sweat began to trickle down their dirt-covered faces. David adjusted his hat, causing more sweat to fall down his cheeks. The sound of cicadas echoed throughout the desert as their horses' hooves clicked against the winding road. Suddenly, a loud noise punctuated the desert air, causing David and Jon to come to an abrupt stop.

"You hear that?" Jon asked.

"Let's go!" David yelled as he hit the side of his horse. The outlaws began to gallop down the road as horses' hooves followed quickly behind. David and Jon looked back to see a band of men on horses. "It's the cowboys!" David yelled as they began to gallop away from the men chasing them. Gunfire followed as the men with bandanas over their mouths began to shout across the road.

"Get 'em!" they yelled. David looked over at Jon and cocked his head. They soon split up, the men split formation, too. David quickly galloped up behind a sand mound before jumping off his horse and pulling out both his revolvers. *Boom boom! Boom boom!* He quickly blew two of the men off their horses before running and jumping off the mound, landing back on his horse.

"Ya!" he yelled as his horse began to chase after the three horsemen following Jon. Several more shots fired as Jon continued to maneuver his way down the road. His eyes focused on the road as he began to focus on a large turn.

One of the men continued to aim at Jon before gunfire brought him off his horse. The horsemen looked back to see David with his black mask following close behind. David dodged several bullets as the men began to shoot at him. More gunfire ensued as David turned off the road to avoid the two men's gunfire. As they turned around, Jon shot them off their horses and came to an abrupt halt. David came back out from outside the road and quickly came up to Jon.

"You see that Jon! We took on the notorious Cowboys!" He rolled up to Jon to see he was hunched over on his horse. "Jon, you alright?" David came up to find blood dripping down Jon's arm as he held his shoulder. David quickly got off his horse and wrapped some cloth tightly around Jon's wound. He grabbed the reigns of his horse and began to drag it with him down the road. He continued for several miles until Jon hunched over and fell off his horse.

"Come on, Jon. We're almost there," David said exhaustedly as he put Jon back on his horse. They continued for several more miles before finally arriving in Tucson. David quickly hopped off his horse and slung Jon over his shoulder. "Stay with me, buddy."

Jon soon woke up in a soft bed with a patch on his right shoulder. "What happened?" he asked as a man with a scruffy beard walked in.

"You got a gunshot wound to your right deltoid. Your buddy over there brought you over to me to help ya out." Jon looked over at David as he tilted his cowboy hat above his eyes. The man placed several fragments of metal on the counter next to the bed. "These are all the pieces from the bullet," he said as Jon began to examine the pieces.

"Ow," Jon held his shoulder pain as he began to sit up.

"You should be fine in a couple weeks. You're buddy here says you gotta long ride back to Tombstone. I'm sure you'll be fine if you don't run into any trouble." He looked over at David with a concerned look. "It's real dangerous out there right now. Them Apaches are startin' to get real violent with all these westerners comin' down." David nodded his head as he walked over to help Jon out of the bed.

"It's alright, Doc. We'll be sure to take the major road."

The doctor looked over at him with one eyebrow raised. "Well, you better load up on some ammo if you're gonna go back down to Tombstone." David nodded as he walked with Jon toward the swinging doors.

"Thank ya, Doc," David said over his shoulder as the doctor nodded his head and waved goodbye.

"You stay safe now, ya hear?"

David helped Jon on his horse while Jon used one arm to hoist himself up. "You ready to look for that church?" he asked. Jon nodded. "The reverend said it was the big church with stained glass windows." They walked their horses down the road as David looked up at all the wooden buildings.

"I reckon' that's it," Jon said as he pointed toward a church with a big cross on the front. They trotted over. David got off his horse and tied them up to the hitching rail. He helped Jon off as they walked toward the front of the big church.

"After you," David said as he opened one of the big wooden doors. The church had several rows of wooden pews lined up with a long red carpet in between leading up to the podium. They walked up the red carpet until a man stepped out from the back wearing a pair of nice pants and a black button down. The white clerical collar on his neck let David and Jon know he was one of the reverends of the church.

"How may I help you today?" The man asked as he carried his Bible in his hand. He reached out his right hand toward David in greeting. "I'm Reverend Tim. Are you here for prayer?" David looked over at Jon before reaching out and grasping Reverend Tim's hand.

"Pleasure to meet ya. I'm David, and this is Jon. We were sent by Reverend Paul to get supplies for the new church in Tombstone." Reverend Tim began to smile.

"Ah, yes! I hope the journey wasn't too hard. I was praying God would send some men to take these supplies back to Reverend Paul. Please, follow me." Reverend Tim began to walk toward the back of the church. He pointed to a carriage with food and different objects in the back. "Take that carriage back to Reverend Paul and give him my best wishes." David nodded his head as they began to walk back toward the front. "Wait!" the reverend said, stopping them. "Let us pray for God's protection in your journey.

"All right," David said as Reverend Tim put his hands lightly on both their shoulders.

"Dear Lord, I pray you be with these two men as they go on a journey to serve you. Be with them in all they do and help them to follow your plan for them. In Jesus's name, amen." David and Jon nodded their heads. The reverend looked at both of them with a smile. "You guys are new at this, huh?" Jon and David looked at each other and back at the reverend. "It's alright. After I say amen, you guys say amen as well." David and Jon turned their head in confusion.

"What does amen mean?" David asked.

"Amen means it is done by the hands of the Lord."

David and Jon nodded in understanding. "Amen," they both said together.

Reverend Tim waved them off as they began to ride the carriage outside the city. "God bless!" the reverend yelled as they waved goodbye. The carriage began to roll down the rickety road as David and Jon sat on top. David held the reigns as they continued back into the scorching desert.

"You ready to see Aida?" Jon said, looking over at David.

David looked at him with a crooked smile. "Oh shut up," David replied, giving Jon a light punch on his arm. They both laughed as the carriage began to bobble up and down through the rocky desert road.

"You think there are any mountain lions around here?" David asked as he looked around the surrounding ridges.

"I ain't seen any yet," John replied as he pulled up his revolver and began to spin it around his finger. "If we do see one," he stopped spinning his revolvers and aimed it forward pretending to shoot, "I'll shoot it down faster than you chug your whiskey."

David looked over with a grin. "I don't even think I can shoot that fast." They both began to laugh until suddenly several rocks appeared in the road causing the horses to stop. "What are these rocks doin' here?" David said as he jumped out the carriage to inspect the rocks in front of the road. As David took several steps toward the roadblock, several men began to rise up from the sand.

"Apaches!" Jon yelled as he jumped up on the top of the carriage and lay down with his gun. *Boom!* A bullet flew into an Apache trying to attack Jon with a knife.

David quickly turned around and pulled out his revolvers. *Boom boom!* He shot one Apache down just as another jumped on his back behind him. David jammed his elbow into the Apache's rib as he tumbled off. David quickly grabbed one of his revolvers and shot the Apache in the head, causing blood to splatter all over. The horses began to neigh loudly from the gunshots as they reared up on their hind legs trying to escape. "No more gun shots till I can—" Another gunshot caused the rearing horses to become even more out of control. David tugged at the reigns as he quickly began to push the rocks blocking the way. The horses then began to run through the opening as David rolled out of the way.

David ran after the speeding carriage as several Apaches latched on. "A little help here!" Jon yelled as he saw David chasing after the carriage. David quickly pulled out his two revolvers as he began to shoot the Apaches trying to climb on the top of the carriage. *Boom boom! Boom boom!* Three Indians fell off as the carriage began to gain speed. An Apache jumped on the back as the distance separating David and the carriage continued to increase. The Apache jumped on Jon with his knife as Jon struggled to hold on with one arm.

Boom! The Apache fell off the wagon as Jon's smoking gun was quickly dropped in order to hold on with both hands. "Ah!" Jon groaned as he pulled himself back up to the front and grabbed the reins. David finally came up in the distance breathing heavily and leaning over next to the stopped carriage to catch his breath. Jon peeked around the carriage to see David catching his breath and pressed his head back. He closed his eyes as he began to say a prayer.

David walked around and jumped up into the carriage. He hit Jon's knee with his hand as Jon looked over at him with a playful grin. "That was one hell of a fight!" David said as he rest his head back and took the reins. "Your shoulder alright?" He looked over at Jon who was cradling his shoulder.

"Yeah, my shoulder's fine," he said as he began to slowly rotate it. "I'm just happy tha—" *Schwuuf!* His voice cut out as an arrow flew straight into his chest.

"Jon!" David yelled as he looked over at an Apache standing on a tall ridge with his bow down. David quickly pulled out his guns and began to shoot, but his shots came nowhere near the Apache who jumped on his horse and rode away. Jon lay coughing as David leaned him against his shoulder and continued to hold the reins. "Ya!" he yelled as he quickly snapped the reins up and down.

The horses continued to bolt down the trail until the city of Tombstone was finally in view. The carriage rolled down the road until it stopped in front of the church. David picked up Jon in his arms and carried him over his shoulder. "Reverend!" David yelled as he placed the coughing Jon in the middle of the church. His breathing began to wheeze as he grabbed onto David's hand.

"It's alright, David," he said as he began to cough up blood. "I'm finally goin' home." David tightened his squeeze on Jon's hand until he felt Jon's grip slowly release. His hand went cold as the reverend ran into the church and knelt down beside Jon's motionless body. David's hands were red with blood as he stood up and turned away, clenching his jaw.

The reverend placed fingers on Jon's eyelids and slowly closed them shut. "Rest in peace," the reverend said as he stood up and looked over at David. David looked up at the ceiling trying to stay strong before looking back at the reverend. The reverend walked over and placed his hand on David's shoulder. "It's alright, David. He's finally gone home."

Part 4: He's Finally Goin' Home

David sat on the front steps of the church staring off into the city. Wind blew across his cold face as he continued to look off into the distance. His gaze didn't move for hours as he silently sat still. He walked over to the graveyard behind the church and began to dig deeper and deeper into the dry dirt. In the midst of the night, the shovel continued to hit the ground as sweat trickled down David's dirt-covered face.

The next morning, several gathered as David stood over Jon's grave. The reverend stood next to him with his Bible in hand looking around at the surrounding people.

"Jon was a good man," the reverend began to preach. "The Lord sent him to save me." The crowd was still in silence as David crouched down beside Jon's tombstone. "Jon wanted to do the Lord's work and died in doing so." He opened his Bible as he began to read. "John 14:1-4, let not your hearts be troubled. Believe in God; believe also in me. In my Father's house are many rooms. If it were not so, would I have told you that I go to prepare a place for you?" He closed his Bible as he looked out into the crowd. "Jon also dreamed of finding a place he could call home. This morning I know he finally rests peacefully with our Lord in heaven. Let us pray." David continued to lock his gaze on the grave of his best friend. "Dear Lord, bless those that mourn for they shall be comforted. Help us to be at peace with the passing of Jon. May he rest in peace as he stays with you. In Jesus's name, amen."

"Amen," David said quietly as he continued to look at the tombstone. David then stood up and turned away as rest of the crowd slowly dispersed. David saw Aida standing among the people as she came over and wrapped her arms around him. He pulled her closer to him as he tried to stay strong. As soon as she let go, David began to walk away from the city.

"Where are you going?" she asked, gently grabbing his arm. He turned his head over his shoulder and looked at her one last time.

"I don't know . . ." he said before turning and continuing to walk down the dusty road.

The sun beat on his black hat as he walked across the sandy desert. Cacti and wildlife ran around as he continued deeper and deeper into the heat of the desert. His legs shook as the hot sun began to take its toll on his sweat-covered body. He trudged several more steps before he finally fell to the ground. His eyes were half open, but he continued to look forward.

A figure began to appear in the distance as he knelt down on his knees and felt the heat of the hot sand burn through his chaps. He was too weak to move as he continued to see the figure coming closer and closer.

Soon an Apache with dark long hair and face paint came into the distance carrying a large knife. He grabbed David's head and began to prepare his knife against his scalp. David was too weak to fight as he closed his eyes and thought about his life.

As he closed his eyes, he saw Aida and her beautiful smile. As the knife came closer to David's hairline, the Apache knocked off David's cowboy hat and pulled his hair up preparing to cut off his scalp. David closed his eyes once more and whispered into the wind. "Dear Lord, have mercy on me so that I may be of service to you."

The Apache's knife began to shake as a strong gust of wind blew up sand into the air. The Apache suddenly dropped his knife and ran off into the desert. David fell back on the ground as the wind began to pick up dust and fill the air. Nothing was visible as he lay down on the warm dry sand.

The dust continued its sight-blinding swirl when a tall figure appeared through the windstorm. David's wavering eyes watched as the figure came closer and closer. Soon a hand grabbed David's and helped him to his feet. David put his arm around the figure as he slowly walked through the desert storm. He continued to walk blindly with the man-like figure until finally he couldn't go on. He fell to his knees and rolled over, closing his eyes and falling asleep.

Splash! Water hit David's face as he opened his eyes. He saw the reverend kneeling over him as he lay just outside the city. "Where did you go?" the reverend asked as David slowly began to stand up.

"I don't know," David mumbled in a voice that was barely audible. David walked toward the church as the reverend slowly followed behind.

David stepped up the steps to the church and walked into the wooden structure, falling to his knees and looking up. "God, by your grace I am saved. I give my life to you. Today I believe in the love you have for me." He closed his hands and bowed his head. "Thank you Lord for sending your son to die for a man like me."

The next morning, the reverend watched as David brought in wood and nails into the church. He began to hammer away at the sides, tearing up old planks and replacing them with new ones. He carried in more wood and began to make pews to sit in. As he grew tired, Aida brought to him his canteen filled with water. He quickly poured it down his throat and softly handed it back to her.

"Thank ya," he said with a smile. He then continued to hammer away at the wood planks nailing down each side. As the days went on, David bought supplies and built up the church. The reverend help as they made sure the wooden planks were set up evenly against the walls. David rolled out a large red rug that stretched all the way down the hall. The Reverend stood at the end of the rug, looking at the now almost finished church.

"There's only one thing missing," the reverend said with a smile as he looked over at David.

"And what would that be?" David asked, looking over at the reverend.

"Doors." David laughed as they walked out the church and began to build some wooden doors.

Once they were finished, David and the reverend began to haul in two large doors. Once they set the doors in place, they both stood on the steps and looked at the now completed church.

"Well David, what now?" the reverend asked as he looked over at David. David gave a smile as he continued to examine the church.

"It's time for you to start your first sermon," David replied, looking over at the reverend with a laugh. The reverend gave a nod as he walked into the church up to the front pedestal. Aida stood next to David. They watched the reverend smile across the room.

"Thank you," she whispered as she grabbed David's hand. He looked at her with a smile, grasping her hand tightly.

As the sun went down, David sat on the steps of the church bowing his head. He felt Aida step up next to him, so he stood up and looked into her eyes. There was a moment of silence as she as leaned her head on his chest. He wrapped his arms around her as she took in a deep breath.

"I'm so happy you came back," she said as she looked into his eyes. He smiled at her and brushed his hand across her cheek.

"I don't think I ever told ya this," he said as he continued to look deep into her eyes. She was quiet as he took a deep breath in. "While I was lost in the wilderness, I thought about seein' your beauty one last time." He closed his eyes and pursed his lips. "I asked God to spare me cause I wanted to be able to see your beautiful smile for just a little bit longer."

Her eyes filled with adoration as she put her hands around his neck. She slowly untied the back of his black mask as he began to close his eyes. His black mask fell to the ground as she looked into his eyes without the mask for the first time. Her eyes were illuminated the by the shining stars until they quietly began to close. David leaned toward her as their lips met. Her hand slid down to his chest as she continued to hold onto his neck. Their lips soon let go as he followed with a kiss her on the forehead.

"Goodnight, m' lady," he said as she slowly walked back into the church.

"Goodnight, cowboy," she said, smiling at him one last time before shutting the door.

As several weeks passed, David spent the rest of his money on a home in town. He started a business hunting for pelts and meat. Each day he would wake up early and hunt different animals around the outskirts of town. He spent most of his spare time helping the reverend with the church and would sit and talk with Aida each day.

"I've got several thumpers," he said as he placed several dead rabbits on the counter.

"I'll give ya ten dollars for these puppies," the man said as he placed several gold pieces on the counter.

David nodded and picked up the gold pieces to put in his pouch. "Thank ya, sir," David replied as he tipped his hat and walked out the swinging doors. He made one more stop before pulling up to the church and getting off his horse. "Aida!" he yelled. The reverend stepped out and walked down the steps. David wrapped his arm around the reverend's shoulders as the reverend walked with him.

"You better take care of my daughter now," he said with a smile as he watched Aida come down in a beautiful dress. He winked at David as he watched him pick Aida up and spin her around.

"You ready, m' lady?" David asked, holding out his arm. Aida gave the reverend a kiss goodbye before grabbing David's arm and walking down the steps.

"You be safe now, ya hear?" the reverend called out after them. David gave a nod as he waved goodbye.

David then proceeded to walk Aida past his own horse. "Where are we going?" she asked with a smile. David let out a quick whistle as a beautiful white horse came trotting out from behind a wooden house.

"This is Estella," he said with a big grin. "She's all yours."

Her eyes lit up as she coursed her hand across Estella's beautiful white mane. "I've never had a horse before." Her eyes began to water.

David quickly helped her mount the horse as she grabbed the reins.

"Follow me," David said as she followed him to the outskirts of town. After they trotted outside the city, they soon stopped on a ridge overlooking the desert. David then got off his horse and pulled out a rifle, handing it to Aida.

"Alright. I'm gonna teach ya how to shoot," he said as he stood behind her and held her arms. "First, you want to put the butt of the gun in your right shoulder so it doesn't knock you in the face." She began to laugh as he helped her place the gun against her shoulder. "Now close your right eye and look through the iron sight on the gun." She began to aim at a running rabbit. "Breathe slowly and time your breaths." She began to slowly control her breathing. "Now once the animal is in the cross hairs, breathe out and pull the trigger." She began to breathe out slowly. *Boom!* The bullet hit the rabbit as it fell over dead.

"I did it!" she said with a smile as she jumped up on David and gave him a kiss.

David smiled at her as he continued to show her how to use a pistol. "This rifle's for you." He pulled out a wooden rifle with a long metal barrel. She held on to it tightly, aiming it at a cactus. "Try and shoot it," he said with a smile as she continued to aim. She tried to pull the trigger only to have it stuck.

"Why is it stuck?" she asked as she opened the chamber of the rifle. Her eyes grew big as a large smile came on her face. She pulled out a diamond ring from the chamber of the gun as David knelt to his knee.

"Will you marry me?" he asked as he grabbed her hand and slid the ring on her left ring finger.

"Yes!" she yelled as tears began to stream down her face. As David stood up, Aida wrapped her arms around his neck.

"I already told your father. He's doing our weddin' in a couple weeks," She looked into his eyes with adoration. His eyes locked on hers as he kissed her forehead. He then helped her on her horse and held her hand as they rode off into the sunset.

Part 5: Too Tough To Die

When they arrived at the front of the church, David took Estella to the back stable. Aida kissed David once last time before she ran up the steps and waved goodbye to him. He smiled at her once again as he looked into her beautiful eyes. "Goodnight, m' lady," he said as he gave her small salute.

"Goodnight, my cowboy," she replied, slowly shutting the door behind her.

David turned around and continued to trot his horse down the town's dirt road. He then looked up to see several lights flickering in the distance. He squinted and began to gallop his horse toward the small lights approaching the city.

"What's your business here?" the sheriff asked as he stood in front of several men holding lanterns on horses. People began to step outside their houses in curiosity. The ringleader looked over at his fellow men before revealing a grin with yellow teeth.

"We're here to take this town." *Boom!* A gunshot pierced through the sheriff's chest as he fell to the ground motionless. David saw the sheriff fall in the distance as people began to scatter back into their homes. "Ride!" the head man said as they began to shoot gunshots into the air.

As David galloped back toward the church, he saw the outlaws begin to scatter into the city, lighting buildings on fire. "Find cover in the church!" David yelled as he pulled out his pistols. *Boom boom!* A bandit fell off his horse causing dust to rise into the air. "Run!" He yelled as he continued to cover several families as they ran to the church. *Boom boom!* He took two more shots as a chasing outlaw flew off his horse onto the cold hard dirt.

Families ran into the church as the reverend held open the door. "David! Hurry!" he yelled as David jumped off his horse and ran inside. He saw Aida sitting on the pew as he walked over and sat next to her.

"Are you alright?" she asked as she looked to see families piling in. David closed his eyes and then looked at one of his holstered guns. She nodded her head in understanding as she grabbed his hand. "Follow me," Aida said as she pulled him toward a back room. He watched as she opened a wooden box and pulled out a familiar object. "This town needs you." She placed a black mask in his hands. David looked at her for several moments before quietly nodding.

"I'll be back," David said as he turned around. He slowly walked across the long red carpet as the townspeople watched him quietly put on his mask. As he arrived at the door, he looked back, tipped his hat, and swung open the doors.

His fingers began to fiddle near his sides as he held his hands an inch away from his guns. His hat covered his eyes as he looked down the steps at several armed bandits ready to shoot.

"What do we have here?" The ringleader said as he got off his horse and revolved his pistol around his finger. "Looks like we found the wild outlaw we've been lookin' for." David eyed each man as he scowled at the approaching head man. "Boys. You know what we do."

Everything went in slow motion as bullets flew toward David's head. His pistols were pulled faster than any had seen as he began to shoot down several bandits into the dirt. The outlaws began to disperse as David hid behind a nearby building. "Where'd he go?" one of the bandits yelled as the gunfire ceased.

Boom boom! Two more shots fired as David stood on his horse's saddle and shot down two more outlaws. He quickly jumped of his horse and knocked another to the ground. "Ya!" he yelled as he got on his horse and galloped away from the ringleader and one more remaining outlaw. David jumped off the horse and somersaulted onto the church property. He ran behind the building as the ringleader motioned for his last bandit to go get him.

The outlaw ran around the building only to receive a boot to the chest as David grabbed his gun and shot him in the head. David ran toward the ringleader with his gun as he began to unload a round of fire. The ringleader shot several rounds toward David as he sprinted toward him. A bullet grazed David's shoulder as he fell to the ground and dropped his gun.

The ringleader got off his horse and walked toward the defenseless cowboy as he held his shoulder. "You put up quite a fight, boy, but today you die." The ringleader held the gun up to David's head as he closed his eyes. *Boom!* The gun flew out of the ringleader's hand as David stood up and punched him across the face. The ringleader held his hand in agony as David picked up his gun. He looked over at the church to see Aida standing on the steps holding the rifle he had taught her to shoot.

"You won't cause this town any more trouble," David said as he held the gun up to the outlaw's head. "By law, you are to be executed for conspiracy and the killin' of innocent people." *Boom!* The ringleader fell to the ground as David dropped the gun and closed his eyes. He walked up the steps toward Aida as she jumped into his arms.

"You saved us," she said as she wrapped her arms around his neck. As he set her down, he slowly backed away and looked up at the sky.

"No, God saved us," he said as he removed his mask and held it in his hands. "There's one last thing I have to do." He took a hanging lantern and walked over to a dirt hole. Aida held his arm as he lit the mask on fire and threw it in.

"Why'd you do that?" she asked softly. He looked up once more at the sky before looking back into her beautiful eyes.

"I was born again," he said, looking back at the mask. "So I'm leaving my life with that mask behind." He leaned in for a kiss as he felt her warm lips press up against his.

Several weeks passed and the sound of wedding bells filled the church. David stood next to the reverend as he watched the beautiful Aida in her white dress walk up the long red carpet. He thought about how he was to be married in the same church he had spent so much time building. The reverend smiled at David and gave him a nod as Aida walked up the steps.

She stood next to David as the reverend kissed her cheek. He opened his Bible and began to read as David and Aida looked into each other's eyes and held hands.

"Do you take this woman to be your lawfully wedded wife?" he asked as David took a breath.

"I do," he said as Aida let go of her breath, releasing her shoulders. Tears began to roll down her cheeks as the reverend looked over at her.

"Do you take this man to be your lawfully wedded husband?"

Her smile grew even bigger as she leaned in closer. "I do," she said as their lips came within an inch of touching.

"You may now kiss the bride," the reverend said as David and Aida's lips met. He wrapped his arms around her and spun her around as the townspeople began to clap and cry.

David picked up Aida and began to walk down the front steps of the church. People came out as he placed her on his horse and began to wave. He jumped up on his horse and felt her arms around his black vest. "Where to now?" she whispered in his ear.

"Time to make this place our home," he said. He then softly nudged the side of his horse as they began to ride off into the sunset, and David and Aida lived . . .

CHAPTER 11
WHERE BEAUTY LIES

". . . Happily ever after." I slowly shut my laptop and watched as Aida lay silently on her pillow. A smile came on her face as she closed her eyes and pushed her head farther back into the pillow.

"That story was amazing," Aida said as tear came down her cheek. She gently opened her eyes. "But still not as good as our story." She looked at me with eyes of adoration as I stood up and leaned over her.

"You're so beautiful," I said to her as I wiped away the tears from her eyes. Her smile grew bigger as she looked deep into mine. "You look more and more beautiful every day," I continued as I kissed her forehead, but she soon turned away.

"How can you say that?" she said with tears in her eyes. Her lip continued to quiver as she looked down at her frail arms. "I grow weaker and weaker every day. I am nowhere near as beautiful as I used to be."

I pulled her chin toward my face as I wiped away another tear. "Baby, you look more and more beautiful every day because although your body grows weaker my love for you grows stronger. True beauty lies in the love I have for you."

Her eyes closed as several more tears fell down her cheeks. A smile began to appear on her face as her lips continued to quiver. "I love you," she said, using all her strength to grab my arm.

"I love you, too," I replied as I pressed my head against hers and held my hand against her cheek.

"Forever and ever?" she asked with a sniffle.

"Forever and always," I answered giving her one more kiss on her forehead.

As I began to back away, her hand slowly released my arm. I picked up my things and walked toward the door as her head rested quietly on her pillow. I took one long look at my beautiful frail wife lying in the hospital bed as my heart began to sink once more. I turned out the light and slowly shut the door behind me.

I walked to my car thinking about my last moment with Aida. Aida had been so strong through it all, but today I saw her struggle. The struggle was finally catching up to her. My heart throbbed as I drove down the long winding roads. My heart continued to hurt until I thought about the way Aida looked at me after I had made her smile. With each story, she saw the love I had for her, and in her eyes I saw she was still completely in love with me.

I opened my car door and grabbed my briefcase as the throbbing emotions continued to make me feel weak. The house was completely silent as I entered. I quickly walked into my room and got into my bed. I looked up at the ceiling still thinking about all that had happened. Then I remembered her telling me the same words after every story, "But still not as good as our story." My eyes closed for several seconds until they jolted open. I jumped up and grabbed my laptop and sat down on my bed. I had been so blind. I now knew what to do. I was going to write her the best story she had ever read: our story.

I opened my laptop as the blinding light illuminated the dark room. My fingers violently tapped the keyboard as I watched words quickly form on the page. I was so weak, but my emotions continued to drive my fingers. I looked at the clock to see the hours continue to pass, but I couldn't stop. I continued to pour out my heart on the page as I remembered the wonderful memories of Aida. My eyes grew weary as I felt myself become dizzy. I shook my head trying to stay awake as I wrote page after page. Soon I looked over to see it was time to get ready for work. I looked up at the ceiling with tired eyes as I shut the laptop. I wanted to continue, but I knew it was time to get ready.

I walked down the hallway to see Aaron walk out of his room. He rubbed his eyes before running over to me. "Daddy!" he yelled as I picked him up and gave him a big hug.

"Good morning, champ," I said as I wrapped my arms tightly around him. I set him down as I walked with him toward the kitchen where Mrs. White prepared our breakfast. "Good morning, Mrs. White," I said as she put down oatmeal in front of me.

"Good morning, David," she said with a smile. Mr. White then walked into the kitchen and rubbed Aaron's head before sitting down.

"Good morning, Mr. White," I said to him as I put a spoon full of oatmeal in my mouth.

"Good morning, David," he said with a smile and a nod. "How was Aida?"

I looked down at my oatmeal as I continued to eat. "She's still feeling very weak," I said quietly. Mr. White nodded his head in understanding. "She very much enjoyed my story, though," I said trying to lighten the mood.

"Very good," Mr. White said as Mrs. White put a bowl of cereal in front of him and sat down. "I've enjoyed your stories as well," he said with a half-smile. I responded with a nod as I looked over at Aaron stuffing his face. He smiled at me as food flew out of his mouth.

"Are we gonna see Mommy, today?" he asked with an excited look.

"Of course, champ. If you're good, we'll see her right after I get off work."

"Okay!"

I slowly pushed myself up from my chair and walked back to my room. I picked up some clothes from the floor and threw them on as I prepared for work. I then grabbed my briefcase and headed toward the front door.

"Bye guys," I said after kissing Aaron on his forehead and hugging Mr. and Mrs. White. I waved goodbye as I got into my car and began to drive. I felt my eyes continue to close causing me to shake my head in an effort to stay awake.

As I arrived at school, I slowly got out and reached for my briefcase. "Good morning, Mr. Benelli!" a student said as I shut the door.

"Good morning, Anthony." I said as I began to walk toward the front office. My vision became blurry as I opened the door to the front office and walked in.

"Good morning, Mr. Benelli," Nancy said, waving at me. Her words were muffled as I continued to wobble in.

"Good morning, Nancy," I said as I leaned up against the front desk.

"Mr. Benelli? Are you alright?" Nancy stood up and took a look into my tired eyes. "Mr. Benelli?" Her voice became fainter as my vision continued to fade. I began to rock back and forth as I held on to the wooden desk. "Mr. Benelli?" Her voice sounded slower as my vision began to turn black. *Fa-thud.* My body hit the ground, and I completely lost consciousness.

"Mr. Benelli?" a man's voice said as I felt myself up against a soft bed. "Mr. Benelli?" The voice became clearer as I opened my eyes. The sound of a heart monitor beeping echoed through the room as I looked around. "Ah, you're awake." A doctor in a white coat stood next to my hospital bed as I examined the IV in my arm.

"What happened?" I asked as I touched the back of my head.

"Mr. Benelli, I'm Dr. Wills. You fainted from dehydration, exhaustion, and lack of sleep." He held his clipboard up as he proceeded to write something down. "You should be alright with rest and water." He began to flick the IV with his index finger as water began to drip. "You need to be more careful, Mr. Benelli. I know you're going through a hard time, but it is extremely important you take care of yourself." Dr. Wills looked at me with a concerned look as I nodded my head.

"I understand, Doc," I said softly as he turned around and walked out the door. The door opened again as my mother and father walked in.

"David!" my mom cried as she ran over to me and wrapped her arms around me. "You need to be more careful." I looked down at my feet under the sheets.

"I know, Mom. I'm sorry," I said as my father examined the IV in my arm.

"Son, I know you're going through a hard time, but you need to stay strong." He firmly held my hand as I nodded my head. I kept my head down as my parents sat down with me in the room.

"Does Aida know?" I asked as they looked at each other.

"She has enough to worry about," my mother said as she softly patted my hand. "Dr. Wills says you will be in here for a couple hours." I looked up at the clock. "We'll come get you before it's time to see her." I looked back at my mother and gave her a nod.

"Now get some rest, son." My father came over and grasped my shoulder as he gave me a small smile. My father slowly let go as my mother and he walked toward the door. I waved goodbye to them as they walked out. I watched the door close slowly as I leaned my head back into the pillow. My eyes grew weary as I felt myself drift back into sleep.

I opened my eyes to see the IV removed from my arm. I looked over and saw my briefcase lying on the floor. I slowly got out of the bed and pulled out my laptop. As I settled back in, I pulled the swinging table in front of me and began to type away. As I continued to type, I heard a knock on the door. I lowered my laptop and looked over. The door slowly opened as Jack walked in.

"How's it going, David?" Jack asked as he sat down in a chair next to me. I slowly closed my laptop as I looked over at him.

"Mr. Oliver, I'm very sorry about what happened," I replied as Jack placed his hand softly on my shoulder.

"I understand, David." He said as he looked down. "I know you're going through a very hard time." His voice was very serious. "I'm giving you leave for a couple weeks," he continued as he pulled his lips in. "You're a darn good teacher. I don't want you to wear yourself out."

I gave him a nod as I looked over at my briefcase. "Could you hand me my briefcase?" I asked. Jack nodded as he turned over and grabbed my briefcase from the floor. As he handed it to me, I opened it up and pulled out the lesson plans I had been working on.

"This should help the substitute through the rest of the semester," I said, handing him the papers.

"Thank you, David," Jack said as he slowly got up. "Your students will miss you."

I gave him a strong nod as I looked straight ahead. "I'm going to miss them, too." I said trying to remain strong.

Jack patted me on the shoulder before walking toward the door. "Get some rest now."

"Thank you, Jack," I said as he gave me one last nod before exiting.

My heart hurt when I thought about how I couldn't finish the semester. Aida's cancer was beginning to wear on me. I took a deep breath before I continued typing.

I continued to type for several hours as I focused on my computer. I felt well rested as I continued to quietly write away. *Knock knock.* I quickly finished the sentence on the page before looking up. "Mom, Dad, nice to see you again." I slowly got out of the bed as a nurse came in behind. She conducted several tests on me before nodding her head and letting me go. As I left the hospital, my parents walked with me. I found my car in the parking lot and looked over at my mother.

"We picked your car up from the school," my mother said as she gave me a quick hug.

"Jack told us." My father said as he put his around my back. "Now you can spend more time with Aida." I nodded my head as I opened my car door.

"Thank you," I said as I wrapped my arms around them. "I love you guys."

My mother gave me a smile as I let go. "We're always here for you and Aida." She said as she pinched my cheek. I gave her a small smile before getting in my car and starting the ignition. I waved goodbye as I drove toward home.

I began to worry as to what Mr. and Mrs. White would think of my exhaustion. As I pulled up into the driveway, I saw Aaron playing in the front. "Daddy!" he yelled when I got out of the car. He jumped into my arms as I hugged him tightly. "Can we go see Mommy?" he asked as I opened the door and put him into his seat.

"Of course, champ," I said before looking over to see Mr. and Mrs. White walking toward me. Mr. White wrapped his arms around me and gave me a small pat on the back.

"It's nice to see you're okay," he said as he placed his hand on my shoulder. He gave me a nod before walking to the passenger seat of the car and getting in. Mrs. White came and wrapped her arms around me as well.

"I know you're going through a hard time," she said as she put her hand on my cheek, "but you need to stay strong for Aida." I gave her a nod as she smiled then got in the car.

"Is everyone strapped in?" I asked as Mrs. White gave one more tug on Aaron's seat belt.

"All set, Dad!" Aaron yelled as I started the ignition.

"Alright, prepare for take-off!" I said as I began to pull out of the driveway.

The car was quiet as we drove to the hospital. I tried to play the radio to ease the mood, but everyone continued to silently look out the window. As I pulled in, Mrs. White unstrapped Aaron as we all got out. We walked through the front entrance as I checked us in.

"We're here to see Aida Hope Benelli," I asked.

"Go on ahead," the woman said as we continued to walk down the hall. I held Aaron's hand as we opened the door to Aida's room. She lay sound asleep as I sat in the chair next to her bed and placed Aaron onto my knee. We sat there for several minutes looking at her rest as Aaron leaned up against the hospital bed.

"Momma," he said softly waiting for her to reply. Her frail body continued to rest peacefully as I pulled Aaron back toward me.

"She's alright, champ. Mommy needs her rest," I whispered as he continued to watch Aida sleep.

Knock knock. We all looked over to the door to see Dr. Hopkins standing in front. Mr. and Mrs. White looked at each other before looking over at me. I nodded as I slowly got up. I gently put Aaron in my seat as Mrs. White walked over to my chair. I gently opened the door and closed it behind me in order to not make any noise. Dr. Hopkins held his clipboard with both hands as he looked up at me with a serious face. My stomach dropped as I waited for what he had to say.

"Mr. Benelli, I have terrible news." His serious tone continued to make my heart drop.

"Yes, Dr. Hopkins?" I replied calmly as he looked back at his clipboard.

"Aida's cancer has entered stage four. There's nothing more we can do." Dr. Hopkins eyes continued to look down as I felt the raging fire in my stomach begin to burn my insides. I couldn't breathe as I leaned myself up against the nearby wall. "I'm sorry,

Mr. Benelli." He said looking into Aida's room. I nodded my head as he looked over at Mr. and Mrs. White. I tried to regain my composure as I opened the door.

"Come here, champ." I picked up Aaron as Mr. and Mrs. White met Dr. Hopkins outside. I saw them disappear down the hall as I sat down again with Aaron on my lap. We sat quietly until Aaron fell asleep against my chest. I looked over at Aida with my burning stomach and held Aaron close to me. I gently grabbed her hand as she continued to rest peacefully. I thought about all the wonderful memories I had with her and how she might soon leave my life. My eyes began to water as my heart continued to thump violently in my chest. I closed my eyes and began to pray.

"Lord, please be with Aida and our family through this hard time. May you continue to have your hand on her life." I tightened my grip on her hand as I ran out of words to say. "In Jesus's name, amen."

CHAPTER 12

NO HOPE FOR A HAPPY ENDING

Aaron fell asleep on my lap as I watched Aida lay calmly in her hospital bed. My stomach raged with fire causing my whole body to feel weak. My eyes continued to lock on Aida as my heart sank deeper into my fiery stomach. The door opened as Mr. and Mrs. White slowly walked in. Mrs. White had tears rolling down her cheeks as Mr. White held her close. They stood next to me as we all looked at Aida peacefully lying in her bed.

I felt Mr. White's hand on my shoulder as he gave me a nod. I gently placed Aaron over my shoulder as I let go of Aida's hand. Mr. and Mrs. White both kissed Aida on the forehead before we went out the door.

After leaving the hospital, we all slowly walked toward the car. I strapped Aaron in his car seat as we all began to get in. The car was completely silent as I started the engine and began to drive home.

The rest of the night was completely quiet as we got ready for bed. Aaron continued to sleep soundly in his bed as I sat on my desk and continued to write. My fingers slowly tapped at the keyboard as my heart began to beat at an even slower pace. The house felt drained of life as silence filled the air. I heard sniffles from the other room as Mr. White comforted his crying wife. All I could do was continue the story. I prayed that Aida would live long enough to hear it.

The hours passed as I slowly typed at the keyboard. My heart continued to pour on the page as I thought about Aida and our beautiful memories together. I felt a soft hand on my shoulder.

"David, it's time to get some rest." I turned around to see Mr. White grasping my shoulder. He looked into my bloodshot eyes as I slowly closed the laptop and gave him a nod. I walked with him down the hall before we began to split ways. "Goodnight, David."

"Goodnight, Mr. White," I said as I opened my door and walked into my room. I slowly took off my shirt and walked over to my bed. I crawled in as my eyes began to slide shut. My head fell into the pillow, and my breathing began to slow. I pulled the covers over my cold body as I began to drift asleep.

"Daddy?" I felt somebody tugging at me gently. "Daddy?" I opened my eyes to see Aaron slowly tugging me. "You were asleep all morning," he said as I looked over at the clock.

"Twelve o'clock?" I rubbed my head as I sat up.

"Come on, Daddy. Get up!" Aaron said before he jumped off the bed and ran out the door. My feet hit the soft carpet as I followed him into the kitchen.

"Good afternoon," Mrs. White said gently as I sat at the table.

"Good afternoon, Mrs. White," I said softly, still trying to wake up. "I slept in today." Mrs. White set a plate with a large sandwich in front of me.

"We let you sleep in. You needed the rest." She gave me a small smile before taking Aaron's hand and going with him outside. I bit into the sandwich to taste the delicious flavor of turkey and mayonnaise. I took several more bites until the whole sandwich was gone. I rubbed my stomach in satisfaction. I then slowly got up from the table and walked over to my office. I sat down in my chair and opened my laptop.

"Now where did I leave off?" I said aloud as I started to type again. The warm sunlight gently pressed against my shoulder as I looked out the window. I was home on a weekday. I heard Aaron outside with Mrs. White playing as I leaned back in my chair. The day was beautiful; the two trees out front began to sway in the wind. I turned back to my computer and continued to write thinking about the wonderful days just like this I had spent with Aida.

Hours passed as I heard people walking throughout the house. The house was much busier during the day as Aaron would either be playing outside or running into his room to play with his toys. I could hear Mr. White on the phone consulting some of the men from the church on a new project while Mrs. White was heard in the kitchen preparing dinner. Time flew by as I continued to write my story. I closed my eyes and remembered special moments I shared with Aida. My fingers steadily hit the keyboard as I continued to type away at our story.

"Dinner!" Mrs. White yelled as I finished several more words. I slowly closed my laptop and walked to the table. Everyone sat down as Mrs. White placed lasagna in front of us.

"Yum," I said as she sat down at the table. "Shall we pray?" We all grabbed each other's hands and bowed our heads. "Dear Lord, thank you for this delicious food and this wonderful family. I pray that you may be with Aida also as we enjoy this wonderful meal. Thank you for all you've given us. In Jesus's name . . ."

"Amen." Everyone said as we opened our eyes. The table was soon quiet with exception of spoons dishing up food. The food was delicious as I shoveled it into my mouth. Aaron gave me a smile before putting a big spoonful lasagna in his mouth.

"Mm!" he said with a smile as he began to chew the large amount of food. His smile was contagious as the rest of us began to slowly smile.

"You better slow down there, champ," I said pointing my fork at him. "You want to be able to chew your food." He nodded his head with a smile as he continued to put food in his mouth. Dinner became quiet as we finished up our food. I helped Mrs. White with the plates as Aaron ran off to his room.

"You better wash your hands, mister!" Mrs. White yelled as he ran down the hall.

"Yes, Grammy!" he yelled back as he turned into the bathroom.

After helping clean the dishes, I sat at my chair and continued to finish the story. I wrote for several more hours until my eyes slowly grew tired. After several more words, I stopped typing at the computer. I clenched my jaw as I looked up at the ceiling in thought. I bit my lip as I tried to think of what to write. My mind was blank. I sat for several more minutes until I became frustrated. I hit my desk in frustration as I quickly stood up. I walked around for several moments looking over at the unfinished story. I took deep breaths as I placed my hands on my waist. "Maybe I just need to rest," I said as I slammed the laptop shut.

I walked to my bedroom and looked over to the clock to see it was two in the morning. I laid my head down as I clenched my jaw in thinking. I stared at the ceiling as my mind continued to think about the story. I soon felt my eyes grow heavy as I felt myself begin to fall asleep.

My eyes abruptly opened as I rolled out of bed. My body still felt weak as I walked down the hallway. I heard the sounds of spoons clinging against bowls as I walked into the kitchen. "Good morning, Daddy!" Aaron said as I sat down at the table.

"Good morning, champ," I said with a small smile as Mrs. White brought me a bowl of oatmeal. "Thank you, Mrs. White," I said as I began to dig in. Mr. White quietly read the newspaper as the atmosphere of the house continued to feel cold. I slowly got up and washed my dish as Aaron got up and grabbed my leg.

"Daddy, will you come play with me?" he asked as I gave him a smile and patted his head.

"Alright, champ," I replied as I followed him to his room. He pulled out a bin of different dinosaurs as he slowly set them up around the room. I quietly listened to him imagine a story of the dinosaurs fighting and communicating with each other. I was amazed to see my son exhibit so much imagination. I played with him for two hours before I finally got up and gave him a hug. "Daddy's gotta go," I said as Aaron nodded and continued to play with his toys.

After leaving Aaron's room, I sat down at my desk as my head began to throb. I closed my eyes tight as I tried to continue the story. I let out a deep breath as I opened my eyes. I slowly closed my laptop once again as my eyes began to water. I walked over to the kitchen table to see Mr. and Mrs. White reading their Bible.

"I'm going to visit Aida," I said as they looked at me.

"Go see her," Mr. White said as he placed his hand on Mrs. White's shoulder and gave her a nod.

"We'll visit her later tonight," Mrs. White said with a small smile.

"Thank you," I said as I waved goodbye. I then put on my shoes and walked out the door. As I began to drive, I looked over at my laptop and began to look down. As I arrived at the hospital, I got out of the car and carried my laptop inside.

"I'm here to see Aida Hope Benelli," I said to the woman at the front desk as she waved me through. I slowly walked down to the hall to her room and gently opened the door.

"David?" Her voice was faint as I slowly shut the door and sat next to her. A smile came on her face as I grabbed her hand and looked into her luminescent eyes.

"Hey, baby," I said with a quivering smile.

Her eyes were slightly open as she looked down at my laptop. "Did you write me another story?" A big smile came on her frail pale face.

My lip began to quiver more as I opened up my laptop. "I did." A tear streamed down my cheek as I quickly wiped it away. "But I couldn't finish it." My lip continued to quiver as my eyes began to water. Aida gave me a concerned look as she continued to lay flat on her pillow. "I just didn't know how to give it a happy ending." I suddenly felt tears begin to run down my cheeks. I tried to hold them back only to have more tears stream down. It was the first time Aida had seen me cry. She squeezed my hand tighter as I set the laptop next to her bed.

"It's alright," she said with a smile. "I have faith that we will have a happy ending." Her strength made me feel more at ease, but my lip continued to quiver.

"How?" I said looking into her eyes for an honest answer.

"You will see," she said with a smile. She soon closed her eyes and began to rest.

As she fell asleep, I pondered what she said. I couldn't imagine my life having a happy ending without her. I looked at my frail wife and her pale skin as I held her hand. Her hand was no longer as warm as it used to be. My heart sank into my stomach as I closed my eyes and prayed.

"Dear Lord, help me through this hard time. Help strengthen me. Help me to have faith in the plans you have for Aida and me. In Jesus's name . . . amen." My stomach felt weak as I opened my eyes. I sat and looked at Aida for several hours before I finally got up and kissed her forehead. "I love you, Aida," I said as I slowly walked out the door. Everything seemed blurry as my heart continued to sink into my stomach. I felt hopeless thinking about Aida and her lying in that hospital bed. She was continuing to grow weaker and weaker. My heart ached as I got in my car and drove home.

As I got home, I walked into the kitchen to see Mr. and Mrs. White preparing to leave. "Here are the keys," I said as I dropped them into Mr. White's hand.

"Thank you," Mr. White said as he gave me a pat on the shoulder. "How is she?"

I looked into his eyes and pulled my lips in. "She was responsive today," I said trying not to tear up.

"That's good," Mr. White said as he let go and walked toward the front door.

"I have food in the fridge if you want to make dinner," Mrs. White said, trying to smile as I opened the door.

"Thank you, Mrs. White. You guys have fun with Aida." I waved goodbye as I shut the door. I walked to the fridge and pulled out a plate of chicken and mashed potatoes. I quickly pushed the plate into the microwave and shut the door. I waited several minutes for my food to warm up. *Beep beep.* I quickly opened the microwave door and grabbed my food. I sat at the table slowly eating my food as I looked at the clock. "Aaron?" I yelled, finishing up my dish.

"Yes, Dad?" he said, coming in with two dinosaurs in his hands.

"You ready for me to tuck you in?" I asked as I put my plate in the sink.

"Yes!" he said excitedly running toward his room. I followed him down the hall until I saw him kneeling next to his bed.

"Alright, champ. Your turn to pray." We both kneeled against the bed as Aaron began to pray.

"Dear Lord, thank you for my amazing daddy and my amazing mommy. Thank you for giving me another day to pray. I pray that you can be with Mommy and heal her. In Jesus's name . . ."

"Amen," we both said. Aaron quickly jumped into his bed and pulled up the covers. "Dad?"

"Yes, son?"

"When do I get to read the stories of you and Mommy?" His eyes looked into mine as I searched for an answer.

"When you're a little bit older," I said finally with a wan smile. "Goodnight, buddy. I love you." I gave him a kiss on his forehead as I got up.

"I love you too, Dad," he said before closing his eyes and turning over. I then slowly shut the door and left his room.

I walked into my room and sat on my bed as the pain in my stomach continued to torment me. I threw my feet up as I laid my head into my pillow. I stared at the ceiling, thinking about Aida as my heart continued to ache. I looked up at the ceiling for several hours until my eyes finally became heavy. I tried to think about a happy ending to the story as my lip began to quiver again. I felt hopeless. I closed my eyes and did a small prayer as the pain in my heart kept me awake. I soon realized I had left my laptop on Aida's counter. I forced my eyes shut as I soon found my breathing begin to slow. I let out a yawn as I finally found myself falling fast asleep.

My eyes opened as I felt the light from my window shine into the room. It seemed so much harder trying to get out bed. I slowly got up and rolled onto the floor. As I stood up, I heard little feet stomp into the room.

"Dad." Aaron opened his arms as he jumped up for a hug. I quickly lifted him up and carried him down the hall. Mrs. White silently prepared food in the kitchen as I sat Aaron down in his seat. Mr. White sat across the table from me continuing to read his newspaper. The table was quiet as we followed our daily routine. Mrs. White placed a bowl of oatmeal in front of Mr. White and me as we begin to eat.

"Thank you, Mrs. White," I said as I put a spoonful of oatmeal in my mouth.

"Thank you, honey," Mr. White said quietly as he set down the newspaper. The table continued to be silent as we all finished up our meal. I got up from my chair and washed my bowl in the sink.

The doorbell rang. Aaron jumped up and followed me to the door. As I opened the door, Aaron jumped into my mother's arms. "Grandma!" he yelled, holding my mother tightly.

"Good morning, Aaron," my mother said as she gently put him down. Mrs. White and Mr. White came behind as they each gave her a hug.

"Good morning, Dana," Mrs. White said as she let go.

"Good morning, Theresa," my mother replied with a small smile as we stood at the doorway. "You ready to go?" I gave her nod as we waved to the family goodbye.

"My keys are on the counter!" I called to them. My mother started the ignition as we began our peaceful drive to the hospital.

My mother focused on the road as we quietly drove. "Are you doing alright?" my mother asked as she squeezed my arm. I gave her a nod before looking back out the window. "Your father and I are praying for Aida." She began to sniffle as a tear fell down her cheek. "She's such a strong woman." I looked back at her to see her eyes filled with tears. I placed my hand on her shoulder in comfort.

"It's hard, Mom," I said, trying to remain strong. She pulled her lips in and gave me a nod as we continued to drive. As we stopped at the hospital, I gave her a big hug over the seat. "Thank you, Mom. I'll see you and Dad later." I slowly got out of the car and walked into the front doors of the hospital.

"Aida Hope Benelli," I told the front lady. She gave me a smile and gestured me toward the hall. As I walked down the hall to her room my heart continued to sink.

"Mr. Benelli," Dr. Hopkins said as he stood next to her with several nurses hooking up devices to her. He let out a sigh as he placed his hand on my back shoulder and walked me outside. "Aida's main organs are starting to fail." We both looked in as the nurses continued to connect wires to Aida. "You can stay the night with her if you wish." I bit my lip and held my head down.

"Yes, Dr. Hopkins. Thank you," my voice squeaked as I held back tears. He gave me a nod before entering back into the room. I waited several moments for the nurses to finish before I walked back in. I sat next to Aida looking at her frail frame as she peacefully lay on the hospital bed. The nurses slowly walked out as I grabbed Aida's cold hand and pulled it to my cheek. I took a deep breath as I quietly leaned against her bed and watched her slowly breathe. I sat for several hours holding her as she lay there completely unresponsive. I waited for her eyes to soon open, but she continued to be in a deep sleep. I continued to think about our life for several hours and how I might be spending my last moments beside her. The pain in my stomach burned as I leaned as close to her as I could.

Knock knock. I lifted my head up to see my parents along with Mr. and Mrs. White at the door. We all stood around her as tears began to form in all their eyes. I picked up Aaron as he began to quietly cry in my shoulder. We stood over her for several minutes watching her frail body continue to slowly breathe.

"Shall we pray?" Mr. White finally said as we all began to hold hands. "Dear Father in heaven, be with Aida as she faces her final days with us." Sniffles were heard around the room as I felt my mother's hand grasp mine tighter. "May she soon rest peacefully with you, free from pain. Lord, thank you for the wonderful daughter you gave us and the wonderful wife and mother she's been." My lip began to quiver as I silently nodded my head. "Dear Father, may you also give us the strength to live peacefully knowing she is with you. In Jesus's name . . ."

"Amen." Everyone opened their eyes and lifted their heads. The room was still as we all stood by Aida. I sat down once more as we all circled her. The room was completely quiet as Aaron sat on my lap looking at his mother. Tears streamed down his face as he watched his frail mother continue to quietly breathe. I saw in his eyes he did not completely understand. He looked at Aida the same way I had looked at her all day. The pain in my stomach continued to burn as I watched Aaron try to talk to his mother.

"Mom," he said quietly with a squeak as he looked at her closed eyes. "Is Mom going to wake up?" He looked up at me with tears streaming down his face. I hugged him to my chest and began to rub his back.

"She's preparing for her journey," I said, holding him close to me.

"Where's she going?" He asked with tears pouring down his face.

"She's going home to be with God." His lip continued to quiver as he looked up at me.

"Why is she leaving so soon?" he asked.

I searched for an answer as my lip began to quiver. "God needs Mommy to be in heaven right now for a special purpose." I clenched my jaw trying to stop my lip from quivering.

"What special purpose is that?" He began to puff out his lip even more.

"I don't know, buddy. I don't know." I held him tightly as I felt a tear slowly roll down my cheek. We sat for several hours more until the sun began to set. I rocked Aaron back and forth in the chair as I continued to look at my beautiful wife. Even though she was pale and frail, she was still the most beautiful woman in the world to me.

It soon grew late as my mother and father slowly got up. "We're going to take Aaron home and get him to bed," my mother whispered. I gave them a nod as I handed my mother the sleeping boy. My mother kissed my forehead as they both stood over Aida for several more moments.

"Bye, Aida. We love you," my father said as he kissed her hand gently. Several tears came down his cheek as he walked over and opened the door.

"Bye, Aida. Thank you for making my son so happy." My mother kissed Aida's hand as tears began to roll down her cheeks. My father comforted her as they walked out with Aaron.

It continued to get late as Mr. and Mrs. White sat quietly in their chair. Mrs. White leaned up against Mr. White as they seemed to be fast asleep. Aida was still unresponsive as I grabbed her cold hand again and felt her soft skin. Mr. and Mrs. White soon awoke as they slowly got up. They looked at me with a nod as I got up and left the room. I watched as they gathered around her and closed their eyes and prayed. After several minutes, Mrs. White burst into tears. I saw Mr. White comfort her as they watched their baby girl lay quietly in the hospital bed. I stood next to the door until it slowly opened and the crying Mrs. White came out. I wrapped my arms around her gently as I comforted her into my shoulder. I felt her face move back and forth as the sound of her crying began to make my eyes water. I held her hand as she looked at me with a nod.

"You take care of Aida," she said as Mr. White slowly put his arm around her and began to walk her out. Mr. White gave me a wave as I walked back into the room. I silently sat in the dark only lighten up by the devices attached to Aida. I looked over to my laptop and put it on my lap. I looked at her resting body one more time before I tried to speak to her.

"I know I didn't finish the story," I said to her, hoping she could hear me. "So I'm going to read to you what I already have." I slowly opened my laptop and took a deep breath. "'Our Story' by David Benelli."

CHAPTER 13
OUR STORY

Part 1: You Remember Jon?

"Wake up!" a voice yelled as my body began to shake.

"What is it, Jon?" I asked slowly opening my sleepy eyes.

"We've got to get up! Lieutenant Carson is coming any moment." My eyes opened wide as I quickly jumped up. "Don't forget your boots!" Jon yelled as he threw my boots to me. We then ran outside into the cold desert as the stars continued to shine bright in the sky.

"Attention!" Lieutenant Carson yelled as we stood straight in salute. The lieutenant slowly walked by each one of us eyeing us up and down until, suddenly, he stopped at Jon. "Private! What is your name?"

"Aaron Jonathan Migliore, but people call me Jon, sir!" Jon stood still in salute as the lieutenant looked up and down at his attire.

"Your shoe is untied! Drop down and give me twenty!" Lieutenant Carson yelled in his face as Jon quickly dropped to the ground and began to do push-ups with a straight back.

"I want you all to pay attention to details!" The lieutenant yelled as he walked side to side with his arms behind his back. "Do I make myself clear?"

"Sir, yes, sir!" we all yelled in unison.

"Details are what keep us alive!" Lieutenant Carson stood still and began to look around. "Do I make myself clear?" he yelled again.

"Sir, yes, sir." Jon quickly got up with sand on his chest as he stood back into position.

"At ease," Lieutenant Carson said as he walked away. All the soldiers began to prepare for breakfast as the cold air of the desert continued to send chills down my spine.

Everyone sat in a large courtyard with tables as they got served scrambled eggs and potatoes. I walked past several people in waiting line before sitting down with Jon at a table.

"You ready for today?" Jon asked as he slurped up a cup of water.

"What's today?" I asked taking a bite of scrambled eggs. I gave him a face of displeasure as he reached for some hot sauce.

"There's been a rebellion in one of the towns," he said as he handed me a bottle of hot sauce. I began to hit the back of the bottle as red sauce covered my eggs.

"Are they heavily armed?" I asked, looking up at him and taking another bite.

"Only AK's but we don't know how many there are." I gave him a nod as we continued to eat.

After we ate, we prepared our gear and headed out of the camp. Several other soldiers followed us as we each got into a Humvee. "I'll man the gun," I told Jon as I jumped up into the cockpit.

"All right," Jon replied with a nod as he opened the driver's seat and got in. I hoisted myself onto the gun as we began to drive down the long dirt road.

As the sun rose from the horizon, the temperature began to heat up and the dust filled the air. Soon a town with several tall brick buildings began to appear in the distance. The helmet on my head continued to bobble around as we rolled over several rocks into the city. Women in burqas began to scurry into their homes with their families as we drove by. Several Humvees followed us as we explored the town.

Ding! Kids began to throw rocks at us as we continued to drive through. We ignored them as rocks continued to hit the sides of our Humvees. I then suddenly looked up to see movement on one of the building tops. "Stop," I whispered to Jon as the vehicle slowly came to a halt. It was silent as I looked around to see the streets soon become empty. *Bratatat!* I ducked my head as machine gun bullets flew toward me.

Budda budda budda! I fired my heavy machine gun at a man hiding on the roof top. *Budda budda budda!* I fired another round as more men began to appear. "Ambush!" I yelled as I continued to shoot down the attacking men on the walls. "Drive!"

The wheels spun up dirt as more fire flew toward our Humvee. *Bratatat!* I ducked down as more AK-47 bullets pierced into the side of our vehicle. *Budda budda budda!* I shot down another man in a headdress as blood splattered from his head. "Another kill confirmed," I said into my radio as I ducked down from more fire. *Budda budda budda!* I continued to fire as men began to fall from the buildings. "Jon, turn!" The Humvee tipped as we took a sharp turn around a building. The Humvee sped up as we drove toward the exit. *Crack!* A bullet hit the Humvee causing the windshield to crack as I fired the gun several more times.

Budda budda budda. I continued to shoot the popping up men until suddenly my bullets hit something unexpectedly. A woman carrying a child appeared around a corner as my bullets flew toward her head. My heart sank as Jon looked in the mirror and saw her fall to the ground. I watched as the little boy she was holding lay on the ground crying in agony looking into his mother's blood covered face. The distance between us slowly grew bigger as the boy's scream echoed throughout the hot desert.

"Man down! Repeat man down!" The radio began to sputter as we drove back to headquarters. We quickly pulled in to find a group of medics waiting to attend to any casualties. They quickly opened the door and pulled out a soldier holding his shoulder.

"I've been shot. I've been shot," the soldier said as they carried him over to the medical tent. I began to breathe heavily as I sat back into the Humvee.

"You alright, Jon?" I asked grabbing his shoulder. I heard him try to catch his breath as he leaned back in his chair.

"Yeah. Are you?" I looked back and closed my eyes.

"Yeah," I said as a medic soon came to our Humvee. We followed him to the medical tent as he flashed his light into each of our eyes and started to check our heartbeats. He asked us several questions as we tried to calm ourselves from the traumatic experience. It was the first time we had been in heavy fire, and I had killed an innocent mother. As the medics walked away, Jon reached over and grabbed my forearm.

"Brothers in arms," he said as I wrapped my hand around his forearm.

"Brothers in arms," I replied, giving him a firm shake.

We did not talk about the incident after that day. It destroyed me inside when I thought about the death of that innocent mother and haunted me most nights as I thought about her child. I saw it also take a toll on Jon as he would moan in his sleep, "Don't shoot!" The pain continued to grow.

As the months went on, the heat began to take its toll on our bodies. The sun caused us to sweat profusely as our uniforms would become drenched from the unbearable heat. At night, the temperature dropped significantly as we wrapped ourselves up on our cots. As winter began to approach, the weather became cold. I felt my fingers grow numb each day while working out in the desert field. We continued to take out ours Humvees and patrol towns. We were always waiting for another ambush as I scouted the rooftops and different alleyways. Our routine continued until January finally came.

"Are you guys ready?" Lieutenant Carson asked as we finished packing up our bags.

"Yes, sir!" we both said with a salute as we grabbed our bags and followed him out of the tent. A large aircraft waited outside as Jon and I hopped onboard. We waved goodbye to Lieutenant Carson as the large door began to shut.

"We're going back to the U.S.!" Jon laughed as he playfully punched my arm. I gave him a smile as I nodded my head.

"Back home to Tucson, Arizona," I said with a smile looking up at the ceiling

The plane's wheels began to roll against the runway until it finally took off. We both fell fast asleep as the plane flew. We were excited to be on leave for two weeks and see our families.

We changed several flights until we were finally on an airplane home. As we landed at the airport, I nudged Jon and looked out the window. "We're home!" I said excitedly as he began to stretch. It was a long wait as we exited the airplane and grabbed our bags. I stood with Jon as we waited for my parents to pick us up.

A familiar car stopped in front of us as my parents got out and came toward us. "David! Jon!" My mother wrapped her arms around both of us and kissed each of us on the forehead.

"Hey, Mom," I said as she slowly let go. We threw our bags into the back of the car as my father came around and gave both of us a hug.

"You guys are so grown up," my dad said in admiration.

"Thanks, Dad," I said with a smile.

"Yeah, thanks Dad," Jon repeated jokingly, giving me a nudge. We drove Jon home as my parents asked us all about our adventures.

"It's a hard life. We don't get much sleep anymore," I said as my parents continued to ask questions.

"You could say that again," Jon said with a laugh.

We drove several more miles until we pulled into a neighborhood. The car slowly stopped in front of Jon's house as his parents waited in front. "Jon!" his mother yelled as he wrapped his arms around her and picked her up. She smiled at him as he put her down. "Oh, and David!" She came over and gave me a big hug. "Is David taking care of you over there?" she said, pointing at Jon.

"Actually he's taking care of me," I said as I wrapped my arm around Jon and pulled him to me.

"Somebody needs to wake you up," Jon said jokingly pushing me off him.

"Mr. Migliore," I put out my hand as Jon's dad wrapped his arms around me.

"It's good to see you, David," he said before walking over to Jon and wrapping his arms tightly around him. "I'm so proud of you, son."

"Thanks, Dad," Jon said as I walked back to the car. I waved goodbye as I rolled down the window.

"'Bye, Mr. and Mrs. Migliore!" I yelled as they waved back. My parents continued to wave as the car started to pull out of the driveway.

"Hey David!" Jon yelled before I could finish rolling up the window.

"Yeah?" I asked sticking my head out and looking at him.

"Let's go to church tomorrow!" Jon yelled as I gave him a confused look.

"Church?" Jon looked at me with big eyes as I began to think about it. "Alright." I said giving him a nod as I rolled up the window.

When I got home I instantly ran over to my room and looked at my bed. My bed was even softer than I remember as I threw my stuff down and jumped on it like a little kid. "Dinner!" my mother yelled as I dug my face into my pillow for several moments. I took a deep breath before answering.

"Coming!" I yelled as I slowly got up from my bed and walked over to the table. I sat down to the smell of spaghetti and tomato sauce. "Mm," I said looking at a large plate of spaghetti and sausage.

"Shall we pray?" my father asked as we grabbed hands. I nodded my head as we bowed our heads. "Dear Lord, thank you for bringing our son back to us safe and sound. We pray you keep him safe and allow us to enjoy the time we have with him. In Jesus's name . . ."

"Amen," my parents said as I kept quiet. I dug into my food as spaghetti sauce began to splatter all over my face.

"Son!" my dad scolded as he handed me a napkin. "Stop eating like a wild animal." He began to laugh as I slurped up the rest of my noodles.

"Sorry, Dad," I said with a smile. "I just haven't had something this delicious in a while." I looked over to my mother with a smile.

"Thank you, son," She said as she took another dainty bite. "I made sure to make your favorite." I continued to dig in until my stomach felt like it was going to explode.

"That was delicious!" I said, leaning back against my chair. "Thank you, Mom and Dad." They gave me a smile as I got up and took everyone's dishes to the sink. "I'm going to get some rest," I said as finished washing off the sauce on the dishes.

"Goodnight," my mom said as I walked toward my room.

"Goodnight, son," my dad said as I gave them a wave.

I slowly opened the door to my room and jumped on my soft bed. I felt my body sink into the soft mattress before I finally turned over and pulled up my blankets. I rested my head on my pillow and slowly began to close my eyes.

Part 2: Jon's Salvation

I heard the doorbell ring as I slowly got out of bed. I heard people talking until footsteps came toward my room. The door quickly opened as Jon jumped on my bed and tackled me. "Come on, man! You just woke up?" Jon slowly got off me as he gave me a light punch on my shoulder. "Get ready! We're going to church." I gave him a look as I slowly got up and rubbed my eyes.

"Alright, man. Let's go," I said as he looked at my hair.

"You didn't even take a shower, did you?" He shook his head before walking out of the room. "What if you meet your future wife today?"

"Ha!" I laughed as I put on my shoes. "It'll be a long time before I meet my future wife," I said, continuing to laugh.

"Man, you never know!" Jon said as we walked toward the front door. "'Bye, Mr. and Mrs. Benelli!" he yelled as we walked outside. Jon jumped into his car as I slowly opened the door to the passenger seat.

"So what's this church called?" I asked as we began to drive down the street.

"Grace Church," he said with a smile as we continued down the road.

As we pulled in, people gathered around the front and continued to mingle. Jon and I walked up the steps toward the church examining the large cross on top of the building. "Good morning," a man said as he handed us both a pamphlet.

"Thank you," I said with a smile as I grabbed one. We continued into the church and sat down in a large hall. The seats began to fill as music played throughout the room.

"Everybody stand up and praise the Lord!" a man said as the choir began to chant a lovely hymn. Jon and I quietly sat down as everyone stood up and sang. I was amazed with the energy of the room. Everyone was so filled with joy as they sang at the top of their lungs. People began to hold up their hands in praise as they looked up to the ceiling with their eyes closed.

"Open the eyes of my heart, Lord. Open the eyes of my heart. I want to see you."

Everyone sang those words as I listened carefully. I looked over to see Jon leaning against the chair in front of him with a large smile on his face. I was confused as to what was going on. It'd been long time since I'd been to church. I sat in my chair observing everyone around me until I looked up at the choir. My eyes opened wide as I saw the most beautiful girl in the world singing in the stands. That was the day I first saw you.

You were so beautiful standing up in front singing. I don't know why you stuck out more than everyone else, but you lit up the room like nothing I'd ever seen. A smile came on my face as I watched you sing in joy. I wanted to meet you, but I was afraid. I nudged Jon on the arm as I pointed at you in the stands.

"Who is she?" I asked as Jon squinted his eyes and looked to where I was pointing.

"Her?" He gave me a small laugh. "That's Aida. She's the pastor's daughter."

My eyes continued to fix on you as the lights illuminated your eyes. "I'd love to meet her," I said in a daze leaning back in my chair.

"Oh yeah?" Jon said as he leaned back with me. "Maybe I'll introduce you."

I suddenly jumped out of my daze. "No way! Look at her. She's way too good for me."

Jon began to shake his head. "You never know, man." He gave me a smile and a playful nudge as everyone began to sit down.

"Let's all bow our heads in prayer," the pastor said as he stood up at the podium. Jon and I began to bow our heads as the pastor began to pray. "Dear heavenly Father, I pray that you be with us today as we receive your message. May you inspire in the hearts of those who are here today your words. In Jesus's name . . ."

"Amen," everyone said as we opened our eyes and looked up.

"Today, I'm going to teach about the reason God sent his Son to die for us." The church was quiet as Jon focused in on the pastor. I sat back in my chair with my arms crossed looking for you in the crowd. "None of us are perfect. We are all sinners in God's eyes." The pastor continued to speak on the podium as he held up a microphone. "It is impossible for one to be saved by good works." He looked out at the audience as he spoke with authority. "For it says, all our righteousness is like filthy rags. We could never make the payment ourselves for the sins we have." He began to step down from the podium. "No amount of giving money to charity or serving others will save you, but I tell you this is not a bad thing. God sent his Son to die on the cross so that we could be saved. Jesus is our salvation." A big smile came on his face as he looked into the audience. "God so loved the world that he sent his only begotten Son to die for us. His Son came down and took the debt of our sin. Whosoever believes in Christ and accepts him as Lord shall see the kingdom of heaven. They shall not be disappointed." Jon watched as the pastor looked straight at him. "There is no need to hold on to the sins of the past. If you believe in Christ and accept him as Lord you can be forgiven of your sins and saved in him." He gave Jon a smile as a tear began to run down his face. I sat back in my chair thinking about what the pastor had said.

As the pastor continued to speak, Jon stayed focused as he wiped away the tears streaming from his eyes. He continued to look at his outline and follow the teaching as I sat back wondering why Jon was so interested.

"Let's end with a prayer," the pastor finally said with a smile as Jon and I bowed our heads. "Dear heavenly Father, I pray you work through everyone's heart today as they hear your message. May you help them to live righteously as they accept your grace. May they hear you call them to you. In Jesus's name . . ."

"Amen," he said as I looked over at him in confusion. As the people began to leave, Jon walked over to the pastor standing at the front.

"Hello there," the pastor said as he held out his hand. "I'm Pastor White, are you both new here?" I nodded my head as Jon shook his hand.

"Pastor White, your message today really touched my heart." He continued to hold his hand. "How does one find Christ?"

Pastor White gave him a smile. "One simply accepts that Christ died on the cross for our sins." He let go of Jon's hand and placed it on his shoulder. "And accepts Christ as Lord of their life, pursuing a life of righteousness."

Jon fell to his knees. "How do I accept Christ as Lord?" Jon asked as tears continued to stream down his face. Pastor White knelt on his knees and grabbed his hand.

"Repeat after me. Dear Lord." Jon closed his eyes and began to repeat Pastor White's prayer.

"Dear Lord."

"I believe your Son died on the cross for my sins."

"I believe your Son died on the cross for my sins," Jon repeated as I watched him close his eyes and look up at the ceiling.

"I accept Christ as Lord."

"I accept Christ as Lord." I was amazed as I watched the emotion channel through Jon.

"I will live a life of righteousness because I know you, Lord," Pastor White continued.

"I will live a life of righteousness because I know you, Lord."

"In Jesus's name, amen."

"Amen," Jon said as he opened his eyes with a smile. "Pastor White, I feel different."

Pastor White patted his shoulder as he helped him up. "Continue to seek the Lord," he said as Jon nodded his head. Pastor White looked over at me as I began to shy away. "It's alright. It's all in God's timing," he said to us as Jon and I waved goodbye. We both began to walk out of the church as I looked at Jon in confusion. A huge smile graced Jon's face as he looked up at the sky in a daze.

"Jon? What happened?"

Jon looked at me with his big smile. "I'm saved from my sin," he said as he began to jump up in the air. I quickly put my hand on his shoulder and looked in his eyes.

"Jon?" He looked at me with big eyes as he continued to smile.

"You remember that day we got shot at in that little town?" I nodded my head. "Well ever since that day I started praying. My heart felt heavy since the death of that woman."

I looked at him in confusion. "But Jon, it was I who killed her."

Jon looked at me with his lips pressed in. "Yes, but it still hurt me that I saw her die. I know it was an accident, but I prayed that I might find salvation and forgiveness from God." He looked up at the sky as he closed his eyes. "Today I found it."

I gave him a pat on the shoulder. "I admire that," I said with a half-smile.

"But David. Why haven't you accepted Jesus?" Jon looked at me with sincere eyes.

I looked up at the sky as I took a deep breath. "I don't believe Jesus would have anything to do with a man who has committed sins like me," I replied as we continued to walk out the church.

"David. Jesus died for all our sins." He placed his hand on my shoulder. I looked away as he tried to give me comfort. "It's alright, David. Just as Pastor White said, it's all in God's timing."

As we walked down to our car, I suddenly saw you standing in the parking lot. "Jon!" I whispered as I nudged him and tilted my head toward you. "It's her." Jon gave me a goofy smile as he began to walk over to you. "Jon! Stop!" I whispered as he continued toward you.

"Hello there," Jon said holding out his hand.

"Hello," you said as you shook his hand.

"I'd like you to meet my friend, David." He put his hand on my shoulder as I walked up next to him.

"Hi," I said shyly as you gave me a smile. Your eyes were so beautiful the first day I met you.

"Pleasure to meet you David. I'm Aida." You looked at me with a smile as we shook hands. Your hand was soft as we looked into each other's eyes for the first time. I didn't know at that time, but I'd get to look into your beautiful eyes for many more years. I tried to speak, but I couldn't get any words to come out.

"We're new here. Only back for two weeks." Jon gave her a smile as he nudged me. "Well, I'll meet you at the car." He gave me a wink as he walked away.

"He's nice," you said with a smile.

"Yeah." I looked over my shoulder. "He's been my best friend since we were kids." I looked back and got lost in your eyes. "Uh, are you busy this week?" I asked with a smile. You looked at me with a white grin as you put your hand on your chin.

"Hmm," you mumbled. I was nervous as to what you would say. "I'm teaching at the church during the week."

"Would you like to go on a date with me on Wednesday?" My voice was a little shaky as I tried to seem confident.

"Depends. Where are we going?" you replied, giving me a smile that made me feel even more nervous.

"It's a surprise," I said, pulling out my phone. "Can I have your number?"

You looked at me for several moments. "How 'bout I get your number and tell you what time I'll be ready on Wednesday, okay?"

My heart beat faster as I realized you had indirectly said yes. "Sounds good!" I said with a smile as you pulled out your phone and took my number. "Well, nice to meet you," I said, opening my arms for a hug.

"Nice to meet you, too," you said as I squeezed you in my arms. It was the first time of many more I would hold you tightly in my arms. I opened your car door as you giggled. "Why thank you." I gently shut the door and waved goodbye as I walked back to Jon's car.

"Wow," I told Jon. "She's so beautiful." I lay back dazed in my seat.

"And you were too nervous to say hi to her!" He gave me a playful punch.

"Thanks man," I said, grasping his shoulder. "Who knows, I'd definitely marry that woman."

Jon gave me a smile as we continued to drive. "I could see it."

"Really?" I said giving him a serious look.

"Yeah, man. I see the way you look at her. I know you'd treat her right."

I gave him a nod in agreement as he dropped me off at my house. "Thanks, Jon!"

"Are you coming with me next week?" he asked, squinting his eyes and waiting for my answer.

"Yeah. I'll check it out again," I replied as he waved goodbye. I walked into my house, sat down on my couch, and thought about how amazing it was that I might have gotten a date with the most beautiful girl in the world: you.

Part 3: The Beginning of a Wonderful Love Story

Beep. My heart pounded against my chest as I looked over at my phone to a text. "Six o'clock tonight?" it read.

I quickly replied. "Sounds good! I'll pick you up at 6!" As soon as I hit send, my heart began to race. "Oh no," I said aloud. I didn't want you to know how excited I was to go on a date with you. I quietly waited for you to text back as I paced back and forth. *Beep.* I quickly flipped open my phone and read your text message. "Her address!" I said aloud pumping my arm. "It's a date!" I jumped up in the air before running over to my dresser and searching for the right clothes to wear.

As the clock hit five forty-five, I quickly got in my car. I wore a green button down shirt and blue jeans. It was the nicest shirt I owned, and I wanted to do anything to impress you. As I drove up to your house, the clock hit five fifty-nine. After I slowly got out, I made sure I was right on time. As soon as the clock on my phone hit six o'clock, I quickly rang the doorbell.

Ding dong! I heard several footsteps patter against the tile floor until the doorknob slowly began to turn. I quickly ran my fingers through my hair one more time.

"Well hello," your father said as he opened the door.

"Mr. White. Pleasure to see you." I shook your father's hand as he let me in.

"Theresa! We have a visitor." Your mom said as she appeared from the hallway and wrapped her arms around me.

"So nice to meet you," she said pinching my cheek.

I gave her a smile as I looked around. "It's a wonderful place you've got here," I said as I examined the décor in the room.

"Ah yes. Many of these decorations are from the different mission trips we've done," your father said. I soon began to examine a decorative vase. "That was from Uganda." I nodded my head in interest as I continued to examine the interestingly designed vase.

"Is he here?" I heard you yell from your room.

"I sure am!" I yelled as we all began to laugh. I stood with your parents for several minutes as they asked questions about my life. I didn't know at the time that one day your parents and I would become very close.

I soon heard the door open as you walked into the front room. I remember that moment like it was yesterday. You had your hair down and a beautiful long dress on. I tried not to stare as you gave me a big smile. "Are you ready?" you asked, looking straight into my eyes.

"Y-yes," I said with a little stutter trying not to act nervous. I shook your father's hand and gave your mother a hug goodbye as we walked toward the door. I opened the door for you as you walked outside. "Shall we?" I said, giving you my elbow. You gave me a smile as you locked your arm with mine. I walked you down to my car and opened the door for you.

"Why, you're such a gentleman," you responded as I helped you in. I walked over to the front and slowly got into the driver's seat. "Where are we going now?" you asked with a smile.

"An Italian place called Caruso's," I said smiling back as I started my truck. I put on some country music as we began to pull out and drive down the black road. It was quiet between us until a song started to play on the radio. I began to nod my head to the music as I looked over at you. "*If there's a want and there's a need,*" I sang loudly as I gave you a smile. "*There's a history between. Girls like her and guys like me. Cowboys and Angels.*" You gave me a half smile as I continued to sing. "*I've got boots and she's got wings. I'm hell on wheels and she's heavenly.*" You began to laugh as I tried my hardest to hit each note. I stopped singing as I looked into your eyes.

"Do you always sing that song to your dates?" you asked raising your eyebrow.

"Nah," I said looking back at the road. "You're the first angel I've ever met." I looked back at you with a grin as you playfully hit my shoulder.

"Are you always this cheesy, too?" you said with a half-smile as we slowly pulled into a parking space.

"Wait right here," I said as I quickly got out and walked around the front of the truck. I slowly opened your door as I grabbed your hand to help you out.

"Why thank you, kind sir," you said, impersonating a British woman.

"You very welcome, darling," I said, pretending to be a British chauffeur. We locked arms as I again opened the door and let you into the restaurant. "Seats for two," I told the host as he motioned us to follow.

"Right this way." He walked us into the restaurant and gestured toward two seats. "We'll seat you right here." I slowly pulled out her chair as she sat down. The host then handed us each a menu. "Your waiter will be with you shortly," he said before walking away.

"I hope you like Italian," I said as I lifted up my menu.

"Mm. Chicken Alfredo," you said as you continued to examine your menu.

"What are you getting to drink?" I asked with a smile looking over at you.

"Coca Cola. My favorite."

"Coca Cola? Dr. Pepper is the real choice here," I said in a teasing tone.

"No. Coca Cola is better," you retorted in a teasing voice.

"No."

"Yes."

"Uh, no."

"Yes!" you yelled as people began to look at us.

"Fine you win," I said laughing as I looked around.

"Thank you," you said playfully as you picked up your menu. A waiter soon came to our table as we prepared to order.

"What would you two like to drink?" the waiter asked as he held up his notepad.

"She'll take a Coca Cola, and I'll take the Dr. Pepper," I said gently. The waiter then gave a nod before walking off.

"Find anything of interest on the menu yet?" I asked as you continued to read through.

"Well, I can't choose between the Chicken Parmesan and the Chicken Alfredo."

"Chicken Alfredo," I said setting my menu down. "Trust me." I gave you a smile as you set down your menu.

"Trust you? Now why would I do that?"

I slowly leaned forward and looked side to side. "You can always trust a cowboy," I said looking into your eyes.

"All right. This will be the first thing I trust you with."

"I'm honored," I said with a grin.

"May I take your orders?" the waiter asked as he came up to our table with a pen and pad.

"She'll have the Chicken Alfredo, and I'll have the Chicken Pesto," I said as I quickly grabbed the menus and handed it to the waiter.

"Thank you. Your order should be out shortly." He picked up the menus and walked off.

You and I continued to talk for hours at that table. Even after we got our food I continued to make you laugh and smile as we ate. As we finished our meal, I paid the bill and we walked back to my car. I opened the door and helped you in once more before we took off.

"Are you taking me home?" you asked as you looked at the time.

"Nope. I told you I have a surprise," I said as we continued to drive into the night. We drove up several hills as we sang together to country music in the car. You had such a beautiful voice.

"Where are we going?" you asked as another song ended.

"We're almost there," I responded with a smile. After several moments, I suddenly turned into a cul-de-sac. Your eyes lit up as I stopped the car, leaving my keys in the ignition. I opened the door and walked up to a low iron fence. You slowly got out and stood beside me as we looked off into the distance. "I know you wanted more of an adventure, but I thought this would do for now." We looked out into wide view of the lit up city. You continued to step up to the nearby railing as your eyes continued to peer out at the view.

"David. It's beautiful," you said with a smile. I slowly grabbed your hand as music began to play on the radio.

"*If there's a want and there's a need. There's a history between. Girls like her and guys like me. Cowboys and angels*," I sang as I took your hand. I began to spin you around as we danced in front of my car to the playing music.

"Do you know how to dance?" I asked as I slowly spun you around.

"Not that well," you said with a little laugh.

"Well, it's like this." I placed my hand on your back as I began to show you the steps. We continued to make a box with our feet as we danced under the stars. "Very good," I said with a smile as I spun you around once more. You were a quick learner as I continued to walk you through the steps. We continued to dance until you finally rested your head on my shoulder.

"Aida. What are your dreams?" I asked as we danced under the moonlight.

"I want to go on an adventure," you said, looking up at the stars.

"An adventure?" I asked as we continued to spin around.

"Yeah. I want to go to New Zealand." You gave me a smile as I looked into your beautiful bright eyes.

"I could make that happen," I said, pressing my hand against your cheek.

"Oh yeah?" you said looking up at me.

"One day. I promise." I put out my pinky as you latched your pinky on mine.

"That's a pinky promise," you said continuing to smile.

"And pinky promises can't ever be broken." You gave me a giggle before closing your eyes and resting your head against my chest.

"David, what are your dreams?" you asked as you pressed against me. I looked up at the sky and closed my eyes.

"I want to be a writer. I want to publish stories about amazing adventures and true love." You looked up at me as the moonlight reflected the beautiful color of your eyes. "My stories are my adventures." I looked into your eyes once more. "Could I take you on an adventure through a story?" I asked as you gave me a smile.

"All right. Tell me a story." You pressed your head back into my chest.

"Well, it started in a kingdom far away—"

"No. Not a kingdom," you quietly interrupted.

"All right," I laughed. "It started on a pirate ship over the vast sea—"

"No. Not on a pirate ship," you quietly interrupted again.

"A tavern in the wild west?" I asked. You looked up at me with a smile as you grasped my chest.

"No. How about on a hill overlooking the city?" I placed my hands on your waist as I looked into your eyes.

"There once stood a cowboy and a beautiful angel on the top of a hill overlooking the lights of the city." You grasped my chest tighter as you nodded your head in approval. "The cowboy thought she was the most beautiful angel in the whole world, but he did not think he was worthy enough." I bit my lip as I continued the story. "You see, the cowboy was wild and rowdy while the beautiful angel was so kind and gentle. There's no way God would allow such a beautiful soul to be with a rowdy boy like him." You grabbed my cheek as I began to look down.

"But what the cowboy didn't know is God gifted him with a heart of gold, and although he did not see he was worthy enough now, he'd found out he would be someday." Those words hit my heart heavy as I lost my breath looking into your eyes. You kissed my cheek as you pulled me back to the truck. "My father will be worried if you don't get me home soon," you said with a smile. I opened the door as you slowly got in.

As we drove down the windy hill, my body felt like I was floating on air. I slowly put my hand on your leg as you grabbed my hand and gave me a smile. I always loved holding your hand in my truck. As we pulled up to your driveway, I got out and opened your door. I grabbed your hand and helped you out as I walked with you to the front door.

"I had an amazing night with you," I said, holding your warm soft hands. "Goodnight, Aida." I kissed your forehead before walking back toward my truck. I watched as you opened your front door and looked back at me.

"Goodnight, cowboy," you said back as you slowly closed the door behind you. My heart began to pound against my chest as I looked up to the sky.

"God. How can it be? A girl like her can't be with a man like me."

Part 4: Jonathan

I stood up in church as Jon began to sing next to me. I continued to look around as I felt my heart continue to sink. Jon had accepted Christ, and I had seen his life begin to change. The memory of shooting that innocent mother replayed in my head as I began to sit down. How could God forgive a man like me? I looked over at Aida singing in the choir as I bowed my head down. "God, I am not worthy," I prayed as the music continued to play around me. As the sermon went on, I thought about the amazing night I had with you. I thought about how I held you in my arms and danced under the stars. I thought about how your beautiful eyes looked into mine with admiration, but I knew I didn't deserve you. I felt so lost in church as if I didn't belong. Pastor White continued to talk about grace and how even the worst of sinners were saved. My heart ached, because I just couldn't believe I was included in God's grace.

As the sermon ended, everyone began to get up from their seats. Jon and I walked over to you as I gave you a wave. "Hey, Aida," I said with a half-smile trying to hide the pain I was feeling.

"Hey, guys," you said with your big smile. You gave Jon and me a hug and held onto me for just a little bit longer.

"David," your father said as he came next to me and gave me a strong handshake.

"Mr. White."

"Jon," your father patted Jon on the back giving him a smile.

"Nice to see you, Pastor White," Jon said with a friendly smile. We all began to talk for several minutes until it was time to leave.

"So when do you both go back?" your father asked as Jon and I looked at each other.

"Tomorrow," we said in unison. You puffed out your lip as you looked straight at me.

"Well, I'll hope to see you guys again," you said giving Jon a hug. As you let go, I wrapped my arms around you.

"I'll see you again. I promise," I whispered as you closed your eyes and hugged me tight. I made sure to keep that promise.

"Bye, Mr. White," I said with a smile as I wrapped my arms around your father. Your father gave me a nod as we walked out of the church. Jon and I walked silently down the sidewalk toward our car until he finally looked over at me.

"Are you alright?" he asked as we approached my truck.

"Yeah," I said, looking back at the church. "I really like being home," I said with a half-smile. Jon began to nod as he looked back at the church.

"Me, too, man. Me, too." We then hopped in the truck and prepared to go home.

After dropping off Jon, I drove home and began to pack my bags. I thought about the night I had with you. It was hard to think that I might not see you for a very long time. My heart began to sink as I thought about how our worlds could never be together. I was a wild cowboy who had done many wrong things, and you were a beautiful angel who deserved so much better. I closed my eyes as my heart continued to ache.

As the next day approached, Jon's parents drove to the front of my house while I waited outside.

"Good morning, Mr. and Mrs. Migliore," I said as I got in the car.

"Good morning, David." I looked over to Jon, half asleep against the window.

"Hey! Wake up!" I gave him a little smack on the face as he wiped away drool from his mouth.

"What?" he said, looking around.

"Good morning, sleepy head," I said with a laugh.

"Good morning, Dave," he said softly as he lay his head back into the window and closed his eyes. We quietly drove down the highway as I, too, rested my head against the window.

I soon felt the car stop as I opened my eyes. Jon and I slowly got out as we held our bags. "Bye, Mom. Bye, Dad," Jon said as he kissed his parents.

"Bye, Mr. and Mrs. Migliore," I said as I gave them a big hug. Jon and I waved goodbye as they got back in their car. I saw Mrs. Migliore's eyes tear up as they drove away.

The journey was long for Jon and me as we boarded several planes flying across the globe. After over a day of traveling, we finally arrived back in Afghanistan at our camp. The weather was cold as we exited the plane to see the dark sky. We walked back into our tents and found our old cots still set up. Jon and I slowly got into our cots and wrapped the covers over ourselves to deal with the cold night. As I lay in bed, I continued to think about you as my eyes became heavy. Jon was fast asleep while I thought about that wonderful night I had with you. I was still torn as to whether I could even think of you. I didn't deserve you, but I felt so close to you on that wonderful night. My eyes closed as I felt myself drift asleep.

We continued our daily routine by getting breakfast and driving our Humvees out into the cold field. As we drove into town, we carried with us a bucket full of water bottles. I slowly handed them out to children as only men stood in the streets. Women with burqas hid inside their homes as the Humvees drove through the town. This continued for several weeks as we investigated each town.

"Here you go," I said to a little boy as I handed him a bottle of water. He gave me a nod before quickly running off. I saw several more kids standing in an alleyway as I grabbed several more bottles of water. I walked toward them as they began to shy away. "Here you guys go," I said softly handing each of them a water bottle. Jon and I continued to look around the city as he followed me down a long alley way.

I carried several bottles of water as I walked down the alley. I then saw a little boy peek his head out from the side of one of the buildings. "It's alright," I said holding out a water bottle. He looked scared as I continued to walk closer to him. I reached the water bottle to him as he grasped it with his little hand.

Bratatat! Blood splattered from his body as I dropped the water bottles and prepared my gun to fire. Jon ran toward me as several kids scurried out from behind the building holding AKs in their small hands. *Bratatat!* I quickly shot several down as they began to aim at me. "Run!" I yelled to Jon as several more children with guns appeared behind us.

Bratatat! Gunshots echoed across the town as Jon and I ran through the alley. I continued to shoot several down as Jon continued to run. My heart throbbed as I watched the little boys drop to the ground. As we ran out of the alleyway, several more shots suddenly fired at us. "Duck!" I yelled as I somersaulted toward a nearby car. I watched as Jon was hit with several bullets. I quickly knelt down and began to shoot several men hiding behind crates. I shot down three of them by hiding behind a wall and shooting in between their rounds. Several more appeared as I quickly took them down. I soon ran low on bullets and quickly grabbed Jon's gun.

Bratatat! My gun shot down several more men in headdresses as I knelt down next to Jon. The area was quiet as I looked over. "Jon?" I rolled him over to see blood seeping from his chest. I pressed down on the wounds as I looked into his half-open eyes. He began to cough up blood as he tried to speak.

"It's alright," he said, barely able to breathe. My eyes began to water until I saw a smile on his face. "Tell my family God's taking me home." He then started looking up at me and then staring up at the sky. I saw his chest stop moving as his eyes continued to gaze forward.

"Jon?" I gave him a shake in desperation hoping he would start to move. I clenched my teeth as a tear fell down my cheek. I slowly shut his eyes with my fingers as I looked up to the sky trying to hold in the pain. Gunshots soon echoed through the alleyway as I lifted up Jon's motionless body onto my shoulders. I ran toward our Humvee as more shots came from behind me. I gently set down Jon's body in the Humvee. As I set him in, I soon felt a warm sharp pain in my upper left thigh. I pressed my hands down on it as I drove the Humvee out of the town. I saw several other Humvees as bullets continued to cling against the back of my vehicle. I finally drove out into the open field as I held my leg. I soon lifted my hand to see blood seeping from a hole in my left thigh. I sped up as I drove several miles back to base. I began to feel woozy as the blood continued to seep onto my uniform.

I soon pulled the Humvee into base as medics waited out front. "Man down!" I yelled pointing to my Humvee as I fell to the ground.

"He's shot!" one of the medics yelled as they began to rush over to aid me.

"Man down . . ." I continued to say as medics opened up the Humvee and pulled out Jon. My eyes became heavy as I watched them carry Jon into the medical tent. They continued to cut up my pants leg as I blacked out on the soft dirt.

I soon opened my eyes to see my leg heavily wrapped and several metal shards lying on a tray. "What happened?" I said as I began to sit up.

"You received a bullet to your thigh. The bullet was several centimeters from your main artery. You're very lucky to be alive," a medic said as I examined my thigh. Pain surged through my leg as I tried to move.

"Agh," I said in agony as blood continued to seep through the wrapping.

"Don't move," the medic said as he continued to sort through his equipment. "You need to rest." I slowly leaned back as I pulled my leg into a more comfortable position.

"Is Jon alright?" I asked looking over at the medic. He took a deep breath as he dropped his items and walked toward me.

"I'm sorry. The man you were with received several bullets to his lungs. We were unable to save him." The medic placed his hand on my shoulder and pursed his lips. "I'm sorry."

I laid back into my medical bed as my lip began to quiver. I couldn't believe my best friend was gone. I continued to replay the last words he said to me, "God's taking me home." It was hard to believe that in his last seconds of life he died with a smile knowing exactly where he was going. His faith in God was so powerful. As I looked up at the ceiling, I closed my eyes and began to pray. "Dear Lord, help me to see you the way Jon saw you. In . . ." I paused for a slight moment, "in Jesus's name, amen."

Several days passed as I lay with my leg bandaged up on my medical bed. Lieutenant Carson entered the room and stood at the foot of my bed. "David, you've served an honorable two and a half years. With this injury, we're going to give you an honorable discharge." Lieutenant Carson looked at my leg as he took a deep breath in. "Thank you for your service." He gave me a nod before walking off. I lay there speechless as I thought about how I could finally go home. I continued to think about Jon and how he had brought me to church. I knew I had to go back. I rest my head back into my chair as I thought about all the great memories I had with Jon growing up. My heart ached as I thought about how Jon was no longer next to me. It hurt knowing he was gone.

Part 5: I'm Coming Home

I slowly walked out of the unloading plane and through the cold walkway into the main airport. I felt alone as I walked out into the open area and saw people begin to slowly pass by, dragging luggage. I continued to walk with my bag slung around my shoulder. I had a slight limp and couldn't completely bend my leg.

As I stood at the airport pick-up, I wondered how I was going to see Mr. and Mrs. Migliore. My heart felt cold as I tried to feel any emotions of excitement about being home. A car pulled up as I dropped my bag and wrapped my arms around my mother. She held me tight as tears began to roll down her cheeks. "I'm so happy to have you back," she whispered. My father soon joined in as I wrapped my arms around the both of them. I still felt cold inside as I let go of them and slowly put my bag in the car.

As we drove down the long desert highway, I pressed my head up against the window and continued to recall the great memories I had with Jon. I knew he was home, but it still ached at me that he was gone. My parents were quiet as I looked out the window. They understood my mourning over my best friend.

The car pulled into our dirt driveway as I got out and slung my bag over my shoulder. My mom gave me a smile. I tried to return it with the best smile I could. It was nice to finally be home.

I walked into my house; I realized I was finally home for good. It made me think about how it must feel for Jon who in his last words knew he was going home. I felt a tear roll down my cheek as I knelt down on one knee. I bent my other knee the best I could as I placed my hands on my bed. I bowed my head in prayer as my eyes continued to water.

"Dear Lord, I pray Jon is enjoying being home in your presence." As I opened my eyes, I felt much more at ease. I began to remember your father's teaching about going home with God. It hurt to know he was no longer with me, but I knew he would go up to be with the God who he had so much faith in. As I stood up, I remembered what I had to do. I walked through the house passing the kitchen as my mom continued to cook.

"I'll be back. I'm going to see Mr. and Mrs. Migliore," I said as my mother gave me a silent nod and continued to stir a large pot of spaghetti. I quickly got in my car and drove to their house. As I pulled in, I slowly got out and walked to the front door. *Ding dong.* The quietness was eerie and cold as I heard Mrs. Migliore's footsteps slowly slide across the floor. The door opened to Mrs. Migliore holding a tissue and tears coming down her face. She quickly wrapped her arms around me. I hugged her tightly.

"It's so nice to see you, David," she said with a squeak as she let me in. Mr. Migliore came down the hallway to join us as I walked in.

"David," he said, smiling with a face red from tears. He quickly gave me a strong hug, softly patting my back. He soon let go as I stood quietly in their front hall. "I know Jon's gone," Mr. Migliore said, wiping away tears. "But you're still family to us." He grasped my shoulder and gave me the best smile he could.

"We would love if you came by and had dinner with us sometime," Mrs. Migliore said as she wiped tears from her cheeks. I nodded my head as I tried to find the right words to say.

"Before Jon died, he wanted me to tell you guys something," I said as their eyes soon opened wide toward me. "He wanted me to tell you that God took him home." I gave them smile as they both hugged me. Tears streamed down their faces as they held me tight. Mrs. Migliore looked up with teary eyes as the light illuminated her rosy cheeks.

"Please be with him, Lord," she said with a smile. At that moment, I felt more at ease knowing God had taken Jon home with him. It had taken some time, but as I waved goodbye, my heart began to feel warm again.

I arrived home to hug my parents as we all sat down at the table. "Shall we pray?" I asked as we all sat around and held hands. My father looked at my mother with a smile as he nodded his head. We all bowed our heads as I began to pray. "Dear Lord, thank you for my family and for allowing me to come home. I pray for Jon as he lives with you that you may be with his family. I thank you for this delicious food and for the hands that prepared it. In Jesus's name . . ."

"Amen." We opened our eyes and began digging into our food.

After dinner, I held my phone in my hand as I tried to build up the courage to call you. I paced back in forth as I thought about what to say. I took a deep breath as I quickly tapped your number into my phone. *Ring ring. Ring ring.* I was very nervous waiting for you to answer my call. "Hello?" My heart pounded against my chest as I heard your beautiful voice through the phone.

"Hello, is Aida there?" I asked trying not to sound nervous.

"David?" you asked as a large smile came on my face.

"Yup, it's me."

"How are you?" you said excitedly as I sat on my bed.

"I'm good. I'm home for good now."

"Really?"

"Yup!" The phone was silent as I waited for you to reply.

"Well, I moved to Ohio with my family." My heart slowed as the smile on my face quickly disappeared.

"Oh," I said as I looked down to the floor.

"It's alright." You still had a smile on your face as you talked through the phone. "I'll be coming back for school this fall."

A smile soon came on my face as I jumped up. "Really? Well I'd love to see you when you come back into town."

I heard you giggle on the other end of the phone. "I would love to see you, too," you said as we continued to talk. We talked for hours as I told you about everything that happened. You were comforting as I continued to talk with you about Jon and his last words to me. As the night went on, I hoped that it would never end. Our long talks on the phone are some of my favorite memories. That night we talked until the sun rose the next morning, and on that day you became my best friend.

After I hung up the phone, I never went to bed. I went out that morning in search for a job. As I scoured the town, I found a job in construction. It was good pay, and I loved the grueling work of lifting heavy things and using my hands. After work I would come home and eat with my family before waiting to talk to you. Throughout the week, we would share stories about our days and talk about our adventures.

"Are you still trying to become a writer?" you asked one night while we talked on the phone.

"Yup!" I said with a smile as I lay down in my bed.

"Have you written anything lately?" I rolled over to my laptop on the side of my bed and opened it up.

"Of course," I said as pulled up one of my stories.

"Really?" you said excitedly. "Send it to me!"

"All right, but you can't laugh."

I began writing a number of stories. You would read them all, telling me how you were my number one fan. You were always excited to read the stories I wrote. As the weeks went on, we continued to talk over the phone almost every night. I always looked forward to hearing your voice at the end of my day then one day everything changed.

"David?" you said over the phone late at night.

"Yeah, Aida?"

"I don't think we can talk like this anymore." Your voice was full of sadness as I kept quiet for several moments.

"Why?" I asked concerned.

"We're very far away, and I've met someone."

My heart dropped to my stomach as I looked up at the ceiling. "I see," I said as I sat down on my bed and put my elbows on my thighs.

"It'd be unfair to him."

I closed my eyes and took a deep breath. "Maybe I'll see you again one day."

"You will," you said quietly. "Goodbye, David." My heart sank even deeper as those words slipped off your tongue. "Keep writing." I took a deep breath before I gave you a response.

"Goodbye, Aida. And I always will."

As you hung up the phone, I slowly closed mine and laid back into my bed. "I didn't deserve her anyway," I said looking up at the spinning fan. "God wouldn't ever let me be with a woman like that." I closed my eyes as the fan continued to blow cold air in my face.

The next morning was hard as I continued to hammer away. I no longer had anything to look forward to. As work finished, I waved to everyone goodbye and got in my car. I drove several miles before I saw a sign that said VOLUNTEER HELP WANTED. As I pulled in, I walked into the double doors of a church to see a man standing in an unfinished sanctuary. "Hello?" I asked, knocking on the doors. The man looked over at me with a smile. "The doors were open so I thought it'd be alright if I came in."

"Please. Do come in." The man gestured for me to walk into the unfinished sanctuary. "Welcome to Faith Community," he said holding out his hand. "I'm Pastor Pearson." I quickly gave him a firm handshake.

"David Benelli," I said with a smile as I looked around. "I saw the sign outside saying you needed help?"

Pastor Pearson's eyes grew wide as he continued to smile. "Yes! What do you do?"

"I work in construction right now," I said as his smile grew even bigger.

He looked up at the ceiling and closed his eyes. "Thank you, Lord!" he yelled before looking back at me. "I was praying you would come!" he said with a smile as he placed his hand on my shoulder. "I need your help building this church." I gave him a smile as I looked around.

"What do you need done?"

After that day, I began to volunteer my time at the church. I began to install carpet and help build the platform for the pastor to stand on. I continued to serve there for several months all through the summer as Pastor Pearson talked with me while we worked.

"So tell me David, do you believe in God?" Pastor Pearson asked as I continued to paint a wooden door.

"I sure do," I said looking up.

"Are you saved?" Pastor Pearson asked as he continued to move several chairs into place. There was a long pause as I continued stroking my paintbrush against the wooden door.

"Pastor Pearson, I'm going to be honest with you." I stopped painting and looked over at him. "With the sins I've committed, I'm not worthy to be saved."

Pastor Pearson soon stopped setting up chairs and sat next to me. "Why do you say that?" he said, looking at me with curious eyes.

"I've done many wrong things in my life. I've killed a lot of people." I looked down and clenched my jaw. Pastor Pearson nodded his head in understanding.

"You know, God sent his son Jesus to die for all sins. That includes yours, no matter how awful they may be."

I gave him a nod before I continued painting. "I just don't believe I'm worth enough for God to send his son to die for me." I closed my eyes and put down my paintbrush. "God doesn't want me."

Pastor Pearson was quiet in his chair as he sat back. "God wants you. It may just take time for you to see." I looked over and gave him a nod as I continued to paint.

Pastor Pearson became a good friend as we continued to build the church. I told him of how I aspired to be a writer, and he told me I should go to college to chase that dream. I took his advice that fall as I attended the University of Arizona seeking a major in English. After applying for school, I continued to work my construction job and save up money. I bought my own place and began to attend Faith Community Church every week. Several days after school started I ran into you.

"David?" you said with a smile as I passed you in the hallway.

"Aida?" I asked, squinting my eyes. You quickly wrapped your arms around me as I lifted you up.

"What are you doing here?" you asked with a smile as I put you down.

"I'm studying English," I said, shrugging my shoulders. "I'm following my dream of becoming a writer." Your eyes grew wide as a smile came on your face.

"Really?" you asked as you grabbed my arm. "Have you written anything new?"

I gave you a smile as I pulled out a folder. "Here. Take this," I said with a smile as you took a stack of papers from my hand. "I wrote this in one of my classes."

You gave me a smile as you looked through the pages. "I'll definitely read it," you said. I waved goodbye as I went to my next class. It was nice seeing you again. You still were just as beautiful as I remember. After seeing you, I went to classes and went through my day. That night I lay on my bed relaxing until suddenly I heard my phone ring.

"Hello?"

"I loved your story!" you yelled in excitement as I began to laugh.

"Hey, Aida."

"Do you have other stories?" you asked as I quickly opened my laptop. I then began to tell you about what had happened since you had been gone. We spent hours talking as you caught me up on your life and how you spent your time up in Ohio. I learned that you weren't seeing anyone, and my heart began to beat again.

"Would you like to come to church with me?" I asked as we talked on the phone.

"Yeah!" you said in excitement. "The church you helped build right?"

"Yup," I said with a smile as I sat on my bed. "I'll pick you up at nine-thirty on Sunday. Deal?"

"Deal," you said with a laugh. We continued to talk for several more hours until I finally had to get off the phone.

"Alright, Aida. I've got to go. I'll talk to you later this week."

"Goodnight, David." These were the same words I remembered except this time I felt as though you were actually falling for me.

"Goodnight, Aida," I said back with a smile before hanging up the phone. I lay back in my bed as my heart began to pound against my chest. You were back in my life.

Part 6: Let the Love Begin

Sunday morning came, and I ran around my house trying to get ready. I finally found my tie and ran out the door. I quickly drove to your apartment as I waited for you to come out. I still remember the beautiful flower dress you wore. You had your hair down, and I couldn't help but smile seeing you walk down those steps. I opened your door for you as I helped you in.

"Why thank you, sir," you said in a British accent.

"You're very welcome, my dear," I said back with a grin.

As we drove to church, I was scared to hold your hand. As we arrived, a smile came on your face as you looked out the window. "Wow. You helped build this?" You looked over at me with a smile.

"Yeah," I said pulling the car into a parking space. "And I enjoyed every moment of it."

We walked up to the church to see Pastor Pearson greeting people in. "David!" he said with open arms as he wrapped his arms around me.

"Pastor Pearson." I wrapped my arms around him and gave him a strong hug. "I'd like you to meet Aida," I said as I let go.

"Aida. Pleasure to meet you," Pastor Pearson said as he shook your hand.

"I've heard many great things about you," you replied with a smile.

"Well, please come in." Pastor Pearson opened the door for us as we walked into the large sanctuary.

You continued to look around as I told you about the many hours I spent helping build the church. I showed you the front platform and what I had to do to build the steps leading to the podium. As we sat down, you grabbed my hand and gave me a kiss on the cheek.

"This church is amazing," you said, squeezing my hand. I gave you a smile as music began to fill the room. "I'd get married in a church like this," you whispered jokingly making me laugh. We then stood up and started to sing for praise and worship.

Your voice was always so beautiful. Singing next to you was always my favorite. Your voice would carry throughout church like a beautiful hymn. Whenever you sang, it reminded me of the first time I saw you. God had really gifted you with an amazing voice. Soon the music began to slow, and Pastor Pearson came on stage. We bowed our heads in prayer as he taught another message. You were very happy with Faith Community. We didn't know at the time, but we would attend that church for many more years.

"Aida, you have such an amazing voice," I told you after church. You looked at me with a smile. "You should join the choir."

"Hm." You placed your hand on your chin as you began to think. "I used to be in the choir at my old church." I gave you a smile as you continued to think. "Alright. I'll do it." You said as you walked over to the information desk. I watched as the woman pulled out a sign-in sheet and gave you information. You talked with her for several minutes as you both began to laugh. "Thank you!" you said to her with wave as you walked back. You had a large smile on your face. "Well, I start practice this week."

"That was quick," I said with a chuckle. "I'll be here watching you sing." You gave me a smile as I lightly kissed you on the forehead.

We continued to hold hands as I walked you to my truck. I opened the door for you once again as you got in and waited for me to start the truck. As I got in, I placed my hand on your thigh and began to drive you home.

Our friendship continued to blossom as we talked on the phone and went to church every Sunday. We always had something to talk about with school or work. It was so nice to have you in my life again. I continued to share my stories with you. You would read my stories and tell me all about your favorite parts. It was the best adventure I could give you at the time. I continued to watch you sing at church in the stands as I listened for your voice in the choir. Your smile on that stage let me know singing was your passion. On the phone you would sing to me the different songs you were practicing in choir. I loved listening to you sing.

After several weeks, you told me how the choir had allowed you to do a solo on a Saturday night. I was very excited. I was several minutes early while I sat in front waiting for you to come on stage. The sanctuary was quiet as the piano slowly began to play. The light shone bright on you as you held a microphone in your hand. My heart stopped as I waited for you to sing.

> "*Amazing Grace, how sweet the sound,*
> *That saved a wretch like me.*
> *I once was lost but now am found,*
> *Was blind but now I see.*"

I fell to my knees as you continued to sing. I closed my eyes and looked up at God as my heart began to release the pain. I had heard the song many times before, but when you sang it, I began to understand every word.

> "*My chains are gone,*
> *I've been set free,*
> *My God, my Savior has ransomed me,*
> *And like a flood His mercy reigns,*
> *Unending love, amazing grace*"

On that day, I finally gave my life to Christ. Your voice captivated me as I listened to every word. For so long, it was hard for me to understand why God would ever forgive a man like me, but now I finally understood why I was forgiven. "Amazing Grace" is what saved me. I finally understood what Jon had seen before he passed. He had seen God's amazing grace.

As you finished singing, I knelt down on my knees and looked you straight into your eyes. I felt as though God sent you to call me to him. Through an angel's voice, I was saved. I stood up and clapped loudly as the audience began to follow. You slowly walked down and wrapped your arms around me as Pastor Pearson walked onto the stage. We sat down as I placed my arm around you. "You were amazing," I whispered in your ear as we began to listen Pastor Pearson teach.

We became very involved in the church. You served in the children's ministry as I helped Pastor Pearson in the men's group. For several years, we continued to serve in the church as we made it our home. You continued to sing in the choir every Sunday as I helped pray for others after church. It was hard at times trying to serve at the church and go to school, but we were very supportive of each other as we continued to fight through. I continued to write you stories as we talked on the phone almost every night. Every Saturday night I would take you out on a date and we would sing together to the radio. I didn't think life could get any better, but then we graduated college.

After our ceremonies, I took you out on another date to a very nice restaurant.

"I have a surprise for you," I said giving you a big smile.

"Oh yeah?" you asked with a playful grin.

"Check under your chair." You slowly leaned over and grabbed a gift bag from underneath your seat.

"What is it?" you said excitedly looking at the bag.

"Open it," I said as you began to pull out tissue paper. You suddenly pulled out an envelope.

"I wonder what's in here," you said with a smile as you began to open it. You soon pulled out two plane tickets as you looked straight up at me.

"I'm taking you to New Zealand just like I promised." Your eyes began to water as you set the tickets down and came over to me.

"Thank you," you said as tears rolled down your cheeks. "I love you." I wiped away a tear as I looked into your eyes.

"I love you, too," I said as I kissed your soft lips.

As the day came for us to go to New Zealand, my parents drove us to the airport and I helped unload the luggage. "You two be safe now," my mother said as she kissed us both on the forehead. We waved goodbye as they began to drive away.

"Bye, Mr. and Mrs. Benelli!" you shouted after them.

"We're going to be Mr. and Mrs. Benelli one day," I said nudging your shoulder. You gave me a teasing smile before giving me a peck on the lips.

"Let's go! We're going to be late!" We quickly dragged our suitcases through the airport and toward the check in.

"Two bags to New Zealand," I said handing the attendant our boarding passes.

"IDs please," the woman said in a monotone. We quickly scuffled our hands into our pockets until we pulled out our IDs. "Thank you," the woman said as we lifted each bag onto the scale. "Okay, you're all set. Have a nice flight." I looked at you with a smile as you grabbed my hand and ran toward the security line.

"I'm so excited!" you said jumping up and down. You were always filled with so much energy. We continued to edge toward the security scanner as we quickly removed our shoes and placed our items into the trays. I had never seen someone so excited to walk through airport security. We quickly walked through the large metal detector as we grabbed our things. You pulled my arm again just as I got my shoe on, and I started to jog trying to keep up with you. I loved seeing how excited you were. As we got to our terminal, we saw people already loading. We quickly hopped in line holding our boarding passes. "You're good." The attendant said as you clapped your hands in excitement.

"Our first plane ride together," you said with a laugh as we waited to find seats. We continued to edge into the plane as people put up luggage in the upper compartments. You continued to hold my hand as you excitedly dragged me to two seats.

"Get ready for a fourteen-hour flight," I said, laying back into my chair. You grabbed my arm and leaned your head against my shoulder.

"Did you bring your stories?" I looked down at her with a smile as I opened the bag on my lap and pulled out my computer.

"Of course. What should we read first?" I opened my laptop and looked through a folder containing all my writing.

"Oh this one!" you said smiling and pointing at the screen.

"'Space Cowboys and the Lovely Alien Princess'?" We began to laugh as I opened up the story and began to read to you. I felt you drift to sleep on my shoulder as I slowly read the words. That was the first time I ever read to you. I soon heard you breathing slow as I closed the laptop and looked over at you. You looked so peaceful on my shoulder. I tilted my head back and began to close my eyes. I felt so comfortable having you right beside me.

"David! Wake up!" you began to shake me as I opened my eyes.

"Yeah baby?" I asked looking over at you. I soon saw the beautiful green of New Zealand as we flew over the lush landscape. The sky was a gorgeous blue as we looked over the beautiful mountain ranges and green hills. You hugged the window as you looked back at me with excitement. The plane soon began to hit the ground as the seats began to shake.

"Welcome to Auckland, New Zealand," the attendant said as we landed. Your eyes were filled with excitement as we debarked the plane. After we got into the main airport, I had to drag you along as you looked around in amazement at the different scenery. We quickly grabbed our bags and took a shuttle over to the car rentals.

"Here're your keys, sir," the man at the front desk said as he handed me a set of keys. "It's the purple Scion." Your eyes grew wide as you took the keys and ran out looking for the car.

Beep beep. "Found it!" you yelled with excitement as I looked over at the man.

"She's really excited," I said as we both laughed. I rolled over our suitcases to the car as we threw them in.

"Now where are we going?" you asked with a smile.

"On an adventure," I said with a laugh as we began to pull out.

We began to drive down the highway as you looked out the window at the lush green hills. We drove for several hours as you rolled down the window and took in the beautiful fresh air. You looked at me with a smile as I grabbed your hand and continued to focus on the road. We soon pulled up to a house resting on the beach as you looked over at me.

"We're here," I said with a smile as you got out and took your shoes off.

"How did you find this?" you asked me while running through the soft sand.

"I knew someone in the army who said he could let us stay for a week." You gave me a smile as you jumped up in my arms and gave me a kiss. I held your hand as we walked up out to a boat resting on the dock.

"A boat?" You looked over at me with a smile.

"Yup. We're going to sail." I pulled you toward the boat as we hopped on. I pulled out the keys from my pocket and started the engine. "You ready?" I asked as you held on. You gave me a nod as I pushed the lever to accelerate the boat. I began to steer it across the ocean as we overlooked the beautiful scenery of the beach. I continued to drive us across the coast as we saw beautiful waterfalls dropping water into rising hills.

"It's so beautiful . . ." you said leaning on the side of the boat.

"Want to drive?" I asked, offering you the steering wheel.

"I don't know how," you said slowly walking over. I slowly brought you over and placed your hands on the steering wheel. I slowly turned the boat with you as you looked over your shoulder with a smile. We continued to drive out in the ocean for several hours before we came back to the house on the beach.

I unloaded our suitcases as you ran into the house and looked around. "This is such a nice place," you said, smiling at me. I put your suitcase in your room as you sat on the couch.

"You ready to go eat?" I asked, rubbing my stomach.

"Yeah, I'm starving!" you said as I opened the door for you. We quickly got in the car.

"My friend told me of a really good place around here," I said as we continued to drive down a long dirt road. We arrived in a small town and pulled into a cabin, NEW ZEALAND FISH AND CHIPS. We sat down as we waited for a waiter to take our order. We continued to examine the menu as we talked about the amazing scenery.

"What can I get you guys today?" the waiter asked.

"I'll take the roasted lamb, and she'll take the fish and chips." She gave me a smile as I handed the waiter our menus. You looked at me with grin as I gave you a confused look.

"What?" I said smiling.

"I love how you know what I want," you said, reaching for my hand. I grabbed your hand as we continued to wait for our food.

"One fish and chips," the waiter said as he put down a big plate of fries and fried fish. "And one order of roasted lamb." The aroma of the lamb wafted up my nose as I closed my eyes and took a big whiff. I grabbed my fork and prepared to dig in when you stopped me.

"David, we need to pray first." I slowly put down my fork and grabbed her hands.

"Dear Lord, thank you for this wonderful time with Aida and this wonderful vacation. Keep us safe as we spend our time together. I pray you also bless our food. In Jesus's name . . ."

"Amen." We both quickly grabbed our forks. You snagged a piece of my lamb and put it in your mouth.

"Oops," you said as you chewed the lamb. I looked at you with my mouth open, then I snagged a piece of one of your fish.

"Mm," I said as I chewed obnoxiously. You began to giggle as we both continued to talk at the table.

I loved how we always had something to talk about. We never had to hide anything. Our conversations would be full of laughter as we continued to tease each other. I never told you this, but I stole several more fries from you while you weren't looking.

After we ate, we drove home and got ready for bed. We brushed our teeth in separate bathrooms as I looked through the doorway to see your mouth full of toothpaste. After we finished brushing our teeth, we both knelt at the foot of your bed and began to pray. After our prayer, I gave you a kiss goodnight and pulled the covers over you.

"Goodnight, Aida," I said, looking into your beautiful eyes.

"Goodnight, David," you whispered as I slowly closed your door. I walked back to my bed and plopped myself onto the mattress. I couldn't wipe off the smile on my face as I thought about where I was going to take you the next morning.

Part 7: Love that Lasts

"Follow me," I said as we continued to walk through a valley.

"Where are we going?" you asked as I opened my map.

"I don't know," I said with a laugh as we continued to walk down. Water ran under our feet as we hopped across the stream. "Come on, babe!" I yelled as you jumped across rocks. "Stop being such a slowpoke!" You gave me a playful scowl.

"Who are you calling a slowpoke? At least I don't drive five miles under the speed limit." I began to laugh as I looked over my shoulder.

"Don't insult my driving! I keep us safe!" I gave you a playful grin as we walked to the end of the valley to a large waterfall.

"Wow!" you said as you came up beside me. Water streamed down several rocks as it splashed into the water. The rocks seemed to gently slice by the blanket of water falling from above.

"We're here," I said as I wrapped my arm around you. We admired the waterfall for several moments as we sat on rocks overlooking the small mouth of the stream. "You ready for this?" I said standing up and taking my shirt off.

"Ready for what?" Suddenly water hit your face as I jumped in.

"Come on in, babe," I said as I continued to wade around. You smiled as you closed your eyes and jumped in. You swam with me to the waterfall as we ducked our heads and went underneath. We came up underneath as the water continued to pound down. "You ever been kissed underneath a waterfall?" I asked as I held you close to me.

"No, I have not," you said with a big smile looking at the waterfall then back at me. I put my hand on your cheek before pulling you toward me. The sound of falling water echoed through the little cove behind the waterfall as our lips began to touch. We held our kiss for several moments before I slowly let go and looked into your eyes.

"I love you, Aida Hope White." You grabbed my chest and pulled yourself closer.

"I love you, David Titus Benelli." We kissed one more time as the musical sound of dripping water filled the cove.

We walked back as the clouds began to cover the sky. Rain began to soak us even more as we ran to the car. "Wait!" I yelled before you could get in. I gave you a smile as you ran toward me and jumped on me. I looked in your eyes and gave you a kiss as the rain continued to drench our heads.

"I've always wanted to do that with you," you said with a big smile as I continued to hold you. I set you down gently as we both jumped in the car. The roads were muddy as we began to drive home. The rain continued to pour as we drove down the long highway. Lightning began to fill the sky as you held my hand in the car.

When we arrived at the beach house, we both ran into our bathrooms and washed off from the journey. The sound of rain continued to pound against the roof of the house as we cuddled next to the fire. I held you next to me as we both relaxed from our long journey. Neither of us said a word, but I knew we both were as happy as can be.

It soon became late, and you fell asleep on my shoulder. I then picked you up and took you to your room. I pulled the covers over you before I stood up and began to walk out. *Boom!* Thunder began to explode outside before I could reach the door.

"David," you said gently before I turned the knob.

"Yeah, Aida?"

"I'm scared." I lay next to you and pulled you toward me.

"Why are you scared?" I asked as I felt you shiver.

"I'm afraid of big storms," you said quietly, grabbing my hand.

"There's no reason to fear," I told you as I held you're hand. "My mom always told me thunder is from God and his angels bowling." You had a little giggle as you held me tight.

"David?"

"Yeah, Aida?"

"Would you still love me if I was bald?" You looked over at me with a half-smile.

"Aida, I will love you no matter what happens to you, because you will always be beautiful to me." You turned toward me as your eyes began to water.

"Forever and always?" you asked as I put my hand on your face.

"Forever and always," I said as you rested your head on my shoulder. I felt you fall fast asleep as I kissed you on the forehead and gently placed your head on the pillow. I slowly got out of the bed and walked toward the door. "Goodnight, Aida," I said as I slowly opened the door and walked to my room.

We spent the whole week going out and exploring. I even took you on a wonderful helicopter ride overlooking the wilderness. The day finally came when we had to pack our suitcases and go home. We drove to the airport. I returned the car. Boarding the airplane was strenuous as we passed through security and walked through crowded lines. I looked over at you with your hair in a bun and no make-up. You were still the most beautiful woman in the world. You were barely able to keep your eyes open as we boarded the early flight. You slept on my shoulder for most the flight before waking me up and having me read you another one of my stories.

"This one," you said as you pointed to the screen.

"'More Beautiful than War'?" I asked as you nodded your head. "I wrote this story about you, ya know." You gave me a smile as I quietly read you my story. We soon hit the ground as the plane began to shake.

"We're home," you said to me with a smile as we continued to fly in. As we debarked the plane, we both dragged our feet toward baggage claim. We slowly waited for our bags to come as suitcases began to appear and fall onto the spinning belt. After getting our suitcases, we went outside and waited for my parents to pick us up. Soon a familiar car pulled up, and we threw our suitcases in the trunk.

"Did you two have a good time?" my mother asked as we got in.

"One of the greatest adventures I've ever been on, Mrs. Benelli," you said as I looked back at you with a smile. We didn't say much more as my mother brought us to your apartment. I helped you with your suitcase before I kissed you goodbye and walked back to the car. As I got back into the car my mother had a huge smile on her face.

"She really adores you, David," she said as I watched you wave goodbye.

"I know. I'm going to marry her," I said as I looked out the window.

When I finally got home, I waved goodbye to my mother and walked with my suitcase into my house. I jumped into my bed and looked up at the ceiling. I closed my eyes as I thought about the amazing time I had with you. "Dear God, thank you for blessing me with Aida and bringing her in my life. In Jesus's name, amen," I prayed aloud then closed my eyes and fell asleep.

It took a while for us to get back in our routines, but we continued to talk about our wonderful adventure in New Zealand. I applied for a teaching job as I continued to write stories. I planned on publishing one of my books, but I was focused on something else. I wanted to propose.

I started my teaching job that fall at Golden Valley High School. You were so excited when I told you how I had gotten the job. We continued to date that year as you kept dropping hints for me to propose, but I just couldn't do it yet. After the semester, winter break came and I had several weeks off. I invited you to go shooting with me as I picked you up and drove you to the outskirts of the city.

"You ever shot a gun before?" I asked as I pulled out a gun.

"No, I haven't," you said with a smile. I set up several bottles a slight distance away as I stood with you.

"All right. Place the butt of the gun here." I put the gun against my right shoulder. "Control your breathing as you aim through the scope." I closed my eye and I slowly took a deep breath out. *Bang!* I shot the bullet straight into a glass bottle as it exploded. "You ready?" I asked.

"Yeah," you said nodding your head nervously. You reached for my gun as I pulled it away. "No, I got you something better." I went to my truck and pulled out a Benelli rifle. "This is yours." Your eyes opened wide as you examined the gun. You then knelt down and placed the rifle against your shoulder. I helped you load the gun as you prepared to shoot a bottle. "Wait," I said before you began to shoot. "Aim for that one." I pointed to a bottle on the far right. I watched as you aimed the gun slowly toward your target. "Remember to control your breathing." I watched as you slowly let out your breath. *Bang!* Your bullet hit the bottle as it exploded. A note flew out from the bottle as you wrapped the gun around your shoulder and walked toward the fallen note. As you picked up the note, you read the words "Be my Benelli." You turned around to me holding a velvet box revealing a diamond ring. "I've already gotten your father's blessing. Aida, will you marry me and be Mrs. Benelli?" I asked as you placed your hands over your mouth and began to cry.

"Yes!" you said quietly as I pulled out the ring and placed it on your finger. You wrapped your arms around me as you covered me in kisses. I picked you up and twirled you around as tears of joy rolled down your cheeks. "I'm so happy," you said as you held your arms around my neck.

We waited till that summer to get married. I asked your father if he would do our wedding, and he happily agreed. We invited all our family as we began to plan for the wedding. I was so nervous waiting all those months to finally marry you. You did most of the planning as I saved up for our wedding and our future home. We planned for the wedding to be at Faith Community, the same church I had helped build. Pastor Pearson was more than excited to help host the wedding as I chose him as my best man. I knew Jon would be happy knowing that I was finally marrying you.

When the day came for us to be married, I was very nervous. I waited for you up on that stage as the piano continued to play. I knew Jon was up there watching us on that beautiful day. The sun was bright and the air was warm as I stood looking at my family and friends. Soon the time came and I saw you in your beautiful white dress walking down the aisle. You were the most beautiful woman in the world, and no one could ever match up to your beauty. My legs began to feel like jelly as I felt my feet glued into the floor. My heart continued to pound against my chest as your father kissed you and released you to me. We walked up to the stage together as your father stood between us. He opened his Bible and began to read passages from 1 Corinthians. I looked up at the ceiling and began to thank God for giving me such an amazing woman. I continued to look in your eyes as you gave me a shy smile. After several more moments, Pastor Pearson soon handed me your ring.

"Do you take this woman to be your lawfully wedded wife?" Mr. White asked.

"I do," I said as I placed the ring on your finger.

"Do you take this man to be your lawfully wedded husband?" I watched as tears began to roll down your cheeks.

"I do," you said as you took a step closer and helped me slide the band on my finger.

"You may now kiss the bride," Mr. White said as we both kissed each other on stage. The music continued to play as I grabbed your hand and walked with you down the steps. I looked in the audience to see my parents sitting with Mr. and Mrs. Migliore. The smile on their faces as they watched me walk with you down the aisle made my eyes begin to water. I couldn't believe we were finally married. I continued to hold your hand as we walked out the double doors into the lobby.

"Well what now, Mr. Benelli?" you asked, looking into my eyes.

"Time to make this place our home, Mrs. Benelli."

Part 8: Aaron Jonathan Benelli

"David!" You opened the door to the bathroom holding a little stick in your hand. "It's positive." I quickly got up from the bed and wrapped my arms around you.

"I'm so excited, baby," I whispered as you held on to me tight. We quickly pulled out our phones and began to call our parents.

"Mom, Dad!" I yelled in excitement as my mother picked up the phone. "I'm going to be a father." My mother began to cheer loudly as she yelled to my father.

"Victor! We're going to be grandparents!" My father quickly grabbed the phone.

"Congratulations, son!" my father said in excitement as I looked over at you. We continued to laugh as we heard both our parents celebrate.

I took you out that night for celebration as I continued to rub your belly. I could barely hold my excitement as I even told the waiter how you were pregnant. After dinner, we cuddled on the couch and talked about the different things we had to do to prepare for the baby. You continued to rant on about finding a school and starting a college fund. I slowly put my finger on your lips as I looked into your eyes.

"Shhh," I said, putting my finger over your mouth. "We don't have to worry about those things just yet." I gave you a smile before kissing you on the forehead. "We can enjoy this time waiting for our child to arrive." You looked down at my hand as our fingers began to interlock.

"Do you think I'm going to be a good mother?" you asked as you continued to play with my hand.

"You're going to be an amazing mother," I said, rubbing your stomach and looking into your eyes. "You're caring, loving, and full of adventure. Anyone would be lucky to have a mother like you." You gave me a smile as you kissed my neck.

"Well, you will be an amazing father." You words made me smile as I thought about how I was going to be a dad.

"I guess I can't publish my book until after the baby," I said with a laugh as I pulled you back onto my shoulder. I felt you close your eyes as you pushed your head into my chest.

"Why is that?" you asked.

"I want to make sure the first story I publish includes our baby." I felt a smile come on your face as you continued to rest against me.

"Am I going to be in it, too?" you asked as I leaned my head back and closed my eyes.

"Of course, baby. You're always the best part of my stories."

As the months went on, your stomach began to bulge out into a rounded ball. Every night after we would pray, I would sing to our baby till both of you fell asleep. I asked to find out the gender, but you wanted to wait till our baby was born. It was hard figuring out what clothes to buy, but I loved the suspense of not knowing.

Our friends and family were also very excited about our arriving baby. Your parents continued to send clothes in the mail and even promised they would be in town for the due date. My parents invited us over for healthy cooking and made sure I was taking care of you.

I continued to work at Golden Valley High School. You came to visit me during lunch. I introduced you to the other teachers as they congratulated me on the soon-to-arrive baby. I loved showing you off as my wife. It was even more exciting to know we were soon going to have another addition to our family.

As the weeks passed, we soon became even closer to the due date. Your parents flew out and stayed at our house to help take care of you and the arriving baby. We all went to the park as you watched your father and I throw the Frisbee.

"Catch!" I yelled as I threw the Frisbee to your father. He quickly jumped up in the air and caught it with one hand.

"Catch this!" he yelled as he threw it under his leg. I quickly ran to the short thrown Frisbee and caught it before it hit the ground. I did a spin and threw it right back at your father.

"Ha!" I said as he dropped the Frisbee. We began to laugh as he threw it again.

"David!" I heard you yell as you stood up. "I think my water broke." I looked at your father as we quickly ran over and helped you to the car. "Our baby's coming," you said in pain as we drove to the hospital. I quickly parked the car and opened your door as your father and me helped walk you in.

As we walked in, the doctors quickly took you in and walked you toward the back. Your parents and I followed as the doctors put you on a hospital bed. The contractions soon began to become closer and closer until the baby was ready to be born.

"Push!" the doctor said as you squeezed my hand. You began to yell in pain as you continued to strain. "I see the head!" the doctor cried as you continued to push. I stood with you for several hours as you continued to push out our baby. "One more push," the doctor said as you began to yell out in agony.

Wahhh wahhh. The doctor held the baby in his hands as he looked over at us. "It's a boy," the doctor said as he handed the baby over to me. The moment I held our little boy was one of the most beautiful moments of my life. I looked down at our crying boy as I realized I was his father. We were going to raise this little boy to be a man someday. I slowly handed him over to you and watched as your eyes opened wide. You looked at our son with adoration as you kissed his little forehead. You held him close to you as you looked at me with a smile.

"What should we name him?" you asked as I got down on my knee and brushed my fingers against his little feet.

"Aaron Jonathan Benelli," I said looking at our little boy.

"Perfect," you said, looking up at the ceiling. You looked back down at our son as you whispered quietly into his ear. "Welcome home, Aaron."

Your parents stood by you as you handed Aaron over to your father. He looked at the baby with a smile as your mother put her finger in his hand. Aaron wrapped his hand firmly around her finger as she looked over at us. "Strong grip," your mother said with a smile as she continued to hold his hand with her finger. Your father handed Aaron over to your mother as she began to rock him back and forth. "Hello, Aaron," she said gently before she handed him back to you.

You held him tightly in your arms as we both continued to look at his adorable eyes trying to open. His crying had stopped as he continued to move his mouth and straighten his fingers. I watched as your eyes became heavy and tired. I gently picked up Aaron from your arms as you began to cough violently. Soon the monitor next to your bed began to beep as your cough became even more violent. Aaron began to cry as I pulled him away and softly spoke to him. "It's alright, buddy. Your mommy's going to be just fine."

Nurses began to enter the room as I placed Aaron in his crib. We walked out the room as we watched the nurses begin to surround you. I was scared. I didn't want the mother of my beautiful child to be gone. I waited several hours in the waiting room with both our parents as we waited for news from the doctor.

"David Benelli?" a doctor asked aloud as he read from his clipboard.

"Yes?" I asked as I walked over to the doctor.

"We have some bad news." My heart stopped as I waited for what the doctor was going to say.

"Your wife has been coughing up blood. We had to run some tests." The doctor put his head down as he tried to tell us the news. "Your wife has cancer." My heart dropped as my knees began to feel weak.

"What?" I asked, confused. The doctor continued to explain the test results and how she would need to seek treatment right away. I nodded my head as I brought the doctor over to the rest of the family. Our parents were both heartbroken when they heard the news. It was so hard to have such a happy moment turn around so quickly.

The waiting was unbearable while we waited to see Aaron again. My mother began to have tears roll down her cheeks when I told her his name. Aaron brought joy to our faces as he lay peacefully in the hospital crib, but the news from the doctor continued to take its toll on all of us. That night, your parents and I took Aaron home as you stayed at the hospital. My heart ached as I thought about how you weren't able to come home with our beautiful boy.

Your parents and I continued to visit you that week as we brought Aaron with us. You were still very lively in that hospital bed as we came to visit. After that week, the doctors released you to come home, and we were able to spend time with Aaron. You still felt very weak, but you continued to stay strong. Your parents soon went back to Ohio as we cared for our baby and continued to watch him grow.

I remember the day you had to shave your head. You looked in the mirror as tears came down your eyes. I put my arms around you as you turned toward me and cried on my shoulder.

"David, I look so sick," you continued to cry as I placed my hand around the back of your neck.

"Baby, no you don't. You look more and more beautiful to me every day." You gave me a smile as I kissed your forehead. "'Sides, now I can kiss you all over your head without your hair getting in the way." I quickly began to kiss the top of your head as you began to giggle.

"Stop that." You laughed as you looked into my eyes. "I love you," you said as you gave me a serious face.

"I love you, too," I replied, looking deeper into your eyes.

"Forever and always?" you asked as a tear came down your cheek.

"Forever and always," I said as I kissed your forehead once more.

As your treatment continued, you began to have more and more energy. As the weeks went by, the doctors continued to give us good reports. Your hair started to grow back as your smile and laugh began to return. I remember coming home and picking up Aaron as we danced around. Both of you would smile as we would spin around. I would rock Aaron in my arms as you would sing songs to help him fall asleep.

"Amazing Grace, how sweet the sound,
That saved a wretch like me.
I once was lost but now am found,
Was blind but now I see."

Aaron always fell asleep right away after that song. Every night after we would tuck him in, I'd hold your hand as we placed our hands on him and prayed for him. He grew up so fast as the years past. Life was amazing waking up to your beautiful face every morning. After two years, I continued to enjoy every morning waking up with you and holding our beautiful son. Our life was filled with love and joy as we continued to be grateful for each day we were given.

Part 9: The Return

"All right, Aaron! Come on!" Aaron continued to walk across the sand toward me as you let him go. Aaron had a huge smile on his face as he stretched his arms out trying to keep balance. "Good job, champ!" I said as I picked him up and twirled him around. He began to giggle as I held him close in my arms. You came beside me and rubbed your nose against his.

"You're such a big boy!" you said as he began to giggle even louder. His smile continued to light up our day as we played with him at the park. You and I took Aaron together twice a week. You were such an amazing mother to him.

Cough cough. Your cough became violent as I walked Aaron up the playset. *Cough cough.* Your coughing became even worse as you fell to the ground. "Aida?" I yelled as you continued to cough on the floor. I quickly picked up Aaron and ran over to you. You lay passed out. I quickly called the ambulance. Aaron began to cry in my arms as they took you onto a stretcher. I watched as you drove away in the ambulance.

My parents took care of Aaron while I drove over to see you. I quickly rushed into the hospital and found you awake in your room. I sat down next to you and grabbed your hand as I looked at the IV connected to your arm.

"Are you okay?" I asked as you pulled your lip in.

"I'm sorry David." You didn't have to say anything for me to know. My heart hurt as I sat next to your bed. We bowed our heads and began to pray as you quietly rested your head on your pillow.

The process started over again. You were able to stay at home with me as you continued to go through treatment. You had to shave your head again and began to tie a bandana around your head. Even though you were sick, I still woke up every morning happy I got to spend another day with you. We still lived happily every day as you continued to get treatments.

I remember my last morning with you by my side. You would smile and make me laugh as we playfully teased each other. Aaron would run in our room as we would go and get breakfast. You made me so happy. I was blessed to have such an amazing woman as my wife. Aida, I love you with all my heart . . .

CHAPTER 14

ONE BIG HAPPY ENDING

My eyes continued to drop tears as I set down the laptop and looked at Aida's resting body. I held her cold hand as I placed it against my face. "I'm sorry I couldn't find a happy ending." More tears fell down my cheeks as I closed my eyes and had my face fall into my hands. I soon looked over to my open laptop and squinted at some writing at the bottom of the screen. I soon scrolled down and began to read unfamiliar writing with the words "The Happy Ending" across the top.

Every day, I would wait in my hospital bed for you to return. Seeing you was always the highlight of my day. You always could put a smile on my face. After we found out my stay here would be longer, you began to write me stories. You didn't know this, but I would read your stories over and over again. I loved the stories you wrote for me. Although I loved those stories, I always believed our story was the best. I was so excited when you told me you were writing our story, but when you came in upset, I realized your story would need some extra help.

You didn't know the ending to our story, but that's all right. I do. Our story is an amazing story, and believe it or not, it has a very happy ending. In our story, we fought countless odds and overcame many obstacles. We loved through the hardest of times and grew closer through the many troubles. You never needed to be a valiant knight, a wild outlaw, or a sly pirate to make me happy. You only needed to be the wonderful man I fell in love with.

Love is like a sword. Through blazing fires and heavy hammers the strongest sword is forged. It is said that this love is the greatest gift God has given to mankind. I believe this to be true for I have experienced it in my life with you. Loving you was the greatest adventure a woman could ask for, but it's time for God to take me home. This may be the ending of my adventure, but yours must still continue.

A long time ago, you once told me you were going to be a writer. Follow your dreams and share your writing for our love will live on through your stories. I know Aaron and you will miss me while I'm gone, but know I will one day see you again. I'll be up in heaven with God watching over the both of you, and don't worry; I'll tell Jon you say 'Hi'.

I love you, forever and always,
Aida Hope Benelli

Aida died on November 11, 2014 at 3:15 A.M. I was by her side when she went to heaven. I continue to think about how she had written such an amazing ending to our story. I took her advice and followed my dreams.

CHAPTER 15
3 YEARS LATER...

"Dad!" Aaron ran down the hallway and jumped up into my arms. "It's bed time!" He said excitedly as he began to drag me toward his room.

"Alright, buddy. Which book do you want me to read?" I asked as Aaron began to look through several books on the shelf.

"This one!" He quickly ran over to me with a large book as he placed it on my lap.

"Alright, but first we have to pray." We both got on our knees as we bowed our heads in prayer. "Dear Lord, thank you for this wonderful night. I pray that we can have a wonderful night sleep and that you can help us become better people. We pray for Aida as she looks over us from heaven that we may one day see her again. In Jesus name..."

"Amen!" Aaron yelled as he hopped into his bed and pulled up the covers.

"Okay, champ. You ready for the story?" Aaron gave me a nod. "Knights, Pirates, Outlaws, and One Big Happy Ending by David Catalano." Aaron gave me a smile as I continued to turn the pages. I opened to the first page of the story and began to read. "Chapter one, the beginning." I smiled at Aaron once more before I continued. "I opened my eyes and turned toward my beautiful wife..."

CPSIA information can be obtained
at www.ICGtesting.com
Printed in the USA
FSHW011958181119
64264FS